THE FINAL PORT

BARBARA HOUTENBRINK ANDREASON

WESTBOW
PRESS
A DIVISION OF THOMAS NELSON

WestBow Press books may be ordered through booksellers or by contacting:

WestBow Press
A Division of Thomas Nelson
1663 Liberty Drive
Bloomington, IN 47403
www.westbowpress.com
1-(866) 928-1240

Because of the dynamic nature of the Internet, any web addresses or links contained in this book may have changed since publication and may no longer be valid. The views expressed in this work are solely those of the author and do not necessarily reflect the views of the publisher, and the publisher hereby disclaims any responsibility for them.

Any people depicted in stock imagery provided by Thinkstock are models, and such images are being used for illustrative purposes only.

Certain stock imagery © Thinkstock.

ISBN: 978-1-4497-9432-3 (sc)
ISBN: 978-1-4497-9433-0 (hc)
ISBN: 978-1-4497-9431-6 (e)

Library of Congress Control Number: 2013908044

Printed in the United States of America.

WestBow Press rev. date: 05/21/2013

TABLE OF CONTENTS

To my husband, Ralph A. Andreason without whose assistance with all things nautical and historical this book could not have been written.

"GOD HAVE MERCY ON US ALL"

July 6, 1653

Whispers sweep through the castle on frosty streams of air.

"He's dead! Mary be Queen."

"Ironic," snickers Lord Buckingham. "After six marriages, Henry left none other than a sickly male heir. He lived longer than expected."

"There is much to fear. Mary's religious fanaticism will be our death." The outcry increases the apprehension pouring into the room. Whispers can be heard throughout the hall. "Protestantism is all but dead. Dissenters will do well to leave the country."

*   *   *

The death of Henry VIII's only son Edward VI makes certain that Henry's oldest daughter will become Queen of England. In an attempt to restore Catholicism, Mary weds the Catholic king of Spain, Phillip II. After a barren marriage Phillip returns to

Spain. Intolerant of Protestantism, Mary begins a wholesale slaughter of non-Catholics. Upon the death of Bloody Mary, her younger sister Elizabeth I succeeds to the throne in 1558. Though not religious, Elizabeth restores Protestantism, persecutes Catholics, and drives Puritans out of the country.

Elizabeth refuses Phillip's offer of marriage. Believing his marriage to Mary gives him claim to the English throne, thirty years after her death, Phillip, in 1588, sends an armada of Spanish warships into the English Channel. With skill, fire ships, and luck, the more maneuverable English vessels, under the superior leadership of Sir Francis Drake, defeat the Spanish. During Elizabethan England, the power of the throne is strengthened, the arts prosper, and piracy on the sea flourishes. Queen Bess never marries, leaving no progeny when she dies in 1603.

James VI of Scotland becomes James I of England and Scotland. The new king writes books, flaunts his divine rights, and constantly fights with a Parliament intent on finding ways to increase its power. Like Mary, James persecutes witches, but ironically, during his reign, he commissions an English translation of the Bible. Some Puritans, an extrazealous group of Protestants, flee to Holland rather than conform to the Church of England. After James's death in 1625, his son Charles I inherits a hunger for absolute power. Constant dissension between Charles and the predominately Protestant House of Commons cause Parliament to adjourn for eleven years. Charles and the royalists lose the ensuing Civil War. In 1649 Parliament holds court and convicts the king of treason, beheading him in front of the Banqueting Hall in London.

When Oliver Cromwell becomes lord protector of England in 1653, the Puritans enforce a more austere style of living, disapproving of any display of gaiety. Sober dreariness outwardly rules their lives, but rumors persist that Cromwell secretly gives parties and attends plays. When he dies in 1658, his son, Richard, rules briefly. Alienated by the bleak, harsh austerity enforced upon them by the Puritans, the people of England invite Charles's son to return from France as the rightful successor to the throne. With the accession of Charles II, London welcomes back the gaiety of the Elizabethan age, the English Navy becomes the Royal Navy, and the Admiralty begins to assume its final form as its central administration.

Chapter 1

GOD'S PLAGUE

London, England

July 25, 1665

Hanging high above the city, the sun sends shimmering glints of light across the river's surface. A mile away, a young lad vaults over the sharp, jagged edge of crumbling plaster that threatens to block his entrance into Cheapside Street. Squeezing close to the wall in the narrow alley, he avoids crossing paths with the shiny black rat scampering across the rough cobblestones. Not moving, the rat stares unblinkingly at the unexpected intruder. Glints of saffron sparkle where pinpoints of sunlight find pathways into its calm, beady eyes. Standing firmly over its meal, the rat fears the trespasser less than the youth fears him.

Shivers run down John's back as he withdraws one step at a time. Pressing his sweaty forehead against the cool brick wall, he tries to erase the unwanted memory of awakening one recent morning to find a rat sniffing at Tristram's face. He had whacked the rat with a piece of firewood—a quick kill. Years later,

1

John could still remember the look of dread on his brother's face, his vulnerability. Tristram was just one of thousands of children bitten by the ubiquitous rodents freely roaming the streets of London. Their numbers had steadily increased since the lord mayor's order to kill all the city's dogs and cats—pets not excepted. With the decrease in the numbers of their natural enemy, rats boldly roam the streets.

The loud wail of a distressed child interrupts his musings. Glancing toward the source of the disturbance, John watches five-year-old Hannah running toward him down the narrow lane near the churchyard of Mary le Bow. Shrugging his indifference, he turns away from her loud cries of protest. After all, she does not differ significantly from the hundreds of other discarded children wandering about the streets of London in 1665.

Teardrops seep from the corners of the child's dark blue eyes. Gray smudges streak haphazardly down her thin face.

"Come now, Kit Kitty. Here, Kit Kitty," she wails, misery wrenching her thin body when the kitten does not appear.

John shows little interest in the child, except as a momentary diversion, taking his mind off his immediate problems. Suddenly the youngster stretches her thin arms toward the empty street in front of her.

A shriveled old man shuffles into view, kicking up whorls of dust in the dry street. Running, slipping like a ship into safe harbor, the child grabs the edge of her uncle's coattails. Clamping his hand tightly on his cane, he avoids the catastrophe of a fall, gratefully leaning against the nearest wall.

"Uncle," she cries, "Kit Kitty! She be lost!"

"Lost, is it?" sniffs the bent-over old man. "More 'n likely the mayor hath ordered it kilt."

With a grunt of pain, he picks up the sobbing child. John watches the man hook his rough walking stick in the crook of his left elbow. Holding her firmly against his shriveled body with his good right arm, the uncle struggles along the street. Speaking more to himself than to the frightened child, he grumbles, "'Tis madness of fools to think poor, scraggly cats be the cause of so much death."

*　　*　　*

Eluding Death
January 1665, Reign of King Charles II

The first death occurred just outside the city proper, near Cornhill, adjacent to Fishmonger's Hall in Black Raven Alley. The Hillman family lived farther down the hill—less than one-half mile away.

In a futile attempt to escape the dreaded plague, a mother huddles with her two small children in the sleeping corner of their small flat. After gently disentangling herself, she cautiously rises and walks to the worn door. She places her ear against the splintered wood and strains to listen for the sound of approaching steps. She gasps, overwhelmed with fatigue and sadness, for instead of her son's footsteps, the clang of an iron bell announces the death cart. Just that morning, the cart had stopped briefly at her door to pick up the diseased corpse of her husband. Now, hours later, she huddles alone with her sick toddlers. The unexpected knock at the door commands her full attention, successfully shutting the mournful sound of the bell from her mind.

* * *

Sleepy, bored, and frightened, the bewhiskered watchman leans his pointed halberd against the building in front of the lane leading to the Hillmans' wretched dwelling. He briefly shuts his eyes, so he doesn't see the dark shadow slip past the barrier, no longer impregnable because of his inattention. Risky business. Under the law, the plague and the death of the husband forces the family to remain quarantined in their rooms for forty days.

Miraculously avoiding the guard, John arrives at his home to find a cross painted on the door, which is nailed shut. Cautious but persistent, he knocks, calling to his mother, "I pray thee, let me in. I have fish."

His mother sternly cries out, "Go! Leave us. You cannot enter."

Yearning for the security of his family, John becomes frustrated. Where else can he go? Fumbling beneath his shirt, he seeks the comfort of a small, coarse bag.

Kneeling by the door, he begs, "I must not leave you without protection. How can I leave my brothers?" Desperation creeps into his voice; he almost sobs when he repeats, "I cannot leave you."

"Go away, John," his mother insists, muffling her tears in the skirt of her soiled dress. Wanting to protect him from the illness within, she lies, "You are no longer wanted here."

Hunger gnaws at his stomach. His back aches after a long day of fishing alone in the river. Numb, threatened by matters beyond his control, his mind is already gripped by loneliness—feelings that will envelop him for an immeasurable time to come.

Aware of the horrific disease gripping the city, he wants to stay with his family. Death threatens. His father has been dead since morning, and his mother's opposition gives him no choice. He will go to the safety of the river for a few days. Certainly this problem will soon go away.

Standing to go, his determination ebbs. He is overcome by conflicting emotions: loyalty versus survival. After slowly banging his head against the thick supporting beam of the building, he traces the irregular heads of the large nails. "Five. Five nails secure the door. Five."

John looks about for a tool to remove the nails. Straining to listen to the hushed tones emitting from the other side of the door, he wants to call out, "Mam?"

Casting a quick look over his shoulder, John can see the guard is still sleeping. He murmurs in a pressured whisper, "How be my brothers?"

A desperate sob precedes his mother's response. "Hot with fever, Tristram is," she whimpers. "Samuel's chest be filled with water, covered with sweat. Thankfully there be no sores on his poor, thin body. The sound of his gurgling breaks my heart." She struggles to hiss through a crack in the door, "Feverish, the babe is coughing up gore, as did your poor papa." In a determined voice, she lies, "I must go. They need me."

Accepting the inevitable, John steps away, but he immediately returns to pound on the door one final time, just as his mother orders, "Go now! Leave. I won't speak to you again."

As if to end their conversation, she shoves a pence under the door. "Take this. Took it from your papa's pocket. 'Tis all I can give ye." Again, she cries, "Run whilst ye can. The plague is here! All are dying! God hath forsaken us!"

John throws his day's catch by the door, ignoring the barricade preventing his mother from retrieving the fish. When she hears the muffled sounds of retreating footsteps, his mother returns to care for her dying children,

Intent on finding refuge on the river, John silently creeps past the snoring guard into chaos.

* * *

"Idiot," bellows the driver of a horse-drawn conveyance racing up the hill away from the river. Forcing his way past other coaches, he pursues a hazardous route, hoping to flee through the nearest city gate. Not considering the safety of others, the coachman savagely strikes his whip against the flank of every horse or human daring to block his path, knowing if he successfully whisks his passengers to the perceived safety of the country, extra shillings will certainly find their way into his poke.

Jumping to safety, John narrowly avoids death beneath the powerful pounding hooves. Sweat pours down his face. He briefly conjures up a vision of his mother riding to a safe haven in such a carriage. How wonderful it would be to carry his family away to a safe refuge in the country, his mother costumed in the finest silk brocade.

*   *   *

Although dying, the aristocratic couple riding in the erratic conveyance took the time to dress according to their station in life. They appear prepared to embark upon an amusing tour of the countryside, not a journey to escape death. The lady might have been an actor in a scene from a macabre play in Drury Lane. Her mascara-smudged eyes reveal open fear as she peers at John across the soft folds of her blue silk handkerchief. She acknowledges him with a refined nod, and her shiny sapphire eyes blink back uncontrolled tears. A coughing spasm threatens to reveal the translucent skin of breasts barely contained within the scoop of her stylishly low neckline. Embarrassed, John averts his eyes, staring at the dark saffron ribbons twisted to create large puffs in the brocaded material of her sleeves. Pale fingers pick at the frill of lace trimming the edge of her sleeve.

A large black ostrich plume droops over the brim of her companion's hat, almost obscuring his face. Black ribbon epaulets sit on the shoulders of the gentleman's stylishly cut jacket, the yellow color closely mimicking the hue of his sickly face. An elegant white wig sits askew on his head. His face is the color of impending death. Pinched skin around his nose intensifies the appearance of illness. Stricken with fear, the man lifts his eyes, as if startled out of an unbelievable dream. Aristocratic fingers nervously knead the puff of fabric above his elbow and then sweep downward to his purse in a compulsive search for gold coins. Neither the coins nor the gold trim on his sleeve will safeguard him from the scourge invading the city of London.

*   *   *

The crack of a whip, the clatter of wheels over aged cobblestones sends John hurtling into a dusty alley near Thames Street. Narrowly escaping death, John heightens his efforts to reach the safety of the docks. A vibrating rumble precedes the arrival of yet another carriage. In the backseat two figures lean against each other for balance. Black hats sit askew on two male heads as their bodies bounce about the cabin. Too weak to push black and red plumes away from their faces, they are unaware of the rearing up of the horses, frightened by the sudden appearance of a child in their path. The driver does not bother to look at the carnage wrought under the carriage. After the horses regain their footing, the driver encourages them forward with a crack of his whip, paying no attention to the battered child in the ragged brown dress.

Although sickened by the sight of the trampled child and recognizant of the horror of death, John shrugs his shoulders and continues down the hill toward the wide river whose serpentine course defines the boundaries of London.

*   *   *

Turning away, John tries to avoid looking at the repulsive sight of a rickety wagon weighted down with unfortunate casualties of the plague. A fatigued old man tries unsuccessfully to prod the horse to move forward. He pauses often to call out, "Bring out your dead," never knowing where his services might be needed. Carelessly tossed atop the cart, an elegantly dressed woman in blue silk ignominiously shares space with the poor. In death they are equals.

"Bring out your dead," he cries, reaching down to the bottom of the heap to pat the hand of his dead wife.

His cart filled to capacity, the driver passes by a pile of human bodies stacked like cords of wood by the side of the road. Grass and weeds sprout around them; crumpled blades of grass steal out from between fingers and toes. Over two thousand corpses await the carts.

John pauses to look at the decomposing heap. Morbidly fascinated by the mass of decaying flesh, he recoils in reaction to a lifeless eye staring vacantly like a bloated fish washed up on the ocean's shore. Never before has he seen anything so repulsive, even in foul seventeenth-century London. Backing away, he comes close to tripping on the uneven cobblestones. Staying in the middle of the street to avoid contagion, he runs past a row of dilapidated tenement houses. More corpses lay decaying under the summer sun, mingled with the bursting carcasses of cats, dogs, horses, and pigs. Unable to tolerate the view of more death, John turns away when he passes a mass grave filled with naked bodies, thrown together for eternity, without benefit of ceremony.

*   *   *

Finally the young man, with life changing beyond his control, arrives at Mr. Hocke's grogshop on Ebbgate Lane.

"What can we do for you?" Mr. Hocke demands in his Norfolk accent.

Knowing he dare not drink the foul water from the Thames River, John places a ha'penny in the proprietor's dirty palm.

Politely, John pleads, "Mr. Hocke, some bread, cheese, a pint of grog, if you please," holding out a ha'penny for inspection. Hocke's grumbling and snorting provide a grim backdrop as John looks around the filthy shop. Cobwebs hang from the ceiling and drape the corners of the dark-timbered room. John idly swishes his foot, concentrating on making patterns in the sand-covered earthen floor. The fireplace contains ashes long cold but not removed. Thousands of tiny glitters of light sparkle through small holes in the window, making pinpoints of light on the blanket of soot. The sun hangs high in the sky, but soon, lengthening shadows will gather outside the door. People hurry by. John worries it might take at least an hour to press through the crowd to his destination. His world has forever changed. He cannot guess what obstacles might delay his trip down to the docks.

Hocke watches John leave and then turns to the bent-over old man in the shadows near the cold blackened fireplace, drinking grog. With a snicker he croaks, "Eh, ye ole sea dog, won't be long. Soon have another willin' crewman for Mr. Morgan."

The old sailor snorts, "Ha, ready, but not so willin', I wager."

Using the hook on the end of his right arm, Hocke prods the misshapen seaman on the shoulder. "Keep a watchful eye. Soon be sleeping like a innocent babe, he will. Wherever he lay his head, ye find him. Do ye hear?" Not waiting for an answer, he orders, "Take him direct to Morgan's barge; they'll put him aboard." Chuckling, he continues, "Why, we be doin' him a favor takin' him away from London!" Clearly threatening the old sailor, he orders, "Follow close. Must not lose sight of him. Bring a few shilling to our purses."

"Aye," comes the toothless reply. "Be glad to go to sea, meself, if'n me old crippled body could tolerate it. Why, I seen one of them *Bills of Mortality.* Pages be full of names. Canna read, but me mate says the plague hath claimed two thousand souls this week, true. Eh, summer ain't even over yet! Not yet. Long time to go."

*　　*　　*

Walking carefully past piles of litter, eyes straight ahead, John intently follows the downhill turn toward the river, not aware of the old seaman following closely behind.

Covering his nose, John passes the hot purifying fires burning in the streets just past St. Magnus Church. The fire does little to mask smells of decay from the open sewer and death. Seeking refuge from the horrors of the day, John steps in the shade of St. Magnus. Cooler air falls sweetly on his skin, lending a feeling of protection. John looks across the small square to the river, hypnotized by the various shapes created in the shadows playing on the irregular gray stones of the London Bridge. Calm water flows beneath the bridge, giving no indication of the tumult to creep in on the incoming tide.

Medieval and Tudor buildings sprawl southward across the bridge, forming a familiar jumble of shapes against the afternoon sky. Buildings, stretching several stories skyward, perch along the entire span, obscuring the Southwark bank from his view. Proprietors in bakeries and stores busily bake and sell a variety of rich breads and cakes; butchers display rich meats for their wealthier customers. Snugly tucked among the houses and stores are shops selling fine frocks.

John imagines Mam, lovely in a green frock from such a shop, bowing to the king, her red hair tied neatly with a pink ribbon atop her head.

"Dress would cost more money than ever I hope to get," John complains. "Even if I ever had an extra shilling," he snarls into the shadows, "Pa would take it. Claim it as rightfully his. "Or"—correcting himself without any regret—"he would take it, if not dead from the plague.

"Cease!" John yells, balling his fists against his ears, attempting to end his melancholy. "What is past can't come back. It's gone."

Squinting, trying to avoid the glare of the afternoon sun, John tries to look past the myriad of aged buildings precariously balanced across the bridge. Decapitated heads rest impaled on poles on the Southwark side—dozens of them. Following a custom of hundreds of years, the skulls, some with dried flesh still attached, serve as a grisly reminder to Londoners of the fate awaiting pirates, thieves, and others who have committed treason against His Majesty's laws.

"Your head be there if'n ye don't behave," Pa had threatened. "Take ye there and leave ye, I will. If'n ye ignore my bidding."

*   *   *

John now has a new set of problems and no experience to solve them. Remembering the years of his father's evil browbeating, John vowed never to use such threats on any of his own future progeny.

He decides to search for Gideon's small fishing boat at the wharf and spend the night in his friend's small craft. "Tomorrow I will float to a spot where I can view the grisly skeletal remains of the pirates. Tomorrow. Not today."

The sound of stomping boots crossing worn cobblestones arouses John from his reverie. Wanting to avoid being quarantined, he plunges into the shadows of the church and listens to the fading steps before the king's troopers file past in redlined blue cloaks. The danger passed, John rushes toward Billingsgate wharf.

Giant tangles of rope hanging from hundreds of masts look like huge spider webs silhouetted against the late afternoon sky—a forest of trees attached to hundreds of wooden boats.

*   *   *

"Them long poles, they be yards," Gideon's voice echoed in his head. "Them," he had repeated, pointing to the poles suspended parallel to the deck, "over there. Them what goes crossways." Seeing the puzzled look on John's face, he patiently explained, "Carries sails slung 'bout the center."

Understanding dawning, John pointed to the horizontal poles, nodding. "Yards stand there, just before the masts?"

"Truth," Gideon responded, "but look there"—he directed with his fingers—"at the end of the yards. If'n not careful, coulds't get yourself strung up out on the yard arm." Laughing at the look of shock on John's face, Gideon pointed to the outer third section of horizontal pole. "Right there, hang ye from the yardarm! Don't take much to condemn a man to hang."

Frightened by the prospect of such a violent act, John wondered how many people had met their end in such a fashion. Seemed to him an end swinging from the yardarms was all that worried the men in his life. Theft of a loaf of bread could get you there.

*   *   *

John quickens his pace to reach the wharf. A fugitive from the horrors of London, he walks alongside the river in the hot sun until he reaches the shelter of a dilapidated warehouse near Billingsgate steps. Even in the shadows, the glare of the retreating sun almost blinds him, blurring the edges of the warehouses. Curious, he shades his eyes, watching the dockside activities.

The slow beat of clomping hoofs announces the arrival of a horse and wagon. Wobbly wooden wheels bent under the weight of a haphazardly piled load of merchandise threaten to collapse with each rotation. Miraculously the load defies gravity, remains upright.

A loader's voice calls across the wharf to his friend, "Not busy today."

"Aye," comes a reply. "Might not earn 'nough for me supper." There is a fierceness in his voice as he explains, "Work as late as I can, I will. A new babe to feed."

A giant of a man, dressed in the distinctive striped shirt of a sailor, adds in an absurdly falsetto voice, "'Twas much busier before the plague."

"Aye," whispers John, not certain whether to cry from the dark dread the message engenders or laugh at a voice incongruous with the man's size.

*   *   *

Wary, fearful of being close to anyone coughing or showing signs of illness, Hillman takes steps to avoid the men on the wharf. From the top of the Billingsgate steps, the sight of the familiar fishing boat comforts him, but he is concerned and wonders, *Gideon ain't been near the wharf in three days. Where can he be?*

Dreading the reasons for Gideon's absence, he also fears Gideon might bar him from the boat if his friend suddenly arrives on the scene. When last they met, John did not notice the small black sores on Gideon's arms, hidden under long sleeves. Remembering how Gideon's violent coughing spasms shook the small boat, John suspects Gideon has the Black Death. *Was that only three days ago?* Probably dead. He sighs, leaning against the ancient walls of the customhouse. The ever-lengthening afternoon shadows slide past.

"Though, if he's dead, who will claim the boat? I will," he boasts without hesitation. To justify this decision, he adds, "Gideon hath no family."

Not eager to spend the night alone on the river, John begins to hope Gideon will appear. "He might force his way onto the boat. Push me out." Ashamed of his thoughts, John admits, "Though he owns it, true."

Delaying getting into the boat, John shifts the package of grog and bread over to his left hand. With the sinking rays of the sun, activity on the dock slows.

The last wagon clanks through the gate to unload its merchandise into a large cargo net dangling from a tall crane. The task completed, men walk away, mopping sweat from their eyes and scratching dark armpits. The river, thick with refuse, becomes opaque in the fading light.

Protected by the wide shadows of evening, John bounds down the steps and leaps into the creaking boat with the agility of a cat. The stale loaf of bread and container of grog tucked under his arm, he casts off the lone mooring line, throwing his bread and grog in before him. In a single motion he grabs the oars. Feeling invisible in the shadows, he fails to see the rummy eyes of the old sailor vigilantly watching him.

"He thinks he be hid in the dark, but I knows where he may be," mumbles his unknown adversary. "I be wise to the ways of young boys. He won't escape."

*   *   *

Thin beams of light stream outward from the few torches strung above the wharf, failing to adequately illuminate the night. The fouled water of the incoming tide courses its way along the southern edge of the city, dark except where an intermittent beacon of lamplight reveals a few bobbing boats. The moon is hidden. Hundreds of other craft remain unseen in the night. A few murmurs, muted sounds, cross the water—telling John he is not alone. Others have also taken refuge from the plague.

*   *   *

The old man moves out of the shadows of the customs house, vigilantly concentrating on the small boat floating in the water directly south of where he stood. An errant beacon reveals John laboring to push the boat beyond the suction of the shore. The enfeebled sailor chuckles with satisfaction as his prey gives a final push, successfully freeing the boat from the bank. The lad's victory will be short-lived; the tide will soon bring him back to shore.

Although surrounded by hundreds of people in nearly as many boats, John suffers feelings of acute isolation and fear. Surrendering his mind to endless memories of his mother and his brothers, he relives recent images impossible to forget. The boy on the verge of becoming a man imagines his mother's thin fingers clinging to the doorframe as she whispered her warnings to flee. John's mind persistently returns to a painful vision of red hair hanging in front of a careworn face on the other side of the door.

*   *   *

Shadows created by the rising moon distort and constantly change the shapes of familiar objects on the wharf. Phantom figures devoid of distinct features move across the dock. Not knowing who or what might lurk in the dark sends shivers down John's spine.

For distraction, John focuses on the silhouettes of familiar buildings standing out against the night sky; dark shapes not fully illuminated by the rising moon. Stone and brick buildings blur with their neighbors, ever changing their shapes. They are but tricks of the mind, victims of time and erosion. Crumbling walls and corners dissolve into the darkness. Fetid odors are the only indication of where an empty slaughterhouse once stood.

John knows the location of every building on the wharf, including a few leather tanneries still making fine products for the rich. The poor count themselves lucky to possess a bit of a ragbag in which to hold their possessions. How fine to keep your treasures in a leather pouch. Like a child holding a favorite toy, the lad fingers the small bag under his shirt, remembering his mam's loving laughter when he begged her for a strand of her beautiful red hair. Without his mam's advice, uncertainty of how to deal with the present situation plagues him. Oh, how he misses her steadying influence, her quiet guidance. He presses the rough material against his skin. Perhaps one day he will be able to keep her tresses in a fine bag—a red leather pouch for red hair.

*   *   *

Masts rise sharply above oak decks, their shadows intermingling with the pointed shadows of hundreds of steeples standing within blocks of the riverbank. Tolling church carillons call the faithful to prayer. Each bell has a distinctive ring recognizable to the members of its congregation. Some ring melodiously, but many not as skillfully cast are loud and harsh to the ear. He changes his position in the boat, bringing relief from the oak splinters boring into his back. The spirited tolling gives John momentary peace. Shutting his eyes, he seeks comfort by focusing attention on his God. "If He does control our lives and destinies," he whispers, "then surely all will be well." Turning his attention to the dark shadows of more distant churches, John points to each house of worship, chanting aloud to assure himself that his world has not really changed as much as he fears. "There be St. Magnus. Over there be St. Botolph, St. George, and St. Dunstan." They are all still there, a hundred count, he would wager—if anyone asked. For the first time in his life he has time to study their varied sizes and shapes as they soar high above the streets of the city of London. Most of the spires carry crosses at their tops, as if trying to touch fingers with the hand of God.

John rubs his protesting stomach. It's been hours since his last meal. Attempting to quiet rumblings and pangs of hunger, he unwraps the stale bread. A chewy object is gnashed between his teeth. Wincing in disgust, he spits out a weevil, quickly cleansing his mouth with a sip of grog. Ignoring the bitter taste, he waits for the warmth of the grog to flow through his body, hoping it will ward off the night chill.

Muted, disembodied voices of fearful men and women drift across the water. Each boat, like John's, tries to avoid intimacy with its neighbor. Voices grumble, complaining about the lack of comfort. Children whimper.

"Hungry they are," he sympathizes. "Poor babes, seeking comfort from their mothers"—comfort that is not always given.

*   *   *

Wondering what he should do next, he decides to float where the water takes him and try to avoid being sucked under the bridge. *Mam told me there be no impossible situation.*

Leaning against the gunwale, John attempts to seek enough comfort to allow himself to think and gather strength. Thus, the boat floats aimlessly while the coolness of an evening dissipates the heat of the day. Some of the more pungent odors fade as a slight breeze follows the tide in from the sea.

Rowing, John tries to avoid running into other river craft floating past him in the evening shadows. Some come adjacent and then abruptly nudge his boat. The increased rocking suggests a change in tide. Expertly sculling his oars against the intensifying current, John skillfully avoids being dragged under one of the fifteen archways beneath the bridge.

Yearning for the warmth of Jack's body next to his, John thinks back to the day King Charles ordered thousands of the city's domestic animals butchered, convinced dogs and cats carried the plague.

"He killed them all, then left the city," John grumbled. "The privilege of royalty."

A bump shakes the boat, intruding into John's reverie. A piece of rubbish grinds itself back and forth against the side of the boat. A flutter of apprehension hits like a fist in the center of his chest.

"Oh, please, God, let it not be Jack." Relief flows over him. "God's mercy, it's not Jack." Seeing a much smaller animal, he covers his nose and mouth against odors even more repugnant than before the plague began to wield its terrible scythe of destruction.

*   *   *

Even during the years of Cromwell's strict Puritan rule, John's mother had never believed that God truly wanted to forbid his children a bit of laughter, a bit of happiness, or a bit of profit for hard work. Mam, in spite of John's father's disapproval, tried to bring fun into their joyless lives.

*   *   *

On the fringe of sleep, John hears Mam's voice tell her children of the beauty of King Charles II when last she saw him in Drury Lane.

"Just back from France after Cromwell died," she described in a dreamy voice. "'Twas then they restored the throne to him. Needed a king who could laugh, we did. Not so severe," she added with a smile. "Tall and handsome—no wonder the ladies trailed after him." Embarrassed at telling her young sons this bit of titillating information, she giggled. "Oh my, not stories to tell such young ears." Her cheeks had colored, red with embarrassment.

"Not a story for young ears, indeed," his father sternly admonished, but John and his two brothers tugged on Mam's dress, teasing for a story about the king.

"Tell us what the king looks like. What clothes does he wear?" they begged.

"Oh my," she said, glad for a break in her dreary existence. Furtively glancing at her husband, she paused before answering. Weary of Puritanism, she ignored his disapproving scowl, continuing her story while she enjoyed a rare moment of amusement.

"Long and curly hair, he has—a thick black wig, I suspect. Most elegantly waved. Thick dark eyebrows sit over twinkling blue eyes. A wee mustache adorns his top lip." With a visible shiver, she sighed. "Oh, such courtly manners. Such fine clothes." She wrapped her arms around her thin body, her voice drifting off, as if trying to keep the dream to herself. "Merry they were, walking down Drury Lane," she added in an undertone. "Better days than now." She continued with a hint of bitterness in her voice, "At least we had a few years of gaiety before the plague came to kill us all off."

"Repayment for frivolity," John's father chided. "Such laughter is out of order. You will go to church and pray for forgiveness. The law requires everyone to attend church. Giddiness is strictly forbidden."

Unruffled by the gruff chastisement, John's mother suddenly jumped from her chair. Grabbing the children's hands, she danced them around the small room, her gaiety a contrast to the dour and severe looks of her husband.

"No, Mam," he laments, knowing too well that she cannot hear. "I will not cry. I am a man. Men do not cry." But inside, he felt like a small boy, younger than his baby brothers.

* * *

Another hour of loneliness passes. Body sagging, shoulders stooped in defeat, John can no longer avoid how the reality of the plague has changed his life. He moans softly so neighboring boaters cannot hear. "I will never see my family again. The Devil brought this trial upon us, certain." Revived by a sudden current of cool air, an unwillingness to be defeated emerges from a strength deep within. At that moment, John changes from a boy into a man. Sipping a bit of grog he begins to formulate a plan.

* * *

A gruff voice startles him. "Back away, blast ye! Stand off." John seizes the oars, barely avoiding capsizing the dinghy in his haste to avoid his antagonist. A child's cry flies across the water, bringing back the memory of his wee brothers and their deadly illness. Reverting to his former fears, John is certain God will punish him for leaving his poor mam to fend with so many problems. Although the law had barred his entry into their rooms, he still condemns himself for not remaining at the door, for not removing the restraining nails, one by one.

"Sick, she is. Without me, no one will help her," he moans. "They'll be locked up for forty days. By then they'll surely be dead."

Halting the rhythmic drumming of his fist against the side of the boat, John rubs a few uncontrolled tears from his eyes and scolds himself for being so weak. He tries to make sense of his predicament. Long influenced by his strong-willed mother, he refuses to be easily defeated and contemplates ways to help his family.

"Mam will scold if I take food back to the rooms. Be angry if I hire on to collect the dead," he broods, "though such a job I could easily get. In spite of the money to be earned, not many willing." It does not matter.

Deciding not to wait until morning to row toward the south shore, he uses the light of the full moon and a few bobbing torches to help measure his distance from other boats. Perhaps Southwark would provide refuge. A cry of frustration and then another vile curse floats toward him from a boat to the east. There are many such sounds on the river. Perhaps the south side will be less crowded.

The old sailor creeps along the dock, searching for his prey, hoping to catch a prize for Mr. Morgan. Determined to find his intended victim, he is prepared to search every boat until he finds the sedated John Hillman.

*   *   *

For three years, John and Gideon fished the river together. Besides the denizens of the deep, they also filled their rickety boat with mankind's discarded items. Shoes pulled off a corpse, reusable wooden barrels, and even furniture was snared in the hopes of finding willing buyers. Busy obeying Gideon's every bidding, John took little time to observe the various interesting aspects of London's waterfront, never appreciating her ugliness nor valuing her beauty. London is simply the place where he lives, where he struggles to earn a few shillings. Often they work in soupy fog, never pausing to dream of better things; he knows of no one who does. There are the rich of the city, and there are the poor. He is poor. His family needs food. That's that.

Two winters ago, the river froze after weeks of intense cold. Unable to fish, except through a hole in the ice, Gideon gave John a rare chance to take a day away from their labors. His mam took him and his brothers to slide about on wooden slates. They smiled each time little Tristram fell and struggled to regain his balance, only to be copied by wobbly Samuel. Mam and John gaily whipped the small children across the ice, savoring brief episodes of laughter, grateful for the good times—as uncommon as they were.

*   *   *

Another sip of grog increases his dizziness. The light from lanterns hanging along the wharf blur in front of his eyes, failing to illuminate the dark shadows lurking between decaying warehouses. The moon drifts behind a cloud; shadows merge and meld, making objects indistinguishable from their background. Above the blackness of London a feeble sliver of moonlight lightly brushes the church spires. Giving variety to the London skyline the silhouettes of hundreds of steeples intermingle with elbow- and spike-shaped chimneys. Other chimneys look like angry clenched fists sticking up into the shadows of night. Along the waterfront, tall, dark masts tower high above the water, commingling with shorter, less dramatic spars. The masts spread across the unlit horizon like the dark primeval forest of the New World across the sea. Anchored ships heavy with merchandise wait patiently to be unloaded.

Low stone arches prevent tall ships from passing beneath the London Bridge, but a gate near the Southwark side allows passage to the West during slack tide. On this night John keeps his distance downstream from the bridge while a high tide swirls beneath its many archways. No craft, large or small, will attempt to cross the barrier during the dark of night.

A few more sips of grog completely fogs John's vision. Ropes dangling down from hundreds of yardarms look like a nightmare of hundreds of deranged webs spun by giant spiders.

More grog—the webs turn into massive sea monsters reaching out their thin, drooping tentacles to pull him downriver toward the great bend. John rubs his eyes in disbelief. The tentacles disappear, metamorphosing back into harmless ropes. Relieved, John turns his attention to the shore.

Like a creeping fog, death slithers into every house, every alley. Like witchcraft it takes control. Shivering, drifting in and out of consciousness, he imagines foul spirits stealing through the night.

*   *   *

John's mam, along with many Londoners, took every opportunity to watch the wealthy stroll along the city streets, wearing Parisian clothes styled after the court of Versailles. John wonders if the return of gaiety brought sin in its wake and thus the plague. Was this the opportunity Satan looked for? Rumors abounded about Charles's sympathies with the French Catholics. Could the plague possibly be connected to a papist plot? Surely this evil does not lie with the God of his Puritan beliefs.

*   *   *

Restless, not quite awake, John peers into the darkness, unable to distinguish the line where the sky meets the water. Silence. Grating. The sound of something being dragged across the wharf. Are men secretly loading supplies into the holds of one of the great ships? The distorted sound, combined with cooling temperature, sends shivers down his back, causing the river of blood in his body to feel as cold as the water on which he floats. Pain stabs deep into his shoulder from being wedged against the side of the boat. Almost waking, he watches the moon climb ever higher above the horizon, lending an eerie and otherworldly feeling to his surroundings. With the passing of time, wispy feathers of fog drift across the water and darken the sky, temporarily obscuring the moon and stars. Hours pass, and occasionally John sips more grog, nibbles the bread. His tiny boat drifts between the wharf and the ancient buildings in the borough of Southwark—an area dark with taverns, vagrants, and brothels. Following the course of least resistance, the boat drifts with the changing tide. He imagines walking along ancient Roman roads, fanning out from Southwark, to the southern parts of England.

Close by, a carriage clanks over ruts etched into the large, rough cobblestone streets over hundreds of years. The clatter almost extinguishes the laughter of men on their way to seek pleasure, unmindful of the plague across the river. The narrow gate scrapes the stones as it opens into a large medieval courtyard surrounded by eight galleries. Grooms secure the horses. A gentleman is quietly escorted up the stairs to a private room in one of the galleries, finding whatever delights and comforts the inn can provide.

Drifting between sleep and reality, John dreams of finding work in one of the stables. He is strong and willing to clean stables or care for the horses. Perhaps he might find a room in the stables while he looks for a gentleman to whom he can indenture himself. Hopefully he can earn a few pence to send home to help his mam and brothers. He had never told his mam, but he once crept into the courtyard of the inn. The galleried porches lent protection from the rain for ladies and gentlemen entering the comfortable private rooms on the second and third floors. Behind ancient rippled glass windows, set into the dark oak exterior on the lower floor, he saw men sitting at tables in front of a lively burning fireplace, discussing important politics of the day.

*   *   *

His eyes increasingly heavy and grainy, he completely succumbs to the welcoming relief of sleep. In the hours before sunrise John pulls his cloak tightly about himself for protection against the falling temperature. In his new dream, he sails on a tall ship to the West Indies and then further west to the vast wilderness of the American colonies. A loud crash from the shore startles him awake. He remembers the freedom engendered in the dream; sadly, such a trip could only be a dream—an impossibility. Without indenture he can never afford the passage. Certain.

Reclosing his eyes he envisions his mother's tired face. John seeks comfort by idly stroking the small cloth bag he wears attached to the inside waist of his trousers. It is too dark to open the bag, but he can feel the lock of his mam's bright red hair tucked safely inside. Having little faith he will ever again see his family, a small tear appears in the corner of his dark eyes. As the craft drifts away from Southwark, he gratefully accepts the unavoidable oblivion of a drugged sleep. He does not feel the bump of the boat when the old sailor reaches out to grasp his arm.

CHAPTER 2

KIDNAPPED

July 27, 1665

Gasping, John desperately struggles to catch his breath.

"Eh, mate," directs a raspy voice, "soak the clodpoll again. Might add a stone to his weight. Bloody skinny. Won't make it a week at sea."

"Ain't much meat on him. Certain," a disembodied voice agrees.

"Not able to pull his weight, I wager. Hope we didn't pay more a ha'penny for him." A laugh follows a second dousing, aimed directly into his mouth. What water doesn't run down his throat courses beneath his strong chin, flowing down his thin chest and finally plopping into a puddle in the crotch of his homespun trousers. Paroxysms of coughing make it difficult for John to push strands of wet hair out of his eyes. Not able to see his tormentors, he wildly swings his arms, ineffectually trying to ward off well-aimed jabs to his head and chest.

Fighting off drowsiness, a fierce pain throbs in his head. He massages his temples in a futile attempt to awake, to get rid of the agony, and the repeated drenchings slowly drive away the drug-induced fog controlling his brain. Cruel words and taunting laughter begin to make sense. To no avail, he attempts to shut out the river of boisterous laughter flowing around him by covering his ears. He tries to resist his antagonists, but numbness squeezes the muscles in his arms and legs, making it impossible to protect himself. Ashamed of his near-nakedness, John wraps his arms around his chest as a shield against countless unfriendly eyes. Rocking on the windswept tide he tries to ignore his situation and pretend he's still floating in Gideon's boat. He isn't.

A glimpse of the ship's rail tells John its height will not allow his escape. Even if he did make it across the gunwale, it would be futile. He cannot swim. A hand tries to yank John to his feet. Fear constricts his throat.

"Up, bastard clod," demands a gruff voice close to his ear.

"Be off," John moans. "How my head does ache." Slowly, reaching for full wakefulness, he pleads, "Where can I be?" No answer quells his worries. High in the sky, the sun indicates he has slept through the night and early morning.

"Who be you?" he blurts. "Who curses me?"

Taunts and a cacophony of laughter accompany a rough voice that commands, "Up, clodpoll. Up or suffer the consequences!"

The drug-induced fog slowly diminishes, replaced by a throbbing pain in his head. Moving to a crouched position, John endeavors to gain a better view of his surroundings. For the first time he notices whip marks across the shoulders of a captive tied to a spar many feet taller than the mast on Gideon's boat. Changing his position causes every muscle in his back and shoulders to scream in pain.

A disembodied voice laughs. "Gentlemen, welcome to our pressing tender."

A gravely whisper warns, "Best stay standing, mate." Reluctantly pulled to his feet, John feels the tip of a long, coarse beard hit his face. "D'ye hear me? Be quick!" The strong arm of the sailor keeps him from crumbling onto the rough, filthy deck of the tender.

"Don't make hem angry," cautions a whisper, "or hang ye from the yardarm, the captain will! Certain."

John stumbles, hitting the deck like a hogshead of beer. The pain in his head makes the simple feat of standing too difficult to accomplish. When he attempts to re-open his eyes, objects and people swim in and out of focus.

"Where be I?" John inquires again, not yet fully realizing his peril. Shivering with dread, he instinctively knows not to waste his breath pleading. A sudden rain shower hits him in the face. When he tries to stand, he slips on the rough deck, scraping his knees in the process.

*   *   *

Eight men stand about the deck, respectfully giving their attention to a tall man wearing beautiful red boots. The man's tones are low, his words obscure.

Occasionally one of the men responds, "Aye, Captain," assenting to a command with a nod of his head, before leaving to do the captain's bidding. John stares intently at the leader's long, curly hair. Each pleat and bow was in place on his immaculate satin suit.

"'Tis the king," he whispers in awe, shocked to see the monarch on this small boat as it navigates down the Thames. Though bearing an uncanny resemblance to King Charles, a second glimpse makes John realize his foolishness. Looking at the ragged clothing and kerchiefs of the other men he suspects that his captors are pirates. King Charles would never be seen in such company. It most certainly is not the king.

Dozens of bare feet—a complete array of white, brown, and black—, line the length of the deck. Feet, ankles, and legs of all sizes and shapes extend upward into the wide openings of short trousers. Rough ropes secure the pants around a variety of fat and thin waistlines. Farther down the line other men stand in clean shirts and trousers, wearing fancy belts ornamented with gold and silver buckles.

John hears a redhead beg, "Make haste, Captain, if'n ye please. The streets be littered with death."

"Quickly, then, hoist the sail! No delay."

Looking past the captain's broad-brimmed hat, John watches the crew hoist a large canvas up the mast into the sky. The flapping sail resonates with a dull thudding sound, grabbing a breeze as it fills. The leading edge billows, reaching out toward the sea, filling the canvases as the ship sails away on the ebb tide.

Glancing astern, John watches the ship slip past the stone walls of the Tower of London on the north side of the river. William the Conqueror built the tower to impress and dominate the population of London after his victory at Hastings in 1066. From behind the high walls the Kentish ragstone of the White Tower rises to ninety feet. Blinking eyes still blurred from the effects of the tainted grog, John strains to get a glimpse of the dark archway he knows passes through the wall from the river.

*   *   *

"Traitor's gate." Gideon chortled, enjoying the effect of this news on John as he related the story of one of the many traitors ordered into the tower in the dead of night. The tower had been witness to hundreds of executions and tortures over the centuries. Gideon delighted in reciting grisly stories, laughing at John's expressed anxiety that some crime might lead to his own imprisonment.

"Relax lad, ye not be so important to be treated to the likes of the tower. Only enemies of the king languish there. Mostly highborn," he continued. "Poor ignorant man that I be, me life on the river hath taught me considerable about the olden days. I watch. I learn. I remember well the prisoners brought here from Westminster for imprisonment and execution. All have passed through that shadowy gate—even a few from the His Majesty's colonies."

A prisoner of the pirates, John feels certain his fate would take him far away from any threat of imprisonment for a very long time.

*   *   *

The river turns southward, sailing gently past the wharves and muddy banks of Wapping dock. Between the high and low watermarks stands the execution dock. The tarred body of a pirate, long dead, rots in a metal harness—a warning of the fate to be suffered by those who follow a life of crime against the king. John turns to see what effect the scene has on the men who have captured him. Not one showed an interest in the specter floating in the breeze.

John's headache returns. Darkness overtakes him once more. Unable to focus, he can barely see the tender moving closer to shore as he descends into unconsciousness. Wooden cranes tower high above, arching over his head like giant birds of prey. The pervasive odor of rotting wood and sewage, always present in this eastern slum of London, fill the air.

*   *   *

Two of the pirates throw John across a plank like a sack of baggage from the tender to the deck of a large, two-masted ship. Landing with a thump, he moans, "Now where?"

Realizing what had happen, he complains, "Threw me from one boat to another like a bag of cargo."

As he tries to raise to his feet, someone kicks them out from under him, and he crashes onto the deck. Several more bodies land on top of him, and he becomes one of a growing pile of torsos, heads, and bent arms and legs, all akimbo.

With a thump, the man with the gravelly voice completes the pile when he lands on top of John.

A black muscular leg whirls around, using his attached pink and black foot to press his bearded victim to the deck.

"Don't be so sweet on him. Hang ye up with the clod, we will," the giant warns. He stands like a statue over the pile of ragged humanity. Huge hands with square knuckles rest on narrow hips. Throwing his head back, he roars without mirth, revealing a full set of strong white teeth in an ebony face.

"Make haste. Captain commands we weigh anchor quick," the giant roars. Satisfied with the men's response he turns to the captain. "Gots a boat full of crew, now. Aye, we do."

Ignoring the giant, another pirate, Mo, turns. In an apparent move to invite friendship, he directs an exaggerated wink at John—as if two men against a common foe. With a toss of his head, the tail of Mo's scarf billows over his right shoulder. Smiling, he squares his feet on the deck as he jerks John to an upright position. Unsteady, drugs still coursing through his system, John's forward motion is stopped by the wood rail of the gunwale, and he just misses ramming his head into the face of his ragged protector.

Mesmerized by the pendulous action, John stares at the pirate's braided beard, which looks strangely like a cat-o'-nine-tails.

Pointing to the black man, Mo cautions, "That be Jeb, lad, the bos'n. Evil-tempered. Of harsh authority." John sees the truth in Mo's claim, easily imagining an evil glint blazing in Jeb's black eyes.

Mo's glance flies between Jeb and the captain. The wind in the sails muffles Mo's voice, forcing John to lean forward to hear more clearly. "And 'tis the Devil's own advocate—though he improves in spirit after his share of rum and beer.

"Captain rescued him off a slave ship, ten-odd years past. Forever at odds with me and me mates. Unhappy devil. Wife died at the hand of slavers. Tried to battle them off, he did. Mutilated the poor man, so they say. His own kind too, don't ye know? Black as ebony."

Seeing disbelief creep across John's face, Mo scowls, gruffly adding, "Give a listen, hear? When done with her—threw her to the sharks. Captain says it took five men to hold Jeb back. Fought to save her, he did." As if toying with John's emotions, for a final horror Mo coldly adds, "To show their power they made him watch the feast."

Relishing the effect of his words on their captive, satisfied with the look of pallor on John's face, Mo shrugs complacently, adding, "Eh, never ye mind, happened long ago. Captain favors him. Faithful like a dog, he is."

"Jeb thinks he be captain," John observes. "Cruel. Screams orders that everyone jumps to obey."

"Oh, ye can wager he be not. Captain be elected by the crew. Morgan be free to pick the best he can to do his bidding. So it goes. We elects Morgan, he picks Jeb to be bos'n. As long as what the captain does be in our best interest, our lot be to obey. That's the power we gives him. If'n he fail, why, we unelect him." Cackling, he adds, "Simple as that." Seeing no inconsistencies in what he is saying, Mo continues, "Course, death to them whats don't obey Captain's orders."

John's look is impenetrable as he tries to listen without expression. He is not convinced a pirate crew could unelect their captain. Waiting for a reaction from John, Mo absentmindedly scratches one of the small patches of hair dotting his chin. The long, thin strands of hair growing out of the patches are braided into a long, scrawny beard.

Mo takes a breath, as if considering what additional information he will give to the prisoner. Making a decision, he hisses across his shoulder, "Calls me Mo, they does." Swaggering across the deck, Mo cackles loudly, his thin chest straining against the red stripes of his soiled shirt. With each step, his tattered trousers droop lower around his hips. When his thin buttocks finally become exposed, Mo bunches the fabric under the rope around his waist.

"Mo is betta then nutten," he brags, motioning John aft along the deck. "Just follow me," he urges. "Show ye the ropes, I will. Act quick. To dally brings the bos'n's starter to your back. Worse yet," he cautions, "string ye up. Float through the air like a feather on the wind, ye will." Happy with the picture in his mind of John hanging, he says, "Lighter than the feather in Morgan's hat. Aye."

*   *   *

Young, inexperienced, John has not yet mastered the art of completely masking his feelings. Viewing his many adversaries, his pressured, bewildered emotions hang raw on his face. Knitting his eyebrows together, John takes furtive looks at the strange men standing around on the deck. He has seen such men down on the docks, but none as barbaric as the cast of characters on this ship. He watches, awed, when Mo sweeps his scraggly beard aside to mime his menacing message—tracing a line around his neck, Mo demonstrates where Jeb will place the rope before jerking John up to the yardarm.

"Float on the end of a rope," he screeches. "Hee, hee. D'ye hear? D'ye see?" Unmindful of the glances directed at him from the other pirates, Mo swings his arms about in wide arcs, jumping up and down in a frenzy. Abruptly, he stops and places two fists under his chin, as if trying to pull an imaginary rope away from his neck. Like a man slowly strangling, he bulges out his cheeks, biting down on his tongue until a small ooze of blood appears. His arms go flaccid at his sides, imitating death.

Alarmed by Mo's antics, John cowers against the ship's rail. Placing his hands over his ears, he closes his eyes, attempting in vain to shut out Mo's raspy giggle. Others on the ship watch him intently. Suddenly aware he is the brunt of a chorus of taunting laughter, John realizes the futility of trying to avoid Mo and his apparent fate. John shrugs his shoulders, reluctantly following aft.

*   *   *

A bizarre patchwork of hair scatters across Mo's scalp; bare patches of skin alternate with scantily seeded tufts. Each patch of hair dangles down to the pirate's midsection. It is unclear if an adversary tore out clumps during a fight or if he lost the hair through disease.

Mo turns. As he races up the ratlines, the aroma of a pig's hovel, not unlike the streets of London, trails behind. Thickly callused toes claw their way up to the yardarm. Looking as if he has lived his entire life in the rigging, Mo hangs like a monkey just above John's head. The skin of his feet is stretched and whitened wherever it presses into ropes. Thick, jagged nails press into filthy nail beds.

*   *   *

Why would God do this—bring me to such a place?
Complying with Mo's orders, John struggles not to sob, certain it is God's punishment for all his past

wickedness. His poor, sick mam is past the age of thirty, maybe thirty-five—at least twice his age. Every exertion brings spasms of coughing and sweating to a woman already worn out from too many babes. Now the plague threatens his family and all of London.

Sick and exhausted, she depended upon him to help with the wee ones when he returned to their rooms each night. He didn't mind, certain she would soon die. Although his da seemed to love Mam, he seldom helped her with any of the labors. Most nights Da sat slumped over the table, seemingly nailed to the seat. His movements are imperceptible until he tips the bottle of grog to his mouth. 'Twas his regular place until yesterday, when, after a few days of illness, he died of the plague.

John misses wee Tristram and sweet little Samuel. "If I could just go home and see me lovely mam, I would go to church with a new devotion." Lowering his eyes, he sadly adds, "Not just pretend to pray." Sliding his fingertips along his hip, he feels the presence of the pouch. It's there, safe. No matter where he goes, a part of his mam will always be with him—in this cloth pouch and in his heart. Irresistible sleepiness overcomes him. Falling asleep, he senses Mo standing over him, grim, without humor.

*   *   *

As he drifts down the Thames, reality mingles with dreams in the mist of John's consciousness. Occasionally he awakes and looks around the edges of the tall mast, where birds soar higher into the sky than any man could possibly go. The sun struggles to burn away the haze drifting across the Thames. Each bend in the river takes him farther away from home, twisting an ache in his heart that exceeds the throb in his head. His fingers trace the rough edges of the clotted blood still clinging to the laceration atop his head and then move to rub the smarting cut on his left cheek. His tongue roams his mouth, seeking the small wound where his cheek has been punctured by a tooth. The pirates ignore him, completely indifferent to whether he lives or dies, certain that escape is impossible. These bronzed men fear nothing, not even pain. As he drifts back to sleep, John feels fortunate that he received as few blows as he did.

Shaking John awake, Mo points out a large man-of-war passing them on its way downriver, toward the sea. Three masts soar into the air. Her bowsprit splits the clear afternoon air as she beats ahead on a tack toward the next bend in the river.

"A ship of His Majesty's Navy," Mo says. "Calls it the Royal Navy. Fancy name for a stink hole worse than the one what carries us. See all the guns? I grant ye they have more 'n us. Guess there be at least forty." Then, concentrating his attention on the sailors, he adds, "Poor bleeders. No one in their right mind wouldst join the navy. Pirates gets the best food." Giggling, he adds, "Course, we captures it from others. Pirates have more to say 'bout where they goes, what they does," he adds.

The navy. John notices the red-and-white-striped shirts worn by the crew and the fine gold trim on the blue uniforms worn by an officer standing at the stern. *What an adventure it would be—life in the Royal Navy. But no, I be a prisoner on this pirate boat, dreading me fate.*

Mo chatted on. "See that hill? Royal Park at Greenwich. Rare for us common folk to get in that place. Royalty parades about at leisure." He points his finger to the south. "Look, there. A fine Lord on horseback. Should dock and relieve them from some of their finery."

Saying nothing, John thinks it unlikely the nearby Royal Navy would allow such antics.

Watching John carefully to see if he believes him, Mo brags, "Lived near here as a child. Just me ole lady and me."

*   *   *

John tenses at Jeb's unsmiling approach. Fists clenched, eyes shifting from side to side, three unsavory sailors swagger boldly behind their boatswain. A giant of a man, towering at least six to seven inches above the others, even Jeb, drags a squirming prisoner along by his convenient pigtail. Mo places a calming hand on John's arm to keep him from pulling away, from looking for a place to hide.

"Steady, lad. Scars ain't lookin' for you."

John could not help but wonder how Scars had earned his spectacular wound. A jagged six-inch scar rips across the giant's bushy right eyebrow, rushing behind the patch over his right eye and finally curving into a shallow jagged cavity just below the bone of his cheek. He gives the appearance of an angry man in continuous pain.

Trying not to draw attention to himself by staring, John furtively looks at the other sailors. A variety of colored scarves worn low on their foreheads do nothing to change their similar appearances. As if they were cut from the same design mold, their muscular bodies move in unison, their naked feet purposefully striding across the deck. The silk kerchiefs partially cover deeply tanned skin, pulling taut over rugged faces. Beards of various lengths hang from determined jaws. None smile. Cold, unflinching eyes examine each prisoner.

John, the youngest of the three captives, wonders why they kidnapped him.

"Curse me," he sputters. "Not wary enough. Too busy with worries about the plague."

Before John has time to repent his blasphemy, strong fingers trace through his long hair. Jerking him backward by twisting a clump at the nape of his neck, one of the men drags John unceremoniously across the deck, flinging him into a growing pile of prisoners strewn under the main mast. Opening his eyes, John finds himself staring up at Captain Morgan. Standing on the hatch, his blue eyes devoid of warmth, Morgan peers down at his captives; a malevolent smile flits across his lips.

To Morgan's side, Jeb leans nonchalantly against the mast, cleaning his teeth with a splinter of oak. When all the prisoners are in place before him, the boatswain confronts each man with a rough piece of paper containing many signatures.

"Here be the rules of the ship. Ye must sign," he orders.

"The pirate's law." Not put off by the confusion crossing the prisoners' faces, he threatens, "Our articles say what ye can and cannot do. Sign," he shouts over the rising wind and the flap of the sails. "Fight with us, ye gets a fair share of the prizes we capture."

John looks at the paper, pretending he doesn't understand the written words. "If I don't sign?" He quivers.

"Chop ye up," taunts a pirate sporting a pitch-black beard.

"Throw ye to the fishes," another jeers, twirling the tail of the bright yellow scarf around his head.

A short, skinny sailor pulls up his low-riding trousers and bullies, "Deserve no better." Grabbing a sword with his right hand, he places the sharp edge just under John's chin. Caressing the blade with gnarled fingers, he pleads to Jeb, "Lets me take a quick first slice."

Captain Morgan watches the unfolding drama. Mocking the prisoners with a satirical grin, Morgan decides his overly enthusiastic crew has gone far enough with their goading—a sport they all enjoy.

*   *   *

Morgan just spent a year furnishing his vast estate in the west of England. On his departure from Cornwall, he assured his mistress, "One more trip will provide enough money to support me in fine fashion for the rest of my life." Returning to London, Morgan quickly secured a sturdy brig and initiated a systematic search for his old crew in the public drinking houses. In less than an hour he found Mo and Jeb in the Crooked Cock, immediately hiring them to snare a band of pirates.

Morgan promised, "Aye, mates, one final voyage, and we all retire richer than your wildest dreams."

Mo and Jeb, sent to locate their old crew, pulled them out of one grimy pub after another. Most of their old mates were found within a few hundred yards of the waterfront, but by the end of a week they still needed three able-bodied men for their planned voyage of piracy. Hocke, a proprietor of a nearby grogshop, eagerly agreed to drug the grog of likely victims and bring their unconscious bodies to the barge. True to his word, Hocke completed the roster for Morgan. When the old sailor from his pub found John insensible, he kidnapped him out of the fishing boat. With the help of Morgan's pirates, they unceremoniously dumped the kidnapped lad onto the waiting tender.

The last recruitment completed, Morgan ordered the transfer of his prisoners to the ship. Not eager to have any of their bloodthirsty crew escape, the boatswain quickly pulled away from shore and guided the small craft downriver to the waiting brig. When everyone had boarded the eight-gun, two-masted ship, Morgan ordered all the sailors to sign the laws by which the pirates lived—the Articles.

*   *   *

Morgan lays a firm restraining hand on the wrist of the pirate most eager to cut John's throat. All the men turn their eyes away from the other two prisoners to focus on John; impatiently, they await his answer. Once signed, the Articles give Morgan complete control of the brig.

"No," John insists, "I cannot."

After an imperceptible nod from Morgan three pirates grab the reluctant sailor, roughly chaining him to the main mast. Jeb brutally brings the bos'n starter down on John's back, and air whooshes from his lungs from the force of the blow. John tightens his muscles in anticipation of another strike. A satisfied smile crosses Jeb's face, as he raises the bos'n's starter. Jeb is more than prepared to demonstrate his power and control. Believing his death a certainty, John gratefully accepts the darkness of unconsciousness that comes with the whip.

*   *   *

Determined to wake John up and for him to sign their paper, the pirates shake his body like a ship in a hurricane. Startled, fully awake, John raises his arms over his head to avoid receiving additional blows. Silently entering the tableau, Mo leads John away from the fray. Surprised at Mo's sudden move, the pirates reluctantly allow John to be pulled from their grasp.

Protectively, Mo sooths, "Don't ye fret. Jest sign with an *X.*" Winking conspiratorially, Mo adds, "Gets the cat off your back. Don't ye know." John listens, trying to ignore his stinging back.

"Sign, fool," Mo insists. "'Tis the smart thing to do. Don't concern yourself. If'n Navy catches us, ye won't be hung as a pirate," he reasons. "Only Captain and bos'n gits hung up. Just claim ye be kidnapped." Adding another lie to his encouragement, he adds, "None will know ye signed a pact with the Devil. D'ye see? Jest makes a *X.* That's all."

John reflects. His refusal to sign the Articles might not be worth this continued intolerable abuse. "I'll think a bit more about it."

*   *   *

Isaac and Willem whisper together at the base of the mast. Even if they sign the pirate's code of conduct, any escape from Jeb's continued lashing will be only temporary. Their reprieve depends entirely upon Jeb's mood. Clenched teeth and tightened jaw muscles attest to their unspoken fear and anger. Both wonder why they have come to such an end: captives on a pirate ship.

Isaac averts his eyes to avoid Jeb's threatening look. Even throwing up his arms to fend off further blows does not save him. Two more strikes of the cat send both Isaac and Willem into the hold, backs streaked red.

After a slight nod from Jeb, Scars leaps forward. Jerking back John's head by knitting his fingers through his victim's unbraided hair, he draws a long, curved machete lightly across John's throat. Bright blood beads up on the cut. Jeb cried out, "Well, what's it to be? Death—or your mark?"

Released, John drops to his knees. Grabbing his throat, choking, John spits out, "What do they say?"

Jeb, patiently controlling his anger, "Well, now, lad, in here ye promise to obey the captain's orders. Simple enough. If ye tries to run away, we maroon ye at the next deserted island. Gives ye one bottle of powder, one bottle of water, one small arm, and some shot." After further thought, he adds, "When and if you're trusted to have such a weapon, that is. Captain ain't likely to give a new man a pistol."

Mo chimes in, "Cap to the pipe, if'n foolish 'nough to smoke in the hold."

John asks, "What happens if its not capped?"

"Ye be lashed. Simple fact. Ye be lashed. Or"— Mo cackles to emphasize the point—"ye blows us up! Wouldn't like that! Devil be blessed, we wouldn't. In no hurry to visit sea serpents down below."

"Ye be marooned or shot if ye steal," Jeb adds, rubbing his hands together gleefully.

Mo leans close to John, trying to whisper. His foul breath makes John draw back. Unperturbed by John's withdrawal, Mo continues, "Marooned or shot. Maybe both. Bad end to be left alone to die on a godforsaken island."

"Fightin," warns Jeb, "gets ye forty strikes from the cat, lackin' one. No shirt. Ye gits it right on your bare back." Giving John a low bow, he adds with malice, "I be most willin' to oblige ye."

"Ask him what ye gits if'n ye sign," Mo encourages.

"And if I sign?"

"Shares in the prizes. Fair and square. Captain gets one full share, plus half. Carpenter, gunner, and me as bos'n each gets a share and a quarter."

Mo counters, "Shares the rest with the others. One share, true count. Fair."

"Course," Mo chuckles, changing his previous statement, "If'n ye agrees you're a pirate, ye could suffer the hangman's noose. Could happen. If'n ye gits caught. But not likely." Warming to his litany of warnings, he adds, "Certain death if'n ye rape unwillin' women. Other mates hang ye. Willing to help, I am! Gentlemen to women, we be."

"'Nough said!" screams Jeb. "Take him below till he makes his mark."

Glimpsing the unsmiling faces of his captors John instinctively tries to bolt over the rail—better to drown than to live with such heathens. Cruel hands prevent his escape, binding his arms tight against his body. A tumble into the gloom of the hold lands him atop Isaac and Willem. The hatch closes, plunging them into darkness.

John whimpers, "Must plot my escape. Need a plan. No help will come from any on this ship." He saw it in their eyes.

*   *   *

Cold, unwilling to face the hopelessness of his situation, John crawls away from his fellow prisoners as far as possible in such a small space. The hold is filled with barrels and rough cloth containers. In the darkness he feels for the edge of a rough sack, pulling it over his shoulders in the hopes of finding a small measure of warmth. Fear fills the air, sucking the warmth from the prisoners' bodies. Even in their enforced confinement, John avoids speaking but can hear Isaac and Willem whispering, discussing their options. John does not speak or touch them, even for warmth. Hunger gnaws, increasing John's fears and rage.

*   *   *

Hours later, under the glow of a rising sun, the crew drags the frightened trio out to stand before Jeb. John tries not to show his fright. Shaky hands give testament to William and Isaac's. Standing over the captives, Jeb pokes each man in turn with the leather tip of the bos'n's whip until they sign their mark. Mo prances about, chanting, "Captain has absolute power. Not one disobeys his orders during hostilities." With a satisfied smirk, he adds, "Death, certain, if'n ye do. Articles be law."

Inwardly terrified, John, again refuses to sign the paper. Impatient, Morgan nods, bringing a disfigured pirate forth to again throw John into the shadows of the hold.

Oh, how he aches. Attempting to ignore the pangs of pain and hunger, John focuses on the constant sloshing of water against the prow as the brig forces its way toward the sea. Above his head, fiddlers play vigorously, unerringly stroking the passage of time. The players seem to follow the cadence of the wind and water. Laughter and the roar of the wind accentuate the rhythm, as if a giant metronome were leading their way.

Sharp nails on tiny paws skitter across his leg, reminding John of his predicament. Certain the scratches come from a rat, he dares not move, afraid he might incite the rodent to chew his leg.

"Keep away," he growls, groping for a heavy object to use as a club. Stomach gnawing, he wonders if he can find the rat's food source. Afraid to move in the dark, he attempts to distract himself from his misery by tapping his fingers in time with the agreeable cadence of the fiddle.

*   *   *

Grating noises announce the sliding open of the hatch. The light of the fading sun dimly illuminates a small section of the hold. John squints at the silhouette of a man in slow descent down the ladder, not recognizing Mo until he creeps up beside him.

Once again, Mo attempts to cajole John into signing the Articles, offering food and drink. John shakes his head slowly at the promise of extra grog. Seeing the futility of his nagging, Mo crows about the wealth to be seized on the high seas.

"Sign on, lad. Great riches, if'n ye sign." Eagerly he urges, "Captain be patient this day. Short of hands. Ye gets equal shares in the prizes we takes as we goes to the Indies." Draping his arm across John's shoulder, Mo cunningly extols the benefits of piracy; his fetid breath in the close quarters of the hold makes John feel nauseated.

"Articles gives us an equal vote about where we goes. What we does." Mo squints his left eye to help him see John more clearly in the beam of light dimming his vision. Without warning Mo raises his right fist and startles John when he proclaims, "Free and equal! Don't ye know? We are! Think, lad, if not here, these men be working as serfs for some lord. Never a chance to do their own bidding, always under the thumb of the master." Then, as if to emphasize his claim, he proudly shouts, "Equal!"

*   *   *

John, determined not to give in to the ways of the pirates, boldly challenges, "I cannot join your ungodly troop."

For the first time, Mo no longer portrays himself as the friendly advisor. An undeniable threat lies behind his words. "I advise ye to sign, lad." Squinting the lids over his pale green eyes, Mo still hopes to make a convert to his way of life without force. Smiling broadly, Mo indicates with his soiled index finger where John must place his mark.

John continues to resist. Mo hisses, "Sign, blast ye!" Drawing back, Mo shrewdly calculates the lack of effect of his forceful words. Changing his approach, Mo makes a surprising announcement. "Soon be captain of me own ship. Likes ye, lad. Ye can be on me crew."

Not able to hide his amazement, John doubts the truthfulness of Mo's bragging. Could this scraggly— indeed, filthy—man have a ship of his own? Morgan looks like a captain with his shiny breeches, glistening hose, flowing black wig, and elegant manner of speaking. What impertinence for Mo to think he could ever compare to Morgan! He does, however, think both men capable of evil doings.

Not easily fooled by Mo's bravado, John is determined to avoid signing the pirate's contract. "It can too easily be broken by Morgan, if it serves his purpose. I trust him not."

Mo shrugs his thin, muscular shoulders, his voice neutral as he pushes John up the ladder to the weather deck. "'Tis time to go before Morgan. Up ye go."

*   *   *

Jeb forces him to his knees, repeating his order that John must sign the Articles. Although seeing no sympathy in the eyes peering down at him, either bravely or foolishly, John persists in his resistance. He fears his God and his mother's disapproval more than death. Life has always been short on the streets of London; another twenty years and he would be dead, no matter what he did today.

"Sign or hang from the yardarm. That be the penalty," threatens Morgan, pointing up to the outer quarter of the yard. "A proper end for foolish men."

"Pardon, sir, I cannot sign," John says, bowing his head.

Raising his head, Morgan blinks his cold blue eyes in disbelief at John's show of politeness and respect. He strolls in a tight circle around John, who tenses under the intensity of the stare. Then a new look, one of surprise, spreads over Morgan's face. Approval follows surprise for the respect Morgan erroneously thinks has been extended to him in the word *sir.* Turning to Jeb, he declares, "Respect comes from this brave lad, even under the threat of death." Turning to the pirates surrounding the scene, Morgan sneers, "Our crew would do well to follow the lad's example. He shows me respect."

Leaning toward Jeb, Morgan whispers, "Could be a possible asset to us, once we win him over to the advantages of pursuing the sea." To Mo, whom he had long considered a trusted associate, he patiently explained, "He resists now because of a natural fear that belongs to one so young—and that blasted religion of his. 'Tis inexperienced. We can influence him."

Morgan grabs the paper and quill, signing John on as a forced man. With a nod, Jeb raises his starter and brings it down on John's back, bellowing, "Now comply with my orders, or ye won't live to see London again."

*   *   *

The brig continues on its journey toward the open waters of the English Channel. A curse from Jeb warns John that the snap of the bos'n's starter will soon meet his back, a testament to Jeb's power. A laugh drifts across the few feet between John and his tormentor. A flash of white teeth and threatening taunts precede the force of the whip. "Watch for the cat. Here, kitty, kitty. Beware the scratch of the cat."

John reaches to finger the bright red furrows streaking across his back. Walking away, Jeb warns, "Caution, ye be on no bloody cruise for the king! Grab them buckets. Gits to work."

"Curse the king," a pirate shouts across the deck. "Just gits to work."

Cowed into submission, John snaps up the bucket. In one smooth throw the slop flies over the side, hitting the water with a heavy plop just barely heard above the wind whispering through the sails. How can they curse King Charles? "He be king, after all—protector of our faith. No one should question his wisdom; 'tis ungodly to revile the king." After a moment's reflection, he reconsiders. "Though true, he lives a merry life."

John heard the gossip about King Charles throughout the streets of London. All know the king is frequently seen with his mistresses, going to the theater on Drury Street or to entertainment in Covent Gardens. Many guessed the king to be secretly Catholic. It made sense—after all, he took refuge with the Catholic French following the beheading of his father, Charles I, and the Catholic king protected him.

*   *   *

By the time of Oliver Cromwell's death, the people of London had tired of his and Parliament's puritanical rule. After the short, bleak rule of Cromwell's son, Richard, the people of England invited the son of the beheaded king to return and restore the monarchy. The English did not trust a Catholic sovereign. Charles II claimed to be Protestant, but claims are one thing and truth another. "Perhaps, as some think, he brought the plague to us all."

*   *   *

John awoke from his reverie, his thoughts intruded upon by Mo's patient directions. "Cease the daydreaming, lad. Empty them slops at the bow of the ship, past the fo'c's'l." John nods. Astonished by Mo's flexible approach, he walks the short distance to the nose of the ship. Looking down, he becomes instantly dizzy from the movement of the water going swiftly past the prow.

"Oh, I'll fall down into the deep," he yells, grabbing at the nearest rope to maintain his balance.

"Gits over there," Mo demands. "Stands on the platform over there." John hesitates but gropes his way to the bow of the ship.

"There," Mo repeats, pushing John toward the small platform. "Stand there, on the beak's head."

John steps onto the landing. When the boat rises on a small wave, he steadies himself by grabbing the edge of the sail.

"Slop goes out over the bow." Mo demonstrates, snatching the bucket before dumping its contents overboard. "D'ye see?"

When the wind changes to port, John again clutches the sail, not resisting when Mo pries away his death grip, patiently placing the new sailor's hand on the thick rope securing the foresail to the forward mast.

"Leave go the sail. Latch on the fo'stay, if'n ye must."

"The fo'stay?" asks John, bewildered by the confusion of the rigging and the man who seemed able to hang from it without effort.

"The rope, fool! Stay what holds the bowsprit to the fo'mast.

Grabbing the heavy rope, John leans out over the water, curling his toes around the edge of the beak's head as he seeks false security.

"Gots your balance, boy?"

John replies with a doubtful, "aye", uncertain how to keep from slipping into the water while he dumps the bucket of slop.

Laughing, Mo calmly points his finger. "Dump it. There. There!"

When John hesitates, impatience creeps into Mo's voice. "Out there, damme."

Reacting to the look of repulsion spreading over John's face, Mo mocks, "Won't stick. Bow be washed as it passes through the water. D'ye sees?"

Closing his eyes, John wildly sends the first bucket of slop out over the beak's head. Flowing down over the starboard bow, it sticks to the ship for a moment and is then washed off as the brig passes through the waves.

Holding his nose, Mo lets out a laugh. "Been on boats long time since. Offal smell always offends." Patting John on the back, he smugly observes, "Ye be lucky. Water smooth today."

John doesn't think the water smooth at all. He is, however, grateful the orders are coming from Mo instead of Jeb, whose wickedness, blackness, height, and physical size frighten him. Feeling it is to his advantage to throw another bucket of slop as quickly as possible—his life is most likely dependent upon it—John extends the bucket far out in front of the beak's head. A shriek halts him midthrow.

"Damme, lad, don't lose the bucket!" Mo screams, forcing John's arm and the bucket back within the confines of the brig. "Dropping it overboard be bad luck." Calming his voice, he explains, "No place to go in the middle of the ocean to replace lost buckets. Ship's carpenter ain't got time to make another. Too busy making spars, mending sails—sharpening swords."

A crooked grin captures the corners of John's mouth as he considers the irony of his situation. He wrinkles his brow, his eyes darkening as he allows his arm to be pulled back. What could possibly be worse luck than what he has already suffered?

*   *   *

A sharp contrast exists between the captain's clean, fashionable clothing and that of the dirty, unkempt pirates. Keeping his eye on John, Mo notices John's interest in Morgan and quietly confides, "Captain's got fine airs, he has! Likes to call himself 'gentleman.' A buccaneer, bleedin' pirate, I calls him."

Although surprised that Mo dares to speak so derisively with other pirates close by, John remains silent.

"An adventurer, give him that," Mo snarls. "Hath his own fine cabin. Granted to him by the suffrage of the majority."

"From whence does the captain come?" John asks. "Have heard that accent in the streets of London. Men from Wales, they say." Lowering his voice, he adds, "Heard it whispered they be the Devil's own. Can put a curse on you."

"If'n ye call being starved, whipped, and hung up the work of the Devil, then the Devil he be." After a pause, Mo adds, "I wager." Rubbing his rough chin, he muses, "Well, we all must die for certain. Maybe death is betta for some than life be for others in this stink 'ole." Wisely, he intones, "Death be the final port of call."

*   *   *

Encouraging Mo to talk about Morgan, John observes, "Well, looks like the Devil to me. Pointed beard. His cold blue eyes drill right through me."

Cautious, Mo lowers his voice to a whisper. "Devil he may be. Some believe so. For certain, he be an adept cheat. I warn ye, avoid playin' him at cards. Watched him, I have. Can shift a card with such address 'tis impossible to discover him."

With his two remaining rotted teeth, Mo mindlessly chews the inside of his mouth. Squinting, he recalls the flash of fire he had seen spit out of Morgan's gun.

"Seen him shoot a man, once," Mo confides. "Captain accused me mate of cheatin' at cards. Some boats outlaws gambling. Wager they have less killin'."

*   *   *

Free of the drug's effects, John is more alert, performs his simple duties, and begins to dream of escape.

Thinking no one is observing his movements, John focuses on Morgan's control of the men, ship, and sails. If he can understand the man's moods, strengths, and weaknesses, John hopes, he can implement a plan of escape. John recognizes that an insatiable need for respect might be Morgan's greatest weakness. *The captain insists the pirates address him as sir.* John will watch and see.

Morgan stands alone on deck, sunlight reflecting off the smooth texture of his clean, well-groomed hair. A red ribbon secures a tangle of long, black ringlets behind his head, a dark contrast to his pink brocade coat. Unbound, his hair would reach below his shoulders. A strong, flowery perfume follows wherever he walks. Two thin patches of hair cover his upper lip, separated by a narrow isthmus of skin. John wonders how Morgan keeps the mustache trimmed, how he maintains the sharpness of the small point of a beard on his chin.

"Ho," Mo informs John, "Morgan hath a slave—well, two, if ye counts Jeb. Takes care of his needs. Lucky he ain't. Suffer he does."

Looking at the captain, John links this bit of information with the man before him, considering how it might enhance his possibilities for escape. He carefully studies the other pirates, not daring to venture a direct look at anything or anyone, fearful someone might decide to blind him for his curiosity. Each pirate carries no less than one sword. Mo says that in battle the toughest pirates carry two or even three. Other weapons abound. All carry knives and daggers—with the exception of the new captives, who are not allowed to carry anything with a sharp edge. The cutlasses stand like soldiers in a rack at the foot of the main mast, sharp steel at the ready in case of attack. Jeb carries the only whip, using it liberally on the newly abducted for minor infractions of the rules.

*　　*　　*

Mo's constant chatter plays like the shriek of a poorly tuned fiddle, constantly bursting into John's thoughts. He is convinced the captain has made his steady companion responsible for his safety. Determined to maintain a truce, John attempts to pay attention to Mo's every word.

It makes sense; the captain of a ship would have a slave. The others certainly have no need for such services; they seem to revel in their filth. So if they don't have servants or slaves, what do the pirates do with their misbegotten gains? "Women, gambling, gold," John murmurs—a spending spree in every port. That's most likely where Morgan bought the thick gold chain he wears, a brilliant stone sparkling in the center of a nugget of gold. Most likely the diamond was yanked from some hapless woman's throat during piracy or gained in payment for a gambling debt.

John mindlessly rubs the rough fabric of his trousers, the coverings of a poor man, and then stares at the remarkably soft fabric of Morgan's breeches. How neatly they tuck inside the tops of his soft leather boots. It doesn't take extraordinary insight to judge the man who rules the ship.

"Full of pride. Easily provoked. Shouldn't want to be near him when he takes offense." John has no idea of the cruelty lying ahead.

The men call him captain, as if he has no first name. "Maybe the Devil has no name. God, protect me."

Although he was elected by the suffrage of the majority, the men remain wary of this man of mercurial moods.

*   *   *

Mo cautions John about the hierarchy of the crew. "We elect Morgan captain. Navigates better than most, with superior knowledge and boldness. Hath great skills in battle. No denying he gots us the brig." Thoughtfully, Mo adds, "Brags he's born of the sea. I've no reason to doubt him."

As an afterthought, remembering John's previous question, Mo nods toward his captain. "Aye, comes from the west of England."

John responds, "As I suspected, a devil."

*   *   *

Quietly looking out to sea, Morgan is unaware that the two pistols swinging from a silk ribbon around his neck frighten John.

"Hadn't noted them before," John chides himself, exhaling a loud whistle of air. "Eyes too cloudy from the grog. From here forward, I must keep a sharp eye and avoid becoming his mark."

Blue eyes ablaze, Morgan disdainfully looks down the length of his nose. Pointing his chin and the tip of his beard toward the sky, he skillfully avoids eye contact with his shipmates. He is a caricature of King Charles, but no one laughs at his haughty manner or questions his control over the ship's occupants.

*   *   *

Deep in thought, John is completely unaware of how long he has leaned against the ship's rail and does not realize he is no longer emptying the pail. During his intense scrutiny, he fails to see Morgan give a curt nod to Jeb. John is unprepared for the downward thrust of the whip across his back and shoulders. Falling to the deck, he stares at the pale underside of Jeb's black fingers as they grip the wooden handle of the starter.

"Up with the slop bucket." Jeb's shattering scream pierces the air. "Gets back to work. Work or death. Your choice." Jabbing the end of the whip under John's jaw, Jeb threatens his victim further by coming almost nose to nose. "No free passage. Nay, not one be concerned with your death." before he turns away. "Ye may soon welcome death more than making the next port of call."

CHAPTER 3

THE PIRATES

At Sea

July 31, 1665

Rivers of crimson streak across the sky, spreading variegated reflections across the white canvases that billow outward from the masts. John's expectation of ever seeing London or his mam again dims. But an interest in the workings of the ship and his new life becomes irresistible as the Braque sails east to the mouth of the River Thames. After passing by the North Foreland lighthouse, the crew turns the ship south. A broad expanse of salt water unlocks before him as the great chalky cliffs of Kent recede into the distance. John is determined to be strong. He vows to survive long enough to again see the legendary waters that separate England from her traditional enemy, France

They sail along the coast on a southwesterly course. Off the starboard the island that is England is obscured by low clouds. A dense fog replaces the clear, cloudless morning. Would the fog ever lift or the sun reappear? It becomes increasingly impossible to tell where the sky ends or the water begins. Then, almost as quickly as it had disappeared, the sun reemerges, flickering upon the water for miles in every direction. There are no dark alleys on the open water in which to hide oneself from the sun's brilliance; sunlight bathes everything not protected by the shadow of the topsails. It will become even more intense after they cross the Tropic of Cancer.

Inflating his lungs with the fresh sea air washes away the memory of the stale, putrid odors of a dying London. Never had he breathed air so pure or seen a sky so clear.

Below the weather deck lies a different situation. Fouled air from unwashed people, chickens, and pigs permeates every crack and crevice. To escape these smells, most men prefer to sleep topside. As night falls again they use their sea chests as pillows, claiming a small space on the upper deck.

*   *   *

Noon. The sun stands at its zenith. Raising the cross staff to his shoulder, Captain Morgan measures the angle of the sun to the sea's horizon, estimating their latitude, or distance from the equator. That completed, Morgan carefully lays six feet of a splendidly carved instrument on the deck.

"Toss the log line over the taffrail," he orders.

Jeb prepares to throw the line, knotted at intervals of fifty feet, eight inches. Grabbing the hourglass, one of the pirates rotates it, waiting until the bottom of the glass fills with sand before flipping it back over, preparing to measure their. Speed over the water's surface.

"Toss," Weasel's voice bellows above the flutter of sails.

Using a thick, muscular arm to cast the line over the stern, Jeb allows it to feed out into the water, counting how many knots on the rope cross the stern before the top of the glass empties of its sand. Curling his thick lips over the stem of his unlit pipe, Jeb chews the stalk and concentrates on the essential task of determining the ship's velocity. "Six knots," he advises Morgan. "We be doin' six knots."

Anticipating Morgan's order, Jeb calls, "Set all sail, Captain? 'Tis a fresh wind."

"Leeway?"

Jeb picks up the log. Heaving it over the stern, he supports the rope, guiding it until it comes to rest across one of the one-hundred and eighty points of a semicircle carved into the wooden taffrail.

"Line taut at one hundred," Jeb calls out.

"Ten points off the wind," Morgan records on the log board. Looking back over his shoulder, Morgan nods at Jeb in the unspoken language of men who have toiled side by side for many years—men who mysteriously predict each other's thoughts and intentions.

"With a fresh following wind and a full sail, we'll be off Weymouth in the blink of a rat's eye." Confident of fortune ahead, Morgan commands, "Set all sail!"

Jeb nods. "Weymouth."

Jabbing his clay pipe into the air, Morgan punctuates his words in his characteristically staccato fashion. "Will make great way today. Wager some unwary merchant ship be waiting down the channel." His laugh revealed a perfect set of small white teeth; none had been lost to scurvy. His jaw set, a determined Morgan promises his crew, "By God, a silver ducat to the sharp-eyed sailor who spots the first sail!"

*   *   *

"Hands to the topgallant," Morgan shouts over the wind.

"Lay on sail," Jeb shouts, urging the men to increase the area of sail available to kiss the wind.

"Send down the yard lines!"

Avoiding the snap of the whip across their backs, John and Isaac hurry to perform their duties. Agile as children, seasoned mariners climb the tarred ratlines to the yardarms, fantasizing about the booty soon to be theirs. Near the forecastle, deck hands loosed halyard and sheet ropes from belaying pins.

Encouraging the crew to haul on the lines that raise the sails, a pirate called Jason sings a chantey tune. "We'll haul the bowline so early in the morning."

Returning his chant, the crew calls out, "Haul the bowline, the bowline."

"Haul!" roars the sail master as each coordinated pull unfurls the topgallant to catch the wind, reaching out like the wings of a giant seabird.

Startled by the sound of the wind smacking the canvases, John covers his ears and wonders if the mast will hold or crack under the intense stress.

"Set taut!"

"Mains'l," Morgan commands. As the crew casts off the gaskets, the mainsail is loosened.

"Let fall," Morgan orders. A soft rumble fills the air as a lusty wind forces the vacuum out of the draped mainsail. Within minutes it billows before the following wind. Dozens of screeching seabirds, forced off their perches on the yardarm when the canvases were released, rise haphazardly to soar hundreds of feet above the foam. The cacophony of the seabirds' strident shrieks follows the speeding ship down the channel. Feathered creatures swoop down in a seemingly choreographed dance, capturing bits of garbage following in the ship's wake.

* * *

To complete the dangerous business of securing the square sails, the free ends of the attached lines are passed through wooden blocks. Making fast the rigging, the sailors twist the ropes in figure eights about the belaying pins.

Breaking through the clouds, the sun spreads a soothing balm across John's bruised face and shoulders. Never before aboard a vessel propelled by more than a small, three-foot sail, he is exhilarated as they fly like a feather before the wind. The mainsail casts a sudden shadow, obliterating the rays of the sun. Shivering, he moves out of the shadow and looks skyward, relieved to see the sun still hanging in the sky.

* * *

"Lovely to see, ain't they?" intrudes a hissed whisper from a small mouth lying below a pair of dark hazel eyes, shaded by bushy eyebrows. As if reading the questions in John's mind, the pirate continues, "Watch close. Addin' the sprits'l and tops'l takes us up on the wind." Not knowing one sail from another, John studies the large sail on the main mast.

"That one be the mains'l," he explains. "We brail up the main course in strong winds. Furling the sails reduces strain on the mast when there's a big blow."

Edging closer, the skinny man nervously makes certain no one sees him standing next to John.

"Name be Weasel," he murmurs, bringing his emaciated face close to John, making it almost impossible for John to move away.

Winking, Weasel speaks in conspiratorial tones. "Captain be protected by Gov'nor of Jamaica. Steals in the name of the king—ha, least Morgan say he do. But none have seen his letters of marque." Shrugging his shoulders, he informs John, "Scarce matters. Morgan be a good leader in battle."

"Where are we going? Will we do battle?" asks John, fear creeping into his voice.

"For now, be headin' for Jamaica." Pausing to scratch his crotch, he boasts, "Maybe catch a merchant or two on our way. Aye, gots a fine, swift ship! A battle royal be in the wind." Rubbing his hands together, Weasel adds, "But no matter. Captain's generous with prize money, don't ye know. Gets our full share, we will! Promise!"

John assures him, "I want nothing of plundered goods. And certain, I want nothing to do with these men."

"Ha. Weathered many a blow together, me mates and me." Swaggering up and down the deck, Weasel proclaims, "Hopes to fetch prizes enough to buys me a wench—in Jamaica." Sticking his chest out, the pirate boasts, "Big Mary be waitin' me return. Round she be. Comforts me. Be assured."

John listens and shrugs.

Grabbing John by the shoulder, Weasel points out John's good fortune. "Lucky ye be. Sail a fine ship. If'n ye minds your business, a good share of a prize be yours. Certain as the sun rises." Squinting into brightness of day, Weasel startles John when he changes the subject. "What kinda women suits ye?"

Except for his mother, John knew little of women. In Fishmonger's Lane, a few had caught his fancy, but mostly they were a passing curiosity. Lowering his eyes, flushing in embarrassment, he changes the subject, carefully asking, "What's a letter of marque?"

"Letter from the king or one of his gov'nors. Gives the captain permission to capture ships from countries England be at war with. Shares prizes with the king, we do. Course, sometimes we breaks the rule and captures ships from friendly countries." Cackling, he adds, "And sometimes we not share. That's what makes us pirates. Not much sharing. Wager, if I gets me share, details not of much interest to me."

John completely stops what he's doing. Leaning against his mop, he looks at the squat, toothless man with new interest. Weasel's skin is tawny, much darker than John's. He is older, shorter.

"How long ye been with Morgan?"

"Taken prisoner off a merchant ship, three years past. Knows how they runs this ship." Weasel brags, "Signed the Articles 'fore they beat me to death, I did. Ye do well to sign. D'ye hear?"

Moving slowly, pretending to tighten up the lines on the belaying pins, Weasel brings his head close to John's, confiding, "He trusts me, Morgan does. Can go ashore when we anchor in Port Royal. Time to rests up, if not carrying out hostilities against the Spanish, Dutch, French, or whatever comes across our path." Weasel enjoys telling the young novice about the lives of the pirates, the ship, and Jamaica. A perfect audience, John doesn't interrupt. Boasting boosts Weasel's sense of importance. "In Jamaica, meets up with old-time mates. Enjoys the grog. D'ye hear?"

Eyes twinkling, a smile of pleasure spreads across Weasel's face. Trying to shock his young student, he points to the south, confiding, "Many ships, pirates, hides out there. Places of sin. Aye, great to be there. Women and plenty to drink." He stops, groans, and complains, "Hotter than the Devil's oven in Jamaica. Sweat pours off ye like rain. Shan't believe it till ye feels it for yourself. Storms brew up fast. Heat, then storms. Heat, then storms. On and on. Plenty of heat follows the storms. Lively place. Not cold and damp like London." A dreamlike distant look enters Weasel's eyes, exposing an inner dream. "One of these days, gets off this ship and catch me a ship to them new colonies in America. Make me way around easy, if'n I gets there. Captain don't know it, but read and write, I can. Pretended me couldn't read the Articles and then signed me *X*." With a knowing look at John, he adds, "Just as ye did. Power in not lettin' no one knows what's ye knows. What's ye can do."

Weasel waves to the southwest with the crooked fingers of his left hand. "For now, Jamaica." Pointing toward the distant shore, he advises, "Watch off the starboard side as we sails by the coast of England. Soon see a big island. English anchor warships on the north side, at the head. Careful as we goes."

John moves away from Weasel, grumbling, "Stinks worse than Mo."

Not hearing the insult, Weasel beams. Using his finger to pull back his cheek, he gives John a look at his foul, toothless mouth. "Lost me grinders to scurvy. Surgeon pulled them out, just afore he got killed with grapeshot. Glad to be rid of the pain." Weasel vocalized his self-satisfaction.

*   *   *

Standing next to Weasel at the ship's rail, John instinctively knows he will never be a good sailor. The brig heaves over the top of a wave, running before a tempestuous wind. His stomach in protest, John stands near the rail as a precaution. Staring off into the distance, he ponders the sights and sounds of the days since being taken captive and idly watches the high bluffs along the coastline, absorbed by their rugged beauty. Not for a moment does he believe Weasel's claims. As sure as the sun rises in the sky at the beginning of each day, Weasel cannot read or write. Certain.

Cautiously, not wanting to upset the pirate who has seemingly befriended him, John asks, "Where did you learn to read and write?"

"Me mum be housemaid for a fine gentleman and his rich wife. Wronged me mum, he did—deflowered her. Lady kicked mum out. Course, the lady let the fat lord of the house stay on. 'Twas me da, I wager. Mum made her way to London, where I be born. Her own sister refused her shelter. Could only earn her keep by being with men looking' to sin with a woman. Cried a lot, but held her head high, and treated me right. Learned me numbers and letters. If'n she'd only lived longer, might of learned more." Reflecting, he adds, "Went to sea. On a merchant ship Morgan captured. Captain be so scared, soaked his pants. Har, har! Signed on with Morgan, then and there." Remembering what he'd told John of his resistance to becoming a pirate, Weasel amends, "Well, signed on after a thrashing smartened me up."

The beat of a drum attracts their attention. Strolling to his position near the quarterdeck, Jeb shouts, "Cannon practice. Places. Quick."

Moving into position, the topmen lower the movable yards. By reducing the size of the canvas, they slow the ship.

Screams pierce the air. Filled with fear, John crouches by the mast. Glancing toward the stern, he sees Jeb drag Isaac off the quarterdeck by his pigtail. Isaac's eyes are blackened, round with fear. His mouth opens in a silent screech as Jeb pulls and bounces him along the weather deck. Of small stature, Isaac has little muscle under his raggedy brown shirt. John stands horrified while a pirate secures Isaac to the forward grating near the hatchway covering the steps leading to the hold below.

"Thinks ye be an officer, eh?" shouts an angered Jeb. "Fool! Crew the like of ye not be allowed on the quarterdeck without invitation. 'Tis the captain's domain, stupid cur."

Morgan stands on the forward edge of the quarterdeck, his long cloak and black curls blowing about him in the wind as he points a long finger at the trembling Isaac. Morgan's mouth is twisted in anger and displeasure; the glint in his eyes almost matches the red of his doublet. He has the look of Satan.

Morgan orders Jeb, "Take care of him, mister. Such indiscretions are not allowed." Turning to face the fearful prisoner, he hisses, "Let this lesson teach ye well. The laws of this ship will be followed, or ye will bear the consequences."

Morgan nods his head. Jeb raises his left arm, bringing the bos'n's starter solidly down upon Isaac's back. The anticipation of the whip seemed worse than

Barbara Houtenbrink Andreason

the reality, as Isaac stops screaming once contact is made with his body. After two additional strikes, Morgan gives the order to cease. Ignoring Isaac's sobs, his captors turn away, leaving him tied to the grating.

John edges up next to Mo. In an undertone, asks, "Whatever did he do wrong?"

"Only Morgan, the steersman, and them with business with the captain be allowed on the quarterdeck." Explaining the hierarchy aboard ship, Mo tells John, "Morgan tends the quarterdeck like King Charles on his throne. We allows the captain one area where no one else goes, where he can think. Abide here, lad, must tend to me duties. Get the cannon ready for firing."

Fearful, John decides to do anything he's asked to avoid another strike from the cat. Fearing it might go hard on him, he does not dare look at Isaac or to show any sympathy. "Hiss!" A familiar whisper causes John to jump in alarm. The friendliness of the tone surprises him, and relief floods through his body.

"Watch me! Learn the motions for workin' the guns. Cannon practice be on the larboard side," Mo explains, pointing to the left side of the ship.

* * *

"Belay the lashings," orders Morgan.

Quickly removing the heavy ropes from the eyebolts below the gunport, each gun crew free their cannon from their lashings to the gunwale of the ship.

80

"Hoist powder and shot."

Shaking his fist at John and the other new crewmembers, Jeb shouts, "Green horns git below. Grab the powder boxes." Using a whiny, condescending tone, he orders, "Now, watch your head, your tiny fingers and toes." John and the other pirates scramble into the dark hold; squeezing past a sailor bringing up wadding to the men at the cannon.

As bidden, John grabs a cylindrical silk bag of powder and returns topside. Ignorantly, he sets the bag of powder on the lee side of the cannon, reasoning it will be protected from air currents blowing gently across the bow.

"No, lad, no!" shouts Mo. "Blow us to kingdom come. Certain! See here. When the piece is lit, if'n a spark floats on the wind, can land on the powder."

"Boom! Boom!" intones Weasel for emphasis, puffing his cheeks out with each word. "Shorten all our lives." Laughing, he adds, "Or just take off a few limbs."

Turning away from Weasel, Mo guides John to where crew members store the shot under tarpaulins. "Waits here. When we needs more powder, I'll let ye know."

"Haul hem inboard."

In preparation for loading the guns, the gunners pull the cannon inboard. Muscles straining with exertion and shiny with sweat, they tug on the train tackle, which is attached to the ringbolt on the rear of the gun carriage.

"Not all brigs have gun tackles," Mo brags. "Keeps the gun from wildly whirling out of control when the ship keels or changes tack."

"Remove the tomkins," Morgan shouts as the gun crews remove the round pieces of wood, flat on one side with domed tops, from the muzzles of the cannon.

"During high seas, the tomkins keep the rain and water from washing into the mouth of the cannon," Weasel whispers.

"Keeps the bore of the gun dry—powder too," Mo wisely intones.

"Raise the gunports."

Six sailors jump to follow Morgan's orders, pulling on the rope that passes through round holes in the gunwales of the ship and fastens to ringbolts above the gunports. The slack in the port tackle reduced, the hinges bend.

"Gunports open," shout six sailors in unison.

"Clear the touchhole," shouts Morgan. Long, sharp picks strike the touchholes, clearing them of the powder and debris from past firings.

"Sponge her well. Strike her good."

Stretching out through the portholes, spongers ram long-handled sponges down the cannons' throats. Without pause, they strike the muzzle several times, knocking out any residue still clinging within from the last firing.

"Ram the cartridge down the lady's throat. Pack it well." Standing to the right of the guns, crews push the powder cartridges down the full length of the bore, making certain they are tightly packed.

"Home the ball," Morgan shouts. Six iron balls of shot are rammed deep into the muzzle of the cannon.

"Snuggle her up with wadding." Pieces of shredded rope are rammed down the muzzle—the crew filling the spaces between the powder, the first wad, the shot, and the last wad.

"Keeps the shot tight," Mo informs John. "Tight in the muzzle on a downward roll."

"Prick and prime." Pricking the powder bag, the gunners stand to windward, filling the touchholes to the base ring with fine powder.

"Run carriages." John follows Mo's direction, hurrying over to help the men tug on a side tackle. Their muscles straining, they push the gun carriages forward. Six muzzles project well beyond each gunport. In spite of himself, John feels the excitement of the action and savors a sense of pride in being a small part of it.

"Cannons placed. Ready to fire," shouts Jeb.

Mo explains, "Gotsta keep the muzzles away from the side of the vessel. When she's fired, sparks shoot out. Ship's dry timbers can get set on fire. Be disastrous." Frowning and stroking his beard down to the tuft on its end, Mo nods his head in concern. "Burn the ship into a watery grave. Us with it."

As the ship begins to rise on a swell, Morgan orders, "Aim your guns."

The guns are raised as much as the limited space of the porthole will permit. Each nose is turned, raised, or lowered, bringing the identified target into within their sights.

"Matches to the touchhole, mates," he calls out.

"Fire."

Long linstocks, holding matches, are grabbed and clamped onto the touchholes. After a brief pause while fire and smoke hiss and spew from the holes, each gun emits a loud blast of fire and iron as the cannons explode. Each gun roars as it releases its load of deadly metal.

John watches as smoke, fire, cannonballs, and bits of wadding disgorge in an enormous flash. Cannonballs hit the water near their intended marks. The ship groans and vibrates in response to the tremendous force.

Powerful guns of destruction spring back, shrieking from the recoil. Tackles, hitched to ringbolts near the centerline of the ship, prevent the cannons from crushing the sailors as they fly out of the gunports.

Scrambling away, John clenches fists over his ears, protecting them from the deafening sounds of firing and forcefully rebounding carriages.

"Wise to be careful. A thirty-two-pounder with a normal charge can recoil fierce. At least eleven feet," boasts Mo. "Tis why we restrain the guns with breeching." He points to thick rope securing each cannon to the ringbolts in the side of the brig.

John fears the ring and tackle will not consistently prevent the guns from flying off in his direction. As the wind clears away the smoke, the crew moves about, looking like specters, ghosts from an ancient time.

With his newly acquired experience, John believes he knows all there is to know about cannons. If he escapes, he is certain to be of use on a gun crew of

His Majesty's Navy—if he can just be rescued from this devil's brig.

Morgan quickly paces the deck, going to each member of the crew and nodding his approval. Fearing Morgan can read his mutinous thoughts, John hurriedly moves away.

"Firin' on the upward roll, takes out a merchant's mast," Mo laughs. "Lays helpless in the water, seriously disabled she be."

"Swab!" The roar of a late firing cannon obscures the command. A thick blanket of gray smoke swirls around the deck, momentarily shrouding the view of the disapproving captain.

Quickly, anticipating the next command, the swabbers scramble to douse and clean the guns, carefully extinguishing any burning fragments that might cause the next charge to explode prematurely.

"Show us again, lads."

Immediately, the crew repeats the procedure, charging, loading, wadding, and ramming the balls into the open neck of the cannon, returning the muzzle of their cannon through the gunport, ready once more to dislodge its fiery destruction.

Morgan, hatless, hair blowing in the breeze, solemnly nods his praise.

"Fire!" All cannons once again discharge their content, this time in almost perfect synchronization. After checking to see how close the balls have come to their mark, Morgan glances at each cannon in turn. After he finally gives the order to swab and stow the guns, they lash their mouths above the gunports.

"Secure the gunports well," Jeb orders. "Open ports reveals who we be to any wary merchant."

Whistling softly, Morgan casually turns and walks to the larboard side of the ship, gazing out over the horizon. With a slight smile of satisfaction, he mutters, "Will do fine in battle. We'll pick those with fewer guns." The swirling smoke continues to drift around the brig. "The lads can hit the mark as well as any."

*   *   *

Opportunity comes quickly. Within two days Weasel whoops, "A sail! Two mile ahead." After a pause of a few seconds, he bellows and points. "There! Off the larboard bow!"

Bowing his head, Morgan salutes Weasel with his right hand, proclaiming, "Good man, Weasel. The silver ducat is yours."

The crew responds quickly to the loudness of the battle rattle. Morgan confidently comments, "Low in the water. Heavily laden. By the gods, an easy catch!"

To Jeb, Morgan orders, "Overtake her. 'Tis a slow moving merchant. A simple task."

"See here," Mo explains to John, "we uses the running rigging to pivot, raise or lower the spars. We raise them now. Wants to get maximum wind into the canvases."

"Prepare for battle!" Morgan's orders filter over the noises and voices on deck.

Crews hurry to the left side of the brig to prepare for the confrontation that is certain to come. Pushing John out of the way, they move into position. Handspikes, rammers, powder bags, and matches are placed in order by the side of each cannon. The gunports are shut, giving the sides of the brig the solid-oak walls of a noncombatant ship. The presence of each cannon is kept hidden. Excited, Morgan paces the deck, intending to keep the guns secured until it's too late for the merchant to escape.

"Cut of her jib?" asks Morgan.

"She be Dutch," bellows Mo. "Certain, I am." His excitement mounts as he anticipates his share of the prizes. His impatience is palpable. "Certain, will think we be countrymen when she sees our flag."

"Patience, lads. Wait till we see her colors," Morgan calls out. Mo pulls a red, white, and blue striped cloth from the flag box. Weasel grabs the flag, ready to attach and raise it on a halyard. Glancing at John, Mo exclaims, "Red, white, and blue stripes. Dutch!"

"Fool them, certain," whispers Weasel, rocking back and forth with excitement. "Fool the merchant, just ye wait." Weasel stands, hand on the halyard, ready to do Morgan's bidding. "When gets the order, will hoists it up the flagpole. Certain."

Trained hands quickly set every available sail, including the main and fore topsails, mizzen, and spritsail. Each sail fills with air. Like a large bird, the ship spreads her soiled white wings in full chase. The *Revenge* briskly bears down upon the target, shrinking the distance between the two ships to a half mile. Finally only a quarter mile remains.

A smile crosses Mo's face, coupled with a look of pride when he explains Morgan's strategy. "Captain wants the gun holes covered. Keep the Dutch flag up till last instant."

Weasel, preparing for his flag-lowering duties, pantomimes pulling down on an imaginary rope with his right hand. With his left hand he reaches up and over his right, pulling down in a hand-over-hand series of motions, as if raising a flag to the top of a pole. "Perfect," he declares to himself.

"When Captain commands, 'Engage,' we hauls down the Dutch flag." He chortles quietly so Morgan cannot hear. "Then hoists up the black flag, the Jolly Roger. Just before we attack." With a laugh, he shouts, "Fools them, it does. Way of the sea."

Raising his voice in defiance to the increasing wind, Mo barks, "Fair chance we catch her. Winds be favorable! If she fails to surrender, we moves in front of her—foul her bow sprint in our main shrouds. Rake her length at our pleasure."

Weasel reaches into a box filled with a multitude of flags from all nations. John doesn't recognize any of them, with the exception of the English ensign.

Attempting to get a clear look through the sails, Mo bellows to Morgan on the quarterdeck, "The old *Seahorse*, I wager." Squinting his eyes for a better view, he roars, "See the cut of her jib? Her figurehead be the head of a seahorse. Gots her before. Seems the Dutch caught her after us. Might have a Dutch name, but she be the *Seahorse*, not a doubt."

To John, he adds, "If'n she hath guns, Morgan will grab them, plus all else of value."

"The crew?" John asked, afraid of the answer. "What happens to the crew?"

"If they's lucky, Morgan leaves the boat to flounder. Might make safe harbor." Mo's face is grim, his mouth turned down at the corners. "Seen him make crews jump into the sea. Poor devils, most can't swim. Doesn't matter. Too far from shore to make it anyway. Drown, they do." Sneering, he adds, "Course, we may sweetly invite some of them to join us." Making a sawing motion with his hands, as if cutting off a leg or an arm, Mo quips, "Needs a surgeon. The merchant may have one to graciously lend us, don't ye know?"

Spotting Morgan watching him from the quarterdeck, like a chameleon Mo quickly changes the subject. "Sometimes me talks too much," he woefully says.

*   *   *

"Move briskly. Unchain that fool from the mast. Time he earns his keep." Releasing Isaac, Mo begins preparing the crew for the upcoming battle.

"John, ye and Isaac get moving. Fetch the boxes of cartridges," Morgan orders.

Isaac, now free of his imprisonment and covered with bruises and welts, stumbles as he follows John into the hold.

"Only twenty-five to man the six guns we be usin'," Mo tells John. "Some mates hath more than one job to do. Best do your part."

Hurrying to retrieve gunpowder from the hold, John clutches his chest as fear grips the center of his body. Silently praying he will not die, he tries not to think of the upcoming battle. There is no escape. Dreading the unknown, he feels incapable of slowing his breathing. Sweat breaks out across his brow, and he is unable to control his shaking hands.

"Any deed they do be evil," John complains in an undertone. "Does no good to speak of good and evil with these men. Must keep my own counsel."

"Bear down," orders Morgan, completely ignoring the prisoners, except to ensure they are performing their duties.

The merchant is not built for speed. Designed to carry merchandise, she loses way. The lighter, more maneuverable *Revenge* easily closes the distance. Keeping close to the weather quarter of the merchant, her mainsail set to their best advantage, the pirates maneuver the forecastle of the *Revenge* abreast the mainmast of the *Seahorse*. Shortening her sails to spill the wind, the *Revenge* slows.

Jeb orders, "Hard a-lee." The pirates close in.

"Two guns facin' us," Mo calls out. He hurriedly explains to John, "We gots six, plus the swivel gun. Not to worry. Not a bit. No chance we be raked with gunfire." With a grin, he says, "They'll back-off. A silver coin says they will. Quick surrender. Only chance they have to survive."

Preparing for battle, each pirate slings a pair of pistols over his shoulders, suspended from colorful red, yellow, and blue silk scarves.

"Change the flag?" Mo inquires.

"No, keep them guessing until the cannonballs fly," commands Morgan. "Send the pressed men below now! Might hinder our progress."

With the *Seahorse* within hailing distance, Morgan grabs his speaking trumpet. Sword in hand, musket nearby, he orders, "Put one across her bow." Speaking loudly, pointing to the ensign, he shouts, "Bring down the ensign. Time to show our true colors. Hoist the black flag."

While the crew waits by the cannon on the larboard side, Weasel hoists the black flag up the ensign staff.

"Excellent shot," Morgan exults as the first ball shoots harmlessly across the bow of the trader.

Standing on the weather deck about four feet from the hatch John is jarred by the unholy sound. Before being shoved below, he grabs a brief glimpse of the merchant as a mild wind clears away the smoke. The hatch just misses his head as it is slammed shut.

*   *   *

Reverberations across her bow cause the merchant to slow her speed. Amid the flap of sails and smoke there is general fear and confusion aboard the *Seahorse*. She does not immediately respond to the signal to surrender.

Standing alone on the quarterdeck as the *Revenge* approaches her prey to the seahorse's starboard, Morgan uses a trumpet to call out.

"Drop your sails. We have the advantage. The superior ship!" Without pausing to gauge the effect of his words, he calls out, "Surrender! Your lives will be spared."

Growling and fearing a broadside, the alarmed captain of the *Seahorse* mutters, "Villains!" Turning to the elegantly dressed gentleman standing beside him, he promises, "Your Lordship, I will not resist a boarding. I must strive to save the life of you and Her Ladyship. I must do whatever is necessary to protect the ship and the lives of my crew."

Having been previously boarded, Captain Clives knows full well the terrible atrocities that pirate crews are capable of inflicting upon an unarmed ship. In the pubs of London and Portsmouth he has heard of the heinous acts inflicted upon ships and their crews.

"We are not equipped to repel pirates and their bands of hooligans." Not trusting the pirates to keep any guarantees of safety, Clives is reluctant to reveal to Lord Ashley their imminent jeopardy. Clives is an old man—what choice has he but to comply? Believing he recognizes two of the pirates, he feels a chill travel up his spine.

"Send your captain across," demands Morgan, who now sports a red hat as large as a topgallant sail. Its great black feather sways in the breeze. A pair of pistols nestled in his belt, he grips the handle of the cutlass, which hangs from his waist, snug in a gold and jeweled scabbard.

*   *   *

When the two vessels are roped firmly together, Captain Clives slowly climbs aboard the pirate ship. Long past his prime, he grips the rope with gnarled fingers and clambers across. He grimaces with each pull across the rigging. Once he is on the deck of the *Revenge* his unkempt gray hair hangs in his face as he painfully makes his way to Morgan.

"Good sir, welcome aboard." Morgan gallantly sweeps off his hat, making a courtly if haughty bow. Void of expression, he lies, "We have no desire to harm your person."

Covering their mouths with their hands, some of the pirates snigger, savoring the thought of expected bloodshed.

"Sir," replies Captain Clives, "we shall give ye no reason to harm us." To himself he mutters, "I trust them not but have few options. I must try to save my ship."

Turning to Jeb, Morgan orders, "Interrogate our guest about his cargo." Fearful of what the pirates might do to the ship's occupants, Clives does not feel the necessity of heroic action. Raising his voice above the flutter of the reduced sails, he admits, "We have arms, gun powder, linen, and woolens for the West Indies." The captain's tired eyes have a sad look of resignation but no fear.

"Picked supplies up at Calais," Clives continues. "Currently on our way to Falmouth to complete the manifest."

Giving a curt nod to Jeb and Mo, Morgan indicates his intent. Pointing to the captured ship with a six-foot-long musket, he orders Jeb, Mo, and Weasel to swing across the ropes into the merchant ship. Besides a sword in one hand and knives in their mouths, Mo and Weasel each have four pistols tied to brightly colored silk cords around their necks.

Knowing that if he is caught he will be whipped, John chances a peak out of the hold, quickly counting the number of arms each pirate is carrying to the merchant ship. Jeb has six loaded pistols and a cutlass. The rest of the crewmembers bear pistols in addition to knives and boarding axes. With his limited view, John is unable to see the atrocities committed by the pirates.

Aboard the *Seahorse*, ragged men tear open all the hatches without regard to extreme damages caused to the doomed merchant.

"Search the cuddy, lads," Jeb shouts, urging the pirates to use boarding axes and cutlasses in opening boxes and trunks.

Slow ocean swells lift and lower both ships in concert with the cries of seabirds. Linens, woolen goods, and barrels of provisions, including ammunition and arms, are transferred to the *Revenge*. It takes a full day to construct a lifting tackle and move large containers of gun powder, hogsheads of water, and barrels of grain into the hold amidships of the *Revenge*. The crew is elated to see a barrel each of flour, beef, and pork, in addition to other items they consider useful for their long journey. Cheers fill the air when Mo discovers four bags each of silver and gold coins. With an exaggerated bow he immediately presents the bags and their contents to Morgan.

Triumphant, Morgan smiles, promising, "We'll divide this up once we're underway."

Two mounted guns are moved next in addition to the *Seahorse*'s rigging, which is received with a hoot of satisfaction by the ship's carpenter. "Getting low, we were. Another storm and we would have suffered. Nuff supplies to take us to Jamaica, no matter how big the blow. Certain."

Weasel takes particular care in choosing which pieces of spare rigging to filch from the hapless ship. Neither the carpenter nor Morgan would have been pleased to know that Weasel had left enough rigging for the merchant ship to make repairs that would possibly allow her to get under way again after the pirate's departure. If questioned, Weasel plans to tell Morgan, "Not be worth the bother. Poor repair."

"We'll have fine goods to trade for rum and sugar in the Indies," Morgan exults. "Unfortunately, we did not get what we need most. The *Seahorse* being almost home, her water supplies are low. Too much linen and wool, not enough food."

Undaunted, he continues, "More to be gotten along the way. After trading, repairs, and a good rest in Port Royal, we'll be well supplied when we go on to the colonies."

To Jeb, Morgan sneers, "'Tis of no consequence what happens to the rubbish on the *Seahorse*. Captain's a sick old man with a crew of incompetents. Be of no importance to me. The world will be well served if it be free of them." Laughing, he adds, "How easily they gave in to our demands." Scornfully, the captain of the *Revenge* jeers, "The pitiful acts people perform in order to save their worthless lives." He shrugs, indifferent, "Well, without their rigging, they'll soon dash on the rocks."

* * *

While the pirate crew crawls aboard the devastated *Seahorse* in their search for booty, John is kept below under the closed hatch. The transfer of all spoils completed, the pirates cut the shrouds and disable the masts.

Ironically, not aware of these acts, John wonders, *Be the stories true about pirate cruelty?* Fearing the reply, John is reluctant to ask Mo about the fate of the victims on the *Seahorse*. Were they butchered? John does not see the pirates use friendly persuasion, does not observe a knife to the captured surgeon's throat to convince the man to change his allegiance. John does not see Captain Clives limp back to the helm of his ship or the pirates swing back onto the Revenge. The *Seahorse* is set adrift.

The sea robbers care not that the passengers and crew aboard the merchant will tragically suffer at the mercy of the sea and fickle currents. It means nothing to them that without repairs to the splintered mast and rigging it will be impossible for the crew to control the ship in the rising winds. The destiny of the *Seahorse* is to wreck upon the savage rocks off England's rugged coast. In the hold, not knowing the dangers faced by a ship without sails, John cannot begin to imagine their fate.

Sailing west-southwest, no pirate looks back to see the horrors faced by their drifting victims—predictable horrors unasked for by the crew and passengers. Only Weasel knows that if the crew of the merchant acts quickly and uses the rigging he left behind, the men might get up enough sail to save themselves. Weasel never told anyone of his altruistic deed. Discovery of such betrayal by Morgan or Jeb would lead to his death. Certain.

*   *   *

Approving *huzzahs* permeate down through the wooden deck to where John lays deep in the hold. As the brig sets off for the West Indies, loud laughter and shouts of satisfaction at their success rise and fall with the waves.

A sudden change in the winds forewarns of a late summer gale. The pirates go back to the tasks that would assure survival in rough seas.

*   *   *

Ragged streaks zigzag across the darkening sky. Rising winds whistle through the rigging as Mo releases the captives from the hold. The now shoreless sea has no discernible boundaries; an ashen sky melds into the graying water. Dismayed, John sees his dreams of escape dissolving with each globule of falling rain. Scudding before rain and wind, the deck sways beneath his feet. The waves already streaking with foam, Morgan gives orders. "Reduce the mainsail; double reef the topsails."

Mo yells out in a voice barely heard above the wind, "Needs to reduce the canvas, lad. Stress makes them rip, splits the mast." From experience, Mo knows sails must be trimmed and furled before any disastrous forces that press on the masts, yards, and endless lines supporting them, tear them apart. In that eventuality, no repairs can be made until the storm is spent—if they don't sink before that.

Before the anticipated orders can be given, topmen sprint up the ratlines to the yards, where they stand on footropes, five abreast on each side of the main mast. Weasel shimmies aloft on the windward rigging to his position eighty-five feet above the pitching weather deck. All eyes watching, he crosses to the leeward side to assist his mates in reducing the expanse of sail catching the wind. Certain that Weasel will not gain a toehold on the footropes, John gasps in fright, slowly releasing his breath in relief when Weasel successfully reefs in his section of the flapping canvas.

"Gits used to it, lad! Topmen have amazing ability to maintain their footing in spite of strong winds and adversity. See, over there," exclaims Mo, pointing to the men in the middle of the yard who were leeching the outer sections of the sail, "They be using gaskets to secure the sail."

John watched, fascinated by the hardy men oblivious to the sea boiling below where they labored.

"Ah, well done," Mo proudly exults. "It be one of the most dangerous duties a man faces at sea."

"Lucky if'n he don't find his self flung into the sea," intrudes Jeb.

"Or pitched to the deck," agrees Mo.

The topmen pull in the topsails while the crew on the deck haul and tighten the loosened ropes. Tying the free ends of the running rigging fast to the pin rails, they twist the tails of the ropes and complete the task by making one or two figure-eight turns about each belaying pin. If a sudden change in the wind occurs, the ropes can be quickly released and the sails unfurled.

*   *   *

The ship and her occupants pass under the anvil head of a great thundercloud. Pellets of hail fall like knives onto their backs, soaking everything on the deck.

"Damme," Jeb shouts. Turning to grin at Morgan, he announces, "All secure."

"Enough sail to keep us fairly and freely before the sea," agrees Morgan.

"Main tops'l will catch the wind well above the waves," shouts Jeb above the mounting winds. Undeterred by the storm, they set their course.

John feels the wind's strength as it begins to toss the brig upon the surface of the sea. He fears that the wind's ferocity heralds hardships. His hope of discovery by an English man-of-war off the coast of England has come to naught. At this point in time, he has one immediate concern: in such a storm would they find a safe shore?

* * *

"Why, lad, we use the sun and stars to guide us," Mo assures him when John expresses fear that they have lost their way. "There be thirty navigation stars all named and measured. We follow them."

"What sun? Where be the stars?" John worries, gazing up at the dark forbidding sky. He feels as witless as his baby brother, Tristram.

"Mind ye well, 't'will reappear," Mo reassures him while lightning sears the sky. "Why, even the sea gives us cues. Teach ye about currents, I will. How to watch the direction and drift of the clouds." Amused at the incongruity of his remarks, he grunts, "When 'tis a bit calmer."

Torrential winds send the raging sea across the gunwales. Spray flows across the deck in uninterrupted surges. Concerned that water might seep into the hold, Morgan orders Jeb to ensure the security of the cargo.

"Mo, assure all below," Jeb screams.

As the ship rises on the crest of a wave, John follows Mo into the dank hold. The men listen for sounds suggesting a precarious shift in the cargo. The ship teeters at the top for mere seconds before rapidly propelling to the downside. John struggles to maintain his balance.

"Ye gits to feel small changes in your body, lad. Know when cargo becomes unlashed. A sixth sense, don't ye know? A barrel can roll over, crush ye, if ye not be prudent."

Scant light in the hold makes it difficult to attend to their tasks. The surging sea rattles the aging boards of the craft, causing the men to bounce off barrels and walls, bruising their bodies as they check the lashings. They move as quickly as diminished visibility and stability allow.

After thirty minutes John returns topside. With the full roll of the vessel across the waves, he experiences his first bout of seasickness. Rushing to the rail, he grips it tightly with both hands. He leans his head over the side, his stomach spewing gore into the percolating sea. Although his body and clothing are sodden he can feel beads of sweat on his brow. His stomach emptied, he continues to retch until weakness overtakes him and he falls to his knees.

Barely aware he is being slapped him on the back, John ignores Mo's soothsaying. "Why, lad, 't'ain't nutten. Wind a mere thirty knots, moderate gale." He points across the gunwale. "See there? The waves be streaked with foam. When she blows a fresh gale, will see spindrift—great globes of foam. Then we close-reef the tops'l—to keeps them from fraying. Why, then ye be knowing you're in a real blow. Ha!"

"In a fresh gale, how strong be the wind?" shouts John.

"Thirty-five knots, maybe more. Ye be knowing. No need to ask."

Swirling darkness commands every inch of the sky. The ceiling touches the surface of the water; rain follows hail. The air and all surfaces of the ship become saturated. John rubs his pale hands together, trying to bring them warmth.

* * *

Dawn. The wind slows. The sun struggles to relieve the clouds.

Wind slapping at their backs, the pirates continue their journey, living the life they love—a life with accountability to few. Here on the ship they are equals, each man to the other. After electing their captain, they believe they can easily discharge him if he rules unfairly. John knows of no one with the courage to attempt such a feat.

Anticipating the coming stay in Port Royal, the men gossip about the abundance of agreeable women. The experienced know where to find wine, grog, gin, and rum to drink. No thought is given to their future; most expect to serve months and years of harsh voyages to distant ports, to live short lives. In Jamaica they will drink their fill and claim a wench upon whom they will deplete their riches within a few days or weeks— destined to set sail again without a bob or shilling in their pockets. Most live out their life in this manner.

Some die by the sword or tumble one hundred or more feet from a yardarm to the deck. Few die ashore in their own beds.

Heeding the boasts, the joys of Port Royal, John complains, "I did not seek this way of life. Intolerable. Impious. Threatens my mortal soul."

He makes a vow to stay true to his mother's ways of prayer and devotion, no matter how difficult the task. John considers his duty as an Englishmen to King Charles, though a pompous monarch given to fancy ways. *He be the king and deserves my allegiance for that reason if no other.* He remembers the viciousness of the plague. Is it God's retribution for the frivolity of the court? Guilty about his faithless thoughts, he whispers, "Who am I to feel so pious? An echo of Da?"

The day wears on, the sea calms, and intrusive thoughts of God fade. The vital realities of daily work and survival are forced upon him.

The storm spent, John crawls up from the hold to find a quiet place on the deck. He gazes at an obsidian sky broken up by small clusters of stars. He feels he has but to reach out to touch the nearest one, to find God. "He must be there," he whispers as awe envelops him. "There he be. Lives in the brilliant red star that hangs so low in the sky."

*   *   *

Teaching him the intricacies of shipboard duties, Mo toils side by side with John to perform the tasks that keep a sailing ship afloat. Prudently trying to avoid the bos'n's starter, John learns to keep tension on the shrouds and the backstays by cinching up the ropes going through the holes in the deadeyes. He thrills at gaining the necessary balance to climb up the ratlines, grateful the distance between each ratline seems to be just the exact height necessary to make an easy climb up into the crow's nest. Telling no one of his ulterior motives, he can now find a place of momentary solitude away from the pirates. With no idea of the ocean's vastness, he dreams of sighting a possible route of escape. In the shelter of the crow's nest he marvels at how far he can see in each direction across the ocean's surface. John feels rather than hears Weasel's ascent to sit beside him in the fighting top.

"Twelve miles, that be how far you can see from up here. Good day, no haze, might see twenty." Weasel informs. "Our marksmen stands here," Weasel points out. With bravado, he adds, "Grand place to pick off the enemy, if'n they be unwary enough to stands out in the open."

Looking out in the distance, John sees great, towering clouds building in the east, moving quickly in their direction. A fearful sight, they warn of heavy seas. Heeding Weasel's warning, John quickly climbs down the ratlines to the deck. Looking up, He views their situation with gloomy fascination. The sun has disappeared, and a column of water appears to rise up from the sea into the clouds—or is the column moving down from the clouds to the sea? The column

stands dark against the rest of the sky. Streaks of
lightning flash within the column and across the sky
in all directions. Anxiously he scans the horizon. A
terrible storm seems inescapable. *God's retribution,*
John thinks.

"Wind makes the waves, me boy," Mo calmly states.
"Greater the wind, greater the wave." Following this
prediction, a monstrous hurricane, more viscous than
any storm John has ever experienced, hits the ship
with a force that seems certain to lift it out of the
water.

"Survived the last storm; hope to do the same with
this one," John philosophizes as immense waves wash
over the brig.

Jeb desperately clutches the helm, struggling to
keep the nose of the ship into the waves. John takes
a rope and ties himself to the mast, not certain he
believes Weasel's declaration that "We be safe if'n
distance between crests remain far apart. Danger
comes when crests occur too close, brig hangs across
the tops. Stresses the keel. Can rip her apart."

Mo adds a bland observation: "Breaks her in two,
almost certain."

"I—I c-can't swim," John stutters.

"Don't matter. Best not to swim. Sink faster. Gets
it over with quick."

Scrunching his eyes each time the sea washes over
the weather deck, John prays for deliverance. Afraid
to go below deck, John is grateful he is tied to the
mast, close to Jeb. He prefers to know his fate when it
comes, not die unsuspecting below deck. Still at the

helm, lashed to the wheel on the poop deck, Jeb yells, "Idiot. Gets below. Wash off the deck, ye will."

Each time the ship is carried up to the crest of a wave, John's stomach remains in the bowels of the last trough. Riding the waves and swells for two days, the tempest at its greatest, John feels certain they will sink to the depths before he awakens from the nightmare, wrapped in this floating shroud.

At times the ocean covers the brig like a wet garment flowing from bow to stern or across the bow. After many hours, the tension becomes almost unbearable, and a dull acceptance of his fate overwhelms John. Almost as fast as they arrived, the winds diminish, becoming less ferocious. John's stomach calms, and he unties himself to join other crewmembers sloshing about with bailing buckets.

As the sun falls below the horizon, the evening brings a sky of unimaginable beauty. Reflections of purple light lie across a low-lying bank of clouds. Enraptured by a spectacularly brilliant sky, sucking in his breath in awe, John watches the sun send thin layers of bright crimson streaks low on the horizon. The sails of the brig stand out, bloodstained against the sky. Great patches of crimson and gold streak like fish flying across the water's surface. The air lies heavily across his body like a burdensome woolen shirt. As they sail farther south, the air becomes heavier and warmer. Rivulets of sweat run down between his shoulder blades and drip off his hair into his face. Some relief lies in the shade of the sails and from currents of air stirring across the sea.

The next morning, with seas as smooth as his mam's small looking glass, John joins Mo to recheck the security of the cargo.

Mo tells him, "Be less shifting of the cargo if'n we hardens up the lashings." Sloshing through burbling water, Mo instructs, "Watch, lad. Best served done this way." So saying, he proceeds to tie the barrels together with some of the ropes taken from the merchant vessel.

Alarmed at the depth of the water in the hold, John calls out, "Water's deep. Past me ankles. Be it possible that after surviving such a storm we might still sink?"

"Lotsa seawater," Mo agrees. "Some from the storm, some through wormholes."

"Will we drown?"

"Nay, lad, boys will keep the elm tree pump a-wheezing. Heaving on the chain pumps should keep us afloat." Looking at John, Mo gave a confident wink. "She not be sinking." It shocks John when he adds, "Have a bit more trust in that God of yours."

Could Mo have a secret belief in God? John wonders.

Taking ropes from the plentiful supply of stolen rigging, they finish lashing down the goods in the hold. "Wish we have as much food and water as ropes," Mo mutters.

The barrels secured to Mo's satisfaction, the pair climb topside to the weather deck. Mo's mood changes when he sees Morgan watching him.

"Scrub her down with seawater," Mo barks, pointing to the deck.

Turning his face to the sun to absorb its welcome rays, John leans into the task of scouring layers of dried blood off the deck—blood still clinging even after the storm. Pausing, he listens as Mo whispers to Morgan, "Fear some food stores and barrels of water have been spoiled. Salt water soaked through it all during the storm."

"Should be able to make Jamaica if all goes well," says Morgan.

*   *   *

John doesn't realize the seriousness of the food problems, the potential for starvation or dehydration. Innocently, he asks Mo about the weather, believing that storms present the most imminent danger to his well-being.

"Weasel told me always be vicious storms this time of year. Even more vigorous than what we've been through. Be it true?"

"Aye, true. Fierce winds seem to spin us about in a circle. Torrents of rain. Seas so heavy ye think might never come out of the trough. Ah, don't ye worry. 'Tis a solid ship. Hath weathered many a storm."

"I prefer a calm sea."

"Oh, can be smooth as glass, water reflecting the blue of a robin's egg from the sky. Like this day. Clouds lay out thin, flat as a horse's tail. Learn to watch the sky, lad. Just watch the clouds. Clouds tell ye kinda weather coming. Certain. Sometimes wish didn't know."

A gentle breeze flowing across a sea burnished as polished metal sends them ever to the southwest.

* * *

During weeks at sea, John learns how to raise and lower sails. One evening Mo approaches, grinning. "Say, mate, learning the ropes, ye be." With a crooked smile on his whiskered face, he adds, "Keep them sharp dark eyes of yours peeled, me boy. Important to know which rope be which when we meets the enemy. Never know when it be necessary to move quick like a spider. Merchant ship might be right over the next horizon."

In spite of the calm seas, when John climbs up the sticky ratlines, he pays strict attention to Mo's warnings. "Always, lad, keeps one hand on the shroud. Hear me, lad. Hear me well. Firm step makes a safe step. Eh! One hand for the ship, one for yourself. A lesson for survival."

"Got no choice but to learn how to survive on this devil ship," John laments. "I've learned to hand and reef, furl the mains'l. Takes no brain to scrub a deck. Most important is to avoid Morgan. Failure be most painful."

Unwinding a length of waxed sail twine from its coil, he threads a needle just removed from the wax-filled needle horn. Sticking the needle through a punctured hole in the sail, he complains, "Sew a sail. Suppose next, before stitching, I be required to use a stabber to make the holes." To himself he thought, *Truth be known, on days there be little reason to change the sails I would go mad without some task to busy me.*

John learns the multitude of tasks needed to run the ship, except those involving weaponry. Morgan does not trust weapons to those he has pressed into service, knowing well they dream of mutiny and escape. Without a weapon or a safe port, Morgan knows dreams of fleeing are but exercises in self-deception. The willing outlaws who joined his ship in London, those with a passion for fighting and acts of piracy, are the only ones trusted with sword and pistol.

John dares not voice his inner thoughts of escape to anyone—not to Mo or even to Weasel, who yesterday had boasted of his planned escape to the English colonies. John, not certain whether he was being baited to reveal any intention he might have to escape, kept his own counsel.

*   *   *

During weeks at sea, John experiences the horrors accompanying the life of a pirate—and some of the benefits. On the way to the pirate's base of operation, there were two additional acts of piracy against merchant ships and none against foreign navies. John wonders how they found any ships to plunder in so vast a sea. It seems to him that their prey should be able to escape into a bank of clouds, a front of fog. Almost before John completes his thoughts, the lookout spots a merchant off the Canary Islands.

"Fore 'n' aft on her mizzen," announces the lookout. "Square, gaff spanker on her main."

"Distance?" inquires Morgan.

"Mile on our st`rb`rd beam."

"Brigantine, perhaps," Morgan speculates. "How big?"

"Hundred ton, be my guess."

"Hopefully she carries but one or two light guns," Morgan says. "The heaviest gun be not more than three pounds."

*　　*　　*

Maneuvering into firing position, the deck is readied for battle; for the first time, John isn't forced to go below deck. Ordered to stand by the starboard cannon, John intensely watches the preparations for firing. In the background, over the noise of the men moving guns, raising canvas, stomping their feet, and bringing wadding and balls to the guns, Morgan's voice grabs his attention.

"Fire."

Interest quickly turns to horror. The *Revenge* sends a shot across the bow of the quarry. Morgan immediately commands, "Surrender."

"The devil I will," shouts her strong-willed captain.

"Then suffer the consequences," Morgan growls. Slamming his clenched fist into his hand, he bellows, "Fire."

A second deafening boom sends ball, fire, and smoke blasting from a starboard cannon.

"Surrender now, certain," shouts Weasel, jumping up and down with excitement.

"Rot in the Devil's inferno." The captain doggedly refuses.

"Fire," trumpets the order over the clang of battle.

A misfire on the upward roll—there is no fire, no smoke.

Jeb strides up and down the deck, shouting blasphemies at the gun crew responsible for the delayed firing.

"Idiots, missed the target, missed the masts."

Finally, the gun discharges on the downward roll; ball and chain strike the merchant at her waterline. Within seconds another cannon fires a shot into the side of the ship. Hundreds of oak splinters fly into the necks and bodies of the merchant's crew. Pierced arteries send spurts of blood across the deck.

A splinter protruding from his eye, a crewmember on the merchant bugles a horrific scream. Shrieks of the injured echo above flapping sail, mixing with the triumphant din of clamoring pirates.

A woman's scream wafts over the earsplitting sounds. John cannot believe a woman is on the merchant ship. Surprised, angered, he yells, "Where is the woman? This be unholy."

After a mere three minutes of intense fighting, the frightened captain of the merchant surrenders to the show of superior force. Swinging aboard, the pirates begin their plunder as the ship begins its slow descent into the ocean's depths. Roughly pushing aside the crew, they take jewels, gold coins, and silver and gold ornaments from passengers, grab bolts of fine fabrics, and then streak across the narrow gap to their own ship.

Floundering, taking on water at her waterline, the merchant sinks quickly, as if striving to escape the horrors floating around her. Dozens of people flail about in the water, looking for floating objects to grab. Their eyes reveal fear and hopelessness. John helplessly listens to their screams and watches as the men struggle to cling to wooden debris only to drown in the end. Racing from the port side to the starboard taffrail, John frantically searches for the woman whose scream is haunting him. Finally, ten yards from the brig, a graceful arm reaches up out of the water. A man valiantly struggles to assist her, but within moments both disappear beneath the surface.

"Wants to be a hero, does ye?" snarls a disembodied voice. "We can quickly send you into the deep with her."

Not looking to see who is screaming the taunts, John covers his face with his hands and runs aft. He is pushed hard against the gunwale by Jeb, who runs past, screaming to Morgan, "No victuals. Condemn these fools to everlasting fire."

*   *   *

Sickened, John spends a restless night constantly replaying the horrors he has just witnessed. As the glow of dawn struggles to control the eastern sky, he sleepily takes stock of his unhappy circumstances. Jeb is manning the helm, but where is Morgan? He has not seen Morgan since he went into his cabin at twilight the day before. John watches the man before him while he considers the other. Jeb and Morgan both dispatch their victims with depraved indifference. Jeb follows Morgan blindly. Morgan leads with assured confidence, certain of Jeb's dependence upon him. Morgan is a ruthless leader, demonstrating over and again his intentional cruelty by taking no prisoners from plundered ships—unless they are of some commercial value. Disabled ships are either released with all hands at risk or immediately sent into the deep. To be certain, John admits, the last vessel was accidentally sunk, all hands lost, fodder for sharks, crabs, and birds. There appears to be no particular rationale or purpose related to which ships are sunk, sent to the mercy of the deep, or left to drift upon the ocean. Morgan's evil mind seems to have no exact purpose; the whim to destroy or save appears to be in the moment. Nor does he appear to suffer any consequences for his corrupt actions. Perhaps that will change in the future.

*   *   *

Another vessel crosses their path. From the crow's nest it appears to be about twelve miles distant. John prays that the occupants will escape unharmed, but all traces of optimism quickly flee. After ravishing the captured ship, Morgan has the men shackled back to back and then tossed overboard like helpless, bound puppies. Arms and legs confined, unable to swim, they float only seconds and then sink beneath the surface. A few have expressions of brave defiance, staring directly at the pirates as they sink. Most show stark fear.

John is sickened by the sight of the scar-faced pirate cutting off the hand of one man trying to save himself by grabbing the side of the ship. Immediately, as if on cue, a snout breaks through the film of crimson spreading over the surface. Unconscious, the passenger no longer struggles and becomes a welcome treat for the shark. As if by invitation, the scent of blood attracts dozens of other shark to the kill area.

His scurrilous undertaking completed, Morgan behaves as if it was simply the moil of another day. Morgan is a chameleon of moods, and John realizes his rapid changes in disposition make him a dangerous adversary.

Ordering a change in course to take advantage of the trade winds, Morgan announces, "Lucky we are. The winds will speed us to the Caribbean."

Water, of prime importance, is one of the first items taken from the ships they attack and rob, but they do not always find potable water. Water is scarce. They must hurry.

Except when cleansed by the torrents of rain hitting the boat during tropical cloudbursts, there are no provisions for cleanliness. Bathing is not considered a priority by most pirates. During gales and rain showers, Mo teaches John to catch rain in the water butt. Working at Mo's side, John justifies their labors. "Me mam always insisted on cleanliness in spite of our rude surroundings. 'Cleanliness is in praise of God,' she told me time and again." With a side glance at Mo, he adds, "Even the poorest of us can find ways to keep clean."

*   *   *

Despite constantly changing tack, high winds and squalls continue to blow the ship off course, dooming them to be at sea longer than planned. With no ships captured, food and water are scarce. Spoilage produced by salt water during past storms plagues them.

Hardtack is now their exclusive diet—hard biscuits divided equally among all, no quarter given to the captain or his officers. All have an equal right to starve. None dare complain. Mixing their scant remaining portions of rum and beer with what little water remains makes them less likely to complain about weevils in the biscuits.

"Boat not as seaworthy as Morgan thought," Weasel dares to complain. "Salt water ruined most everything. We be down to eating weevils. Little to wash them down."

Making light of the situation, Mo sarcastically remarks, "Weevils be so active ye must catch them fore they carry the biscuit away. Welcome relief, the grog is. Without it, we would suffer. Best to drink well. Sober men cause trouble."

Hunger looms. A calm sea is something for which to be thankful. They're pleasant times for men not born to the sea, but without the wind they make scant headway. Unexpectedly, a favorable breeze speeds the ship along without effort. Changing from a starboard tack, they fly on a reach before the wind. John loves the feeling of the freshening air upon his face and body. Instructed by Mo, John watches the sky for signs that might portend changes in the weather.

Hunger is not a new phenomenon to John. Thirst is a new experience, more difficult to withstand. Anxiously awaiting their daily rations, each crewmember sips on his daily quarter liter of red wine. On days brandy is allocated they receive only half that amount. Even in the best of times they typically have very little water, for water quickly becomes undrinkable on a long voyage.

Morgan's furious screams fill the air when Jeb and Mo report salt water has seeped into the six barrels of water secured by John and Mo during the storm. Reduced to their last hogshead of water, and with most of their wine and brandy mutated into undrinkable vinegar, John realizes his peril. Rationed to one cup of water per day they are faced with overwhelming thirst in the middle of a wide, saline ocean.

No rain falls during their continuing journey to the southwest. Although hungry and thirsty, the men are still required to run the ship, to keep her afloat. Sails need to be filled and slackened, ropes tied, untied, and retied. Available food is dispensed while they seek the familiar landmark of the Blue Mountains on the east coast of Jamaica. Morgan keeps the men occupied, but they don't forget their thirst.

*   *   *

The cook slowly crosses the deck, hesitating before announcing to Morgan and Mo the unspeakable. Shocked, Mo turns to relate the news to the rest of the men. "Cook just met with Morgan. A grave situation, full of peril. Dire it is."

Seeing that Morgan is about to speak, Mo holds up his hand for silence and harshly demands, "Listen!"

Morgan voice is firm. "Although we have carefully measured our resources for several days, we are down to one-half hogshead of water. Lucky we are to have captured it in our last raid. We must decrease the water restriction to one single mouthful every four hours. The weather has finally permitted us to take measurements with the astrolabe. Our location be directly to the west. I am confident we will make land fall in less than two days."

Groans forthcoming from all of the crew, Morgan reveals a gentler side to his character, showing he understands the discomfort plaguing them. "Now then, lads, a bit more effort, and Jamaica be ours. First call of land, we take our fill of water. Keep a sharp eye—she rises like a vision, hundreds of feet above the horizon." With confidence, Morgan adds, "There be a steady wind abeam. Our luck will hold."

*   *   *

Tom, one of the gun crew, grumbles, "Certain, hath a secret supply of water for his own use, I wager. He don't seem to be sufferin' much."

"Tom, be warned. Such talk is mutinous," whispers Weasel. "He hath no such store." His whining voice causes others look in his direction.

Once said, Tom fearfully looks around to see if anyone else has heard. Such talk would be taken as insubordinate.

Not the praying type, Weasel nonetheless surreptitiously bows his head. "Deliverance, Lord, if'n ye please." He has been with Morgan a long time, and though well aware of his sharp tongue and foul moods, Weasel really does not believe Morgan would partake of a luxury not available to his men.

* * *

His tongue sticking to his dry, cracked lips, John looks at the others. Cracked lips reflect the pangs of thirst he suffers. Mouth parched, John's tongue searches his thick and scaly mouth. His skin is dry and rough. Seeking the shadow of the sails, he begins to hallucinate and absentmindedly pinches the skin of his forearm between his thumb and forefinger. Softly he remarks, "It does not spring back into a soft smooth surface."

Although he knows nothing of human physiology, John is certain the cause is lack of water. Leaning up against the main mast, in his delirium a laughing demon appears, urging him to forsake his weakened

God. As the apparition leers, it grows larger, threatening, curling its claws. When the phantasm beckons with a long thin finger, John's eyes grow wide with terror.

"Come then. Ye be with us soon. Nay, not long now."

Shrinking back from its leering face, John squeezes his eyes and tries to shut out the laughing vision, the gapping white teeth, and the small pointed beard. Closing his eyes fails to make the face disappear. It whirls, twirls, and turns in front of John's face until pushed aside by a beautiful lady with long red hair. Feasting on the vision of his mother, John grasps the small pouch holding a lock of her hair before mercifully losing consciousness.

* * *

Awaking in the night, he retains only a faint memory of the loathsome specter. Head aching, he cannot rid himself of a feeling of extreme loss. He idly watches Tom pick at the air with his thumb and index finger, seemingly unaware of his surroundings.

An intolerable hour must pass before he is given his ration of water and sour wine. Determined to quench his thirst, John grabs the rim of a bucket containing salt water. Before he can scoop the water toward his mouth, a hand fiercely grabs his shoulder. A shake and a scream brings him roughly back to reality.

"Warned you, I did. No seawater. Death, certain," Mo admonishes for the third time that day. But it is not long before some of the crew, suffering inextinguishable thirst, begin to ignore Mo's warning. The following morning, three less hardy sailors surreptitiously dip their hands into the bucket again and again in attempts to assuage their thirst. By evening they suffer severe cramping and vomiting and die. Lacking emotion, the surviving crewmembers toss the victim's bodies into the sea. No ceremony marks their passing, no prayers except for a silent petition given by John. Apathetic, most of the crew show little interest as each hour passes without adequate liquid.

"Ah, well," reflects Weasel, "three less to share the precious few drops we have left."

*　　*　　*

Farther south the sun now climbs higher above the horizon at noon. The cross-staff is no longer useful in determining the ship's latitude. Morgan, his back to the sun, measures its altitude with a backstaff and determines that the ship is about eighteen degrees north of the equator. With this information, Morgan calls out, "Sail due west and we should collide with Jamaica."

The ship flies full sail before a meager breeze. Weakly, John observes, "Sun disappears quick here in the warmer waters. Why be that? Some evil spirit?"

"No. Morgan tells us 'tis but a sign we be below the Tropic of Cancer. Sun sinks quick, for sure. One minute be here, then she be gone below the sea. Not much twilight."

That night a surprise drop in temperature produces a small amount of dew. John eagerly sucks his damp shirt, licks the ship's rail for the life-giving moisture. With little residual strength, the men moan as they struggle to keep the ship moving on a westerly course.

*　　*　　*

The morning of the fifth day of rationing, with just a trickle of water remaining in the barrel, John hears Mo call out, "Land to starboard."

"Land starboard," Weasel whispers, "The southeast coast of Jamaica. Thar, see, be mountains ahead?" As if to verify his claim, sailing before the wind he sticks the fingers of his right hand in his mouth, coughing up just enough spit to moisten them. Raising his index finger, Weasel is encouraged. "Wind be out of the north-northeast, filling the sails proper. A good wind. A few tacks, and on to Port Royal faster than Jeb can flick the cat on your back."

"Fool he be," mocks Mo, "sticking his finger into the air. Ha! Scant feel the wind in the sails." Taking a deep breath of gratitude, Mo calls out, "For once a rocky coast be a welcomed sight." Pinching the bridge of his nose, Mo squeezes his eyes shut, slowly opening them to assure the mountains are not a mirage. The gesture seems to relieve the pressure in his head. Less than twelve miles away stands an island. It is not an illusion.

Morgan repeats, "Gentlemen, the southeast coast of Jamaica. Certain." As if of one body, the men inhale, filling their lungs with warm, tropical air, less ominous with land in sight.

"We anticipate a quick arrival into the protected harbor of Port Royal. Bear up, gentlemen. It be the fastest way to water." The men become increasingly animated, weakly punching the air with joy while they envision fresh water, wine, and grog.

*   *   *

Hours before reaching the safety of the protected harbor, the crew conjures up the pleasures awaiting them—jugs of grog, a rich variety of foods. Minds and bodies grown weary of the treacherous sea dream of women willing to provide them with pleasures of the flesh. Pretty or ugly, it really doesn't matter. It is, however, important that each man receive his long-dreamed-of welcome.

Each man has different expectations. Some falsely thinking that their reception at a house of ill repute is heartfelt and honest desperately feel that someone has missed them. Others who do not mislead themselves have never had enough affection in their lives to recognize the difference between lust and caring. To a man paying for these services, money is of no serious consequence. Most have money in their pockets.

"A sight that pleasures the eye," agrees Morgan. "Drink up the last drops of water and grog. We'll have plenty later this day. Slowly now, lads," he warns. "Start with just one cup each; then in turn have another. The stomach is certain to rebel if ye drink too quickly."

To emphasize the warning, their newly acquired surgeon adds, "Drink down quick, comes up even quicker. Quick toss over the side of the boat if ye be imprudent. Seen it many a time."

"Thank you, sir," says Morgan. "We'll rest a bit and indulge ourselves. Now, lads, to necessary duties. Let us sail proudly around the inlet into the harbor."

*   *   *

Relief overcomes John as they approach the safety of the harbor. However, his anxiety returns as he begins to consider he might be destined to remain on this boat for years. He may never be able to change the direction in which his life now seems fated. He is thousands of miles away from London, in a strange land surrounded by people with different ways. He fears that within the passage of a year, even less, he will become a different person. He frowns as he contemplates the possibility of a different man emerging out of his experiences, a man vastly different from the boy who lived for sixteen years in London. He makes an oath: he will emerge as someone his mother could still love and admire, if she ever sees him again—and even if she doesn't.

*   *   *

Morgan warns the crew against ignoring the work ahead, the toil necessary to keep the ship seaworthy. Gathering them together on the weather deck, he declares, "In a few weeks we'll careen and repair our fine Barque. Turn it over on the beach. It be important we remember our lives are only as solid as a trustworthy ship. The ship and the sea she sails on allow for no dishonesty."

As he walks up and down the deck, the feathers on his hat blow in the wind. Stopping to inspect the anchorage they have selected, he imagines the excitement of the upcoming chase and capture of Spanish ships. A smile spreads across his face as he slams his fist into his open palm. "Then off we go to seek treasure. Certain to be a ship, heavy with silk and silver, bound to Spain from South America! Eh, lads?"

"Huzzah!" they shout in approval.

The *Revenge* makes her way along the south side of a long spit of land in the late fall of 1665. Thirst quenched, hunger soon to be a distant nightmare, the pirates speak of their dreams of conquest as the English fort comes into sight. Sinking below the sea in shades of blazing reds, the sun makes a rapid descent. There are few bounds to their fantasies and excitement.

Sweeping his arm out over the rail, Mo boastfully announces, "Here she be, lads—one of the richest and busiest ports in the Americas. 'Tis this place that allows us to be what we be, do what we wants. Certain."

Most of the crew has never seen the island before. Except for the captives they all expect to go ashore.

"Will I be allowed to go ashore?" John asks Mo.

Mo spit out an honest reply. "All's that have signed the Articles can be trusted to go ashore. Changed your mind on that count?"

Mindful of his resolve, John answers, "I will not sign—not now nor ever."

"'Tis a fact. Certain, ye shan't be allowed to go ashore with these fine gentleman." Mo gestures to the other pirates. "Unfortunate, but simple as that," he says firmly, making no effort to conceal a cruel taunt.

CHAPTER 4

PORT ROYAL, JAMAICA

November 1, 1665

The hurricane season over, the *Revenge* tacks on the incoming tide across deep turquoise waters. John stares at the high mountains as the ship glides into the sheltered harbor of Port Royal, and his gaze then falls on the astonishing number of ships before him. Some drift quietly at anchor while others arrive through the channel with reduced sail. Some begin to raise sail as they prepare to launch.

"Why, there be at least four hundred ships here," John marvels. "Never before seen such a great harbor, so many ships. Although not really a harbor," he admits, "the River Thames always had hundreds of ships from many nations anchored along its length."

"Move on! Spill the canvases," Jeb bellows. Bringing his starter down, he strikes the mast just inches from John's back. "Free time be over. Earns your keep now, ye will. Time to bring the ship into port."

Moving aside, John narrowly misses a jarring impact with Morgan as he strolls aft to take command.

Standing near Mo, Morgan takes his familiar stance of authority: hands clasped behind him, head thrown back. Tilting his chin toward the sky he pulls his hat low over his forehead in an attempt to protect his eyes from the bright glare of the Caribbean sun. A sharp nod indicates their intended course toward the northern shore.

"Lay her for the harbor," Morgan calls to Jeb. "Not a minute to spare. This night we sleep soundly in Port Royal." He adds, "Bring her into the wind."

Scrambling to their assigned positions, eight abreast on the yard, the topmen await their command before hauling up on the reef points to begin shortening the canvas. With less sail exposed to the wind, the *Revenge* slows. Morgan searches for a place to drop anchor among the ships already in the harbor.

In less than forty-five minutes they reach their intended anchorage. After a command of "Let go" the anchor splashes to the bottom of the harbor.

"Beautiful execution." Morgan addresses his men with a sharp salute.

"Hands to mooring stations," Jeb yells. The ship drifts in response to the breeze while the crew plays out the anchor cable. Sails secured, the topmen climb down the ratlines and hurry over to gain a position on the leeward rail. Pushing, shoving, and craning their necks, the men all try to achieve an unobstructed line of vision to the shore. They have survived the voyage and are finally safely at anchor. Their thirst will soon be relieved from the barrels of fresh water being fetched from the shore by Tom and Weasel.

*   *   *

In the lee of the mountain, on the near shore, a woman slowly rises from her sitting position on a small wharf. The men push each other to vie for a place at the rail to ogle her.

"Round in the hips, she is," a topman shouts his approval.

"Tries to gits her attention," urges another.

The maid waves in response to their hoots and obscene gestures. The cacophony of cheers and jeers increase in response.

"Eh, lady, give ye piece or two. What say?" Weasel shouts.

At first, teasing the sailors, the woman waves and twirls about in her bright colorful clothing, wiggling her ample hips in a teasing manner. She calls out, but the men are too distant to hear her response. As abruptly as the game began she turns and walks away. Aware that none of these men will immediately be coming ashore, she tires of a game that is no longer entertaining or profitable. She lives in the present to survive. Waving good-bye, she hurries a few yards to grab the arm of an interested sailor. The men of the *Revenge* bellow in sorrow when the woman saunters off with a tall mariner not known to them. Knowing the futility of their game, the crew jeers in unison to the sway of her generous derrière.

*   *   *

"All right, ye curs, the harlot be gone," Mo trumpets into the breeze. "Help Tom hoist that barrel of water aboard." Then he adds, "Why does ye not gits ready to go ashore?"

Seeing that they were going to abandon the barrel halfway between the brig and small boat, he roars, "Wait, wait. First, gits more water and drink. Then be shore time."

So directed, the seamen turn their attentions to the duties they must complete before they cross the water to the tropical paradise.

Morgan directs the men who are pulling the barrels onto the deck. "Sort out the barrels needing repair. Tend to them later. For now, fill the small boats with enough good barrels to last us a week. We will fill the rest after we careen the ship."

*   *   *

"Go ashore. Find what help ye can. Quick, now, lads," Mo orders. "Cast off."

Rehydrated, the work crew quickly rows to shore. Necks swiveling, they search for women, hoping for a few lewd exchanges.

At the wharf Mo hires sufficient hands to assist in loading hogsheads of water into the launch. His men so occupied, he purchases extra barrels of wine and beer, but water is the priority. They then comb the market for fruit, meats, and fish. There are men to be fed—men who will remain confined to the brig until

Morgan decides they are no longer an escape risk. The last task is to hoist the barrels aboard the brig.

Morgan begins preparations to visit the local governor. Typical of his aristocratic bent, he considers this rendezvous to be a social pastime—beyond the ken of his crew. Having spent years establishing a life of ease in Port Royal, he has an open invitation to visit numerous plantations as often as he pleases. Dressed in finery carefully selected in London, he plans to live like a lord on the grounds of the governor. His uncouth crew will not fit into this social milieu.

Mo and John stand together on the larboard side, keeping an eye on the bantering of the crew. Speaking of days past and days to come, Mo tells John, "Some ships carry women. Not so Morgan. Captain believes women on board makes for fighting among the men. Anticipation of things to come in Port Royal keeps them in line. Better sailors."

"The men have no say in the matter?" asks John.

"Morgan's opinion be law. Captain he be, after all. Further," Mo continues, "women turn men against each other in unhealthy ways. None onboard have known comfort for many months, since London. They know well their fate if they force their will on the women from a captured ship." Pausing with a grin, he adds, "Lacking her consent, of course."

"Have not seen any women survive capture," notes John.

*   *   *

Mo makes an attempt to shout instructions above the bantering among the men. Oblivious to what is being said for their benefit, they mostly ignore him.

Anxiously awaiting a ride to shore, a pirate grumbles, "No women for months."

"Patience, my man. Not long now."

"Well, damme, not much interested in else but women."

"Too busy for women," another argues. "Anxious for a good fight, I am. Shows me a worthy opponent, see a battle ye will." Ducking, he avoids a fake jab to his stomach by one of his crewmates.

"Gives ye a fight, we will. Hack ye right up," they snigger in chorus.

Shouting above his competition, Mo, taking pride in his past experiences in Jamaica, describes this mysterious port of call. Mo hopes that Morgan will hear him and recognize that he is capable of leading the men, even if to a public house. Intent on hearing his own voice, Mo pays no attention to the crew's restless comments.

"Years past, island be Spanish. Now English she be. Lotsa pirates takes refuge here, with government approval. One hand washes the other," Mo chuckles. "Watch yourselves, men. Lotsa thieves and pirates onshore. Some not as genteel as ye lads may be. Ha!"

"Seek out the Green Parrot," a gravelly voice calls out.

"Gits your throat cut there, if'n you're not careful," shouts another. "Faster than can gits your knife out of your pants."

"Greedy vultures abide there. Finds yourself drugged, robbed, if'n you're lucky. Dead if not."

Frustrated, Mo tries to hold the men's attention. "Avoids fights, please to do," he pleads, volume rising. "Lives longer, if'n ye do. Avoid gaming. Here be as crooked as a snake escaping over hot tar." Calming his voice, he warns, "Stays away from the English fort, mind ye, lessen ye wants to end up confined." Pointing his finger, "Fort be on that narrow spit of land. See how the spit curves out to the southeast? A jewel set in the clear blue waters of the Caribbean." Tilting his head back Mo shades his eyes in an attempt to reduce the bright glare of the sun. Looking out through slits, he points toward the fort. "See the sparkles in the sand where the sun be focused? Like diamonds. Look sharp, lads. Tis the English ye find there. Guns, not diamonds."

*   *   *

Elegantly dressed, preening with self-satisfaction, Morgan emerges from his cabin. Soft, wide cuffs trimmed with fine white lace ring the tops of his red leather boots. John looks with envy at the embroidered braid decorating the edges of the creamy silk lining of his red damask waistcoat.

"Would aspire to that," John mumbles. "Hmm, looks exactly like King Charles. Hath almost as much power." Disapprovingly, he mutters, "Plain clothes are enough for a godly man." John tries not to admire the straight-cut legs of the white breeches that are worn loose without garters. Atop Morgan's head sits a tall red hat crowned with a narrow brim. At the apex is the omnipresent feather.

*   *   *

Pacing the deck, white feather blowing in the wind, Morgan stops to inspect the anchor and assures himself that all is properly secured. Anxious to get underway, Morgan hurries to his rendezvous with people he considers to be of a more genteel persuasion. Remembering the many reasons for leaving impoverished Wales, a smile spreads across his face.

"A month here, more or less," he speculates. "Then a few days making repairs before we go back to chasing wayward ships." Laughing with pleasure, he imagines his crew boarding unsuspecting Spanish merchants or capturing a Dutch ship at war with England. "Treasure, easy money be mine—with the correct strategy." Stopping midstride, he slams his fist into an open palm and brags to no one in particular, "Sure to be a treasure ship bound for Spain with riches from South America." He turns to his men. "Eh, lads?"

Pausing in his speculation, he reminds the crew, "Labor ahead before we rove. Not all leisure, me lads. Fun first—make the ship seaworthy. Then, mayhap, more fun." Looking about at their questioning faces, he adds, "In a month, or a bit more, we'll careen on the beach. Repairing our fine brig, 'tis our first priority.

Our lives be only as certain as a trustworthy brig. A boat and the sea she sails allow for no dishonesty, no inattention to necessary details. Found that out on this trip to Port Royal, did we not? But for now enjoy the time here, lads. Then ye be ready to work again."

"Careful now. You know what you must do. Be certain to have enough men." He looks at Mo with meaning.

Waving his adieu, he laughingly reminds the men, "Remember now, save some coin for your dotage."

They stare at Morgan in disbelief.

*   *   *

Weasel begins to dance an Irish jig across the deck, singing, "Mary waits for me onshore, tra la!" A few men clap their hands as he sings out with joy, moving his feet in time to the rhythm. "Waits for me, she does, she does! Tra la, tra la."

"Your dreams will be awash in the sea, Weasel," says the bleary-eyed old surgeon, who has already started to imbibe his daily ration of brandy. "Now why and forever wouldst she wait for the likes of ye?"

"A secret twix me and me ladies," smirks Weasel. "Something ye wilst never knows."

Ribald jokes about "ugly Mary" were quickly followed by an increase in snickers and hearty laughter from his companions. "While the fair moon arises above his fine Mary, her wide bottom sinks to the depths of the sea."

"Won't matter," Weasel boasts. "Always another where she be from, one broad in her stern. Wants somethin' to hang on ta."

"Whoever the lass may be will first soak ye in a tub," Jeb interjects. "Clean ye up. She will."

"Women likes manly men," retorts Weasel. "Real men don't wash. Women, neither."

* * *

As they complete their shipboard duties, the sun, well past it zenith, shimmers in the southwest sea. Anchors set, water barrels stored, sails tightly furled, and slops emptied, their last duty is to scrub the decks with the seawater.

A few men fight over a bucket of water, making an attempt to be more presentable by standing under the tipped bucket to wash their face, hands, and bodies. After a few strokes of their hands to smooth their hair, they are ready and anxious to go to town. Torn shirts and trousers do not matter. None have ever owned a pair of stockings; in rough contrast to Morgan they stand barefoot inside their soft leather shoes.

* * *

Envious of their freedom, John watches the crew set off in the small boats. A captive, he is not allowed to leave the brig. Long weeks have passed since he last stood on firm ground. His eyes wander around the anchorage as he questions, "This great southern harbor looks calm. Is this truly a tropical paradise? Is this calmness a deception? What of storms?" He imagines he can smell the sweet scent of the brightly colored flowers and tropical trees lining the shore. Leaning across the rail, he can see the tops of palm trees swaying gently in the tropical breeze.

The mountains to the east give the harbor a sheltered appearance, but he knows that frequent hurricanes visit the island without warning during the late summer and fall months. Winds tear up trees, destroy shanties along the beach, and toss ships about as if they were toys. These lacerating winds do not spare the elegant homes of the wealthy.

* * *

A blanket protecting his fine clothing, Morgan encourages his men to row to shore as swiftly as possible. The men strain, pulling hard on the oars to make progress against the offshore wind.

"Quickly now, mates. Make haste. Sooner I make shore, quicker ye have free time."

Once Morgan's feet touch solid land, it takes but a few steps for him to regain his land legs. Even after months at sea, his balance is certain. Before striding toward the governor's villa, he turns once, bows, and bids the crew adieu.

* * *

After obtaining the ship and most of his crew in London, Morgan used his abilities to subtly control the men with his wit and intelligence, influencing them to elect him captain. Most of the men had sailed with him on other voyages. They recognized the advantages of having a leader clearly under the protection of the islands' administrators.

There are many governors throughout the English-controlled islands of the Caribbean. By guile and good manners Morgan has curried a close association with the most influential, exerting his influence when in their ports.

Anticipating a warm welcome, Morgan strolls immediately to the governor's villa. Across the years, these two men have developed a satisfying relationship. In this isolated part of the world each man carefully plays his part to his own advantage in a game of mutual protection.

Morgan seeks good company, fine food, selected wines, and the indulgence of the governor's daughter, to whom he has hinted, but successfully avoided, marriage. For his part, the English governor takes advantage of the pirates' ability to help protect Jamaica from hostile French and Spanish military forces while awaiting the English army and navy to capture other previously lost Caribbean islands.

Although the island's society is less cultured than London, it is a refuge for the pirates. Morgan is satisfied no one will attempt to convict him of piracy and hang him.

An elaborate meal is served by slaves. After dinner the ladies are excused, and the small, elite group of white men leisurely smoke pipes, enjoying the fine wine carried across the Atlantic by Morgan in his cabin. He smiles at the success of his deception, having successfully hidden the wine from his starving, dehydrated men.

*   *   *

Surrounded by an appreciative audience of local landowners, Morgan relaxes on a veranda encircled by lush tropical flora. Swirling a glass of fine wine, Morgan tells the governor of the harrowing experiences on the way to Jamaica. Elaborating on how they had run short of supplies and their usual menu of meats, he relates about how they had been forced to eat hard tack. His listeners express sympathy, dismayed by the alarming stories of days without sufficient fluids.

"Gentlemen, ye cannot imagine the untold horrors the crew suffered for lack of water and spirits. Terrible tricks their minds played on them, hallucinations of imagined devils and serpents—most appalling, but now history. After a short pause, he continues with a laugh, "Now that I've plenty to eat and drink, life is much improved." Leaning closer, Morgan bows to his host, "Sir, thoughts of your table kept me alive. That and, of course, the extra skin of wine hidden in my cabin, most beneficial in a time of need. Tragic for me it would have been had the crew discovered it." With a wave of his hand, Morgan dismisses the importance of his betrayal. Without apology he murmurs, "Ah, but a small amount, I swear." A smile causes his tiny mustache to curve up with mirth. "Well, a near tragedy, but not comparable to months without a fetching damsel. Gentlemen, the terror of both stations be overwhelming to the tender disposition of one unlike myself who is not truly an adventurer."

Seeing the looks of disbelief passing between the men, he ruefully amends, "'Tis true. An adventurer is what I be."

The flickering candles cast glimmers of light across the veranda, causing Morgan to suggest one further toast, "To sweethearts and wives. May they never meet." In response to a spattering of laughter, Morgan admits, "Ah, never suggested it was an original toast. A man should never hesitate to borrow that which fits the situation."

"Spoken like a true sailor of the realm," yields his host. The men join in derisive laughter. With good humor and wry grins, the men raise their glasses in a salute.

*   *   *

After delivering Morgan safely ashore, the men jostle for position, awaiting their turns to climb into the boats that will take them to a night of revelry. Boisterous, anxious to disembark, each jokes, companionably clamping a hand on the shoulder of the man closest to him.

"Remember, what sign leads ye to women?" one asks.

"Shan't forget. Sign in the road shows the stiff part of a man," several recite in unison.

"Carved in stone. Points the way," another says. They all agree they will have more fun than their captain, whom they see as restrained by his straight fashionable appearance and prissy ways. Nervously, each man becomes aware that it is not wise to ridicule Morgan. They might be overheard, appear disloyal— could be dangerous.

"Allows, he be good captain," one interjects. "Can be trusted."

The *Revenge* anchored, supplied, and secured to Jeb's satisfaction, the most senior of the crew climb into the shore boats. After quickly rowing to shore, Weasel and his mates mix with pirates from many lands. Converging on Lime Street, they vie for the services of women whose livelihoods depend upon meeting a seafarer's needs. Not needing a symbol of male virility to show him the way to Mary, Weasel arrives at his destination to find her gone.

"Sophia, where is Mary? Weasel hopefully asks.

"Gone. With an English seaman," her friend explains.

"Left more 'an a month ago," jeers Ruthie, with a great deal of satisfaction.

"Broke away from His Majesty's ship," adds Sophia, a beautiful woman with long red hair and a decidedly Irish look about her. "Left on a ship bound for Portofino, in Italy."

Weasel yells out, "What the hot blazes? How dare she?" With a hoot, his protest and sadness last only to the end of his sentence. It is not the first time a woman has disappointed him. Immediately Weasel tosses a silver coin and catches it again, looking around at other prospects. The coin quickly catches the eye of Lilly, a beckoning wench leaning out a second story window. She invites Weasel up to her room.

"Sailed off with another gent, she did," taunts one of his mates. But already Weasel has fixed his thoughts on other opportunities.

"Found me another twat quick enough," Weasel boasts, starting up the stairs. "Money enough in me poke. Waste no time, I won't. To the devil with Mary."

*　　*　　*

Morgan, considering him a high escape rise, left orders for John to remain on the ship, suspecting he would seek out the British navy if set free in town.

Jeb had argued, "Crew needs free time. Shouldn't be responsible for John."

"John and the other captives stay aboard. All others will seek their pleasures ashore. Someone must remain with the prisoners at all times."

Mo and Jeb assign John numerous duties to occupy his time and alert the others to be aware of any warnings of imminent escape. Compared to the amount of work Morgan requires of the men at sea, the labors performed while at anchor are simple. Josh, the sail maker, is assigned to teach the captives how to apply seam rubber to the creases in the lower fold of a canvas. Under the hot sun, the noxious fumes under the hot sun, make them lightheaded.

*   *   *

"Old sails needs a patchin'," Josh says. "Use patched sails where sturdier sails not be required, such as in light air."

Against Jeb's orders, taking a chance he won't be attacked, Josh hands John a needle and teaches him how to repair sails.

Although spending hours using a needle to loop twine through the canvas, John still finds time to climb into the rigging, where he sits on a yardarm, watching the distant activity onshore and dreaming of escape. There are no sails to hoist or trim and fewer slop buckets to empty. Most of the men are ashore; the rest expel their slop directly into the harbor.

For the first time in his life, John relaxes under the soothing rays of a hot sun. Hundreds of miles away from the fumes of London, he worries about the fate of his family while his body thickens and tans.

Toward evening, the shadows lengthen, and the gray shape cast by the main mast appears to caress the far shore. John contemplates the carefree lives of the pirates, who seem to be obsessed with action, drink, and adventure. In spite of their evil, the pirates eat and drink better than ever he did in London, unless of course they run out of supplies. They have no concern for the inescapable fate dealt their captives or the horror of their deaths.

*   *   *

John is startled by a presence close behind him. Mo whispers, "Enjoy your leisure whilst ye can. Soon we heave down. Careen. Cleans the barnacles off her fine bottom." Making pushing motions against John's shoulder, he demonstrates a boat being turned over on the beach. "Over on her side she goes."

Mo's fingers begin stroking, moving slowly down John's arm to his hands. Repulsed, John pulls back. Ignoring John's shutter, Mo continues rubbing, "Smooth hands ye 'ave. Smooth, like a lady's, even after all these months." With a friendly laugh, he adds, "Waits till ye really works up a sweat. Scrape and rub. Toughen ye up, for certain. Ye 'ave fine hands for the job."

After his revulsion at the touch passes, John turns and stares in rapt amazement at Mo. There has been a complete metamorphosis, His clothes and hair are clean. His braided beard shines, free of grease and debris. And more, Mo's bearing reminds John of a dandy walking the streets of London, the scent of floral perfume wafting after him.

Mo seems to take no notice of John's bewilderment. Rubbing his hands together, Mo visualizes the new scars soon to disfigure John's hands.

"A week scraping the ship's bottom will take the softness away," he vows. An onlooker would see two very different men standing within a few feet of each other, almost sharing the same space—one ragged, one elegantly dressed. Each man has his own thoughts, his own plans. Different agendas. Both need Morgan's approval.

Patiently Mo explains Morgan's reasons for careening the ship, "Needs to clean her. Barnacles, cracks, bumps slows her down. Won't catch a merchant. Certain."

Noticing John's furtive glance toward shore, Mo assures, "Patience, lad, soon as he trusts ye, ashore ye go."

Looking idly into the clear cerulean water, John complains, "Not much to do, sitting in the harbor. Idle hours." He does not tell Mo about how he spends his days alone on the ship.

* * *

After two weeks of near starvation, an unrestricted amount of good food has restored John to good health. Lost body weight is being replaced.

Confined to the anchored ship, little more than one hundred feet long, John mends sail, swings in the rigging, and climbs the ratlines into the tops, where he scans the horizon for possible paths of escape. Absently probing his upper arm, he idly traces newly formed biceps and triceps, contours emphasized by skin made brown in the sun.

John has fantasies about parading his changed body before his mother. "No one in London be this dark. Wouldn't be recognized." In awe, he studies his reflection in the smooth water. "How strong I am since they captured me."

John has grown tall, his chest measuring at least two inches higher than the ship's rail. "Near as tall as Jeb," he marvels, surreptitiously peering back at the stern, where Jeb is staring hypnotically at the water. "Another three inches and I'll top him." Wishfully, he adds, "Perhaps then he'll leave me in peace. Wonder—could I beat him in a fight?"

Most sailors fear Jeb and are reluctant to be within his reach. Some, certain the Devil lives in his black body, wisely dread the power conferred upon him by Morgan.

"No question he hath their respect, but do they respect his ability to lead them into battle, or fear his unpredictability and cruelty? Cannot be certain. Jeb is indispensable to Morgan. He never expects another man to stand alone against any threat or danger—insists on leading the way into battle." John wishes he had someone in whom he could safely confide.

Again, he peers down into the water, pleased to see the reflection of a strong male, dark hair streaked with red and pulled back into a pigtail. "Can that truly be me? Gideon would laugh in wonder at how I've grown." Sadly remembering Gideon sitting in the boat, coughing, he declares, "Dead, no doubt."

*   *   *

Having learned enough seamanship to survive, John must find an escape route that will take him directly to the English Navy. Sitting on the yard, he pretends to tighten the ropes around the canvases while again searching the harbor for possible avenues of escape. Sails furled, it would take no effort for someone below to see what he is doing; no one bothers. Suspended one hundred feet above the water, John has an excellent view of ships coming into and leaving the harbor.

"Very soon, be certain to make it to shore. Find a way out." John finds himself lethargic, unaccustomed to the heat, and his thinking becomes sluggish. After three weeks of plotting, John now believes his plan may be futile. "Beyond the shore, there be nothing but jungle. Spirits reside there, certain. I hear them moaning across on the wind."

Close inspection of the hundreds of ships and sails anchored within line of sight of the *Revenge* fails to reveal the presence of an English man-of-war. Lacking an eyepiece, he sees nothing of interest and begins to drop small stones into the water. The sea is smooth, glassy enough for John to study thousands of mirrored reflections. The ripples the stones create fascinate him. Images of clouds appear to scatter like a flock of sheep under the ship. Remembering Mo's advice that he should learn to predict the weather, he begins to study the sky. Towering clouds begin to drift across the horizon. Their soft edges indicate the clouds are no longer building.

"Dying thunderclouds. Threat of a storm be not imminent—at least for now. But Mo says that here in the tropics conditions change quickly."

*   *   *

Rubbing his gums with his forefinger, John detects no soreness. "Most satisfactory."

He recalls Mo's words: "Gums gets sore, bleed. Great relief when they fall out." He knows that scurvy is a terrible malady. "Assaults the body. No energy. Pain. Sores in your limbs. Can't eat. Mouth gits soft, like a sponge."

"Da had sores," John told Mo. "Burst forth just before he died. Later, poor Tristram had one arise in his armpit."

"'Tis a different disease. Man can suffer scurvy whilst none of his mates suffer from it. Your teeth don't have time to fall out in the plague."

*   *   *

Grimacing as he balances his hips over the rail, John stretches downward toward the water and grins broadly, satisfied when his reflection mirrors strong, even teeth. After a tug on each one he jubilantly proclaims, "All fast."

Most of his shipmates are as toothless as Tristram and Samuel were when Mam bore them. John thinks; *perhaps better to have no teeth than to be left with one or two black stubs. Makes for foul breath. True, it be just another odor on a ship that already hath so many other unpleasant smells.* He considers Morgan's good fortune in having a place onshore where he can escape the vile odors of his shipmates.

Schools of colorful parrotfish quietly parade beneath the brig in a silent underwater dance among the clouds. Disrupting the ship's reflection, they float above a pink coral bed surrounded by brilliant red and pink lace fans that sway in the current.

"A demon!" John howls, pointing to a fin creasing the water. Remembering the attacks of sharks on helpless victims during their voyage, he jumps back, his heart feeling as if it will burst out of his chest. Running amidships, he escapes from the evil apparition. Sprinting to see who has screamed, several sailors push him aside.

"Looky there," one yells, pointing to a long, black shadow casually swimming away. The men snicker at John to cover up their own fear.

The sail maker places his thumb on his head, fanning his fingers in the shape of a shark's fin. "Here be a real shark to gits ye," he cries, charging John while wagging his tongue back and forth. "Hee, hee, see him run," he shouts. A few men begin to form a circle around John, attempting even further humiliation, by intimidation.

Shunning them, John walks quietly away. Bravely attempting to appear unconcerned, he keeps his eyes directed ahead. Ignoring their jeers, John resolves not to be frightened by this group of heathens.

"Loathsome creatures. Soon, have my turn."

*   *   *

As the sanguineous sun sinks below the horizon, John climbs down to the weather deck, surprised to find fresh fruit lying on the hatch. Remembering Mo goading him into eating a green banana the previous week, he laughs. Not recognizing it was not ripe, he bit into the fruit, skin and all.

"Phooey," he uttered as he unsuccessfully tried to spit out the bitter residue sticking to his teeth. Laughing, Mo and Weasel slapped their legs and then danced with glee.

The banana is bright yellow, but John sniffs it with suspicion.

"Try again, lad," Mo hectors. "'Tis a ripe one. Sweet as honey, it be."

Trying to restore John's trust, the two men turn away, leaving the fruit lying atop the cabin.

"Like this one better, ye will!" they shout over their shoulders. "Certain."

Curious, John presses on the fruit to test its ripeness.

"Not to be fooled twice," he shouts.

Easily peeling off the skin, John tastes the sweet ripe banana that seems to melt on his tongue, and groans with pure delight, "Oh, so sweet!" A heavenly reprieve, a most welcome change from the hardtack with its wriggling insect occupants.

Two more weeks pass. As John grows increasingly restless, it is difficult to take his eyes off the brown path leading through the trees.

CHAPTER 5

ASHORE

January 1666

Motionless in the shadows, Jeb stands, his muscles twitching in response to his increasing rage. "Mo been acting as though he be second-in-command. And now this! Weasel and Mo bragging, telling the men they be Morgan's equals. What 'bout me?" he mutters.

*   *   *

Morgan, rarely aboard, leaves the responsibility for discipline to Jeb or Mo—not to Weasel, who seems free to be gone for days at a time, a laxity in surveillance John hopes might work to his advantage. Unseen, John crouches on the maintop above their heads. This first sign of competition between these three men might be a break in the pirates' strict code of loyalty to each other. Could this tension build to his advantage? Other crewmembers might well be tired of being treated with disdain. Will they revolt? Perhaps the new clothing worn by Mo and Weasel is a sign they are taking power away from Jeb.

Each man depends upon an intact system of mutual defense for his protection, and intact it has always been. Although John has seen signs of kindness in Mo and Weasel, the other pirates remain aloof, showing no signs of comradeship. To them, John remains invisible, an unsigned man. No one seems willing to take the risk of befriending him.

*   *   *

John suspects Mo has an ulterior motive for his kindness: a desire to weaken John's reluctance to sign the pact that will make him one of the pirates.

"Maybe part of a game. Mo pretends to be someone I can trust, gives favors with ill intent. Tries to influence me into becoming a voluntary recruit." Mulling this over, he wonders, *But then, what does it matter to them? How is it to their advantage? Me mum understood people's motives. Would that she were here.*

Deep in thought, John rests his arm on a starboard cannon, idly swatting at a mosquito. *Not a healthy place, the West Indies. Some be plagued by mosquito bites, ugly red welts.*

In spite of the pleasant warmth of the sun, John hopes the day is close at hand when he will sail away from this insect-infested stink hole. Slaps punctuate the air, the sounds of futile attempts to kill the annoying insects.

*   *   *

At the first symptoms of the fever, Jeb has the surgeon send a warning to Morgan. "Belay coming aboard. Your good health be vital to our financial success. Crew agrees your health must not be compromised."

Morgan has already been at the governor's villa for a period exceeding three weeks. He does not argue or express disappointment. "I shall remain at the villa until the pestilence hath run it course," he informs the messenger. "Only fair to warn others away. Raise the Q flag. Bring it down only when safe for me to return." He tells himself, "Lucky, I am."

Weasel hastens to raise the yellow flag that shouts to all others of the quarantine.

At least ten crewmembers languish in the extreme tropical heat, victims of the fever.

"Stricken in town," John speculates to Josh. A shiver scrambles down John's spine when Isaac begins to retch black vomit; his yellow-tinged body shimmers with sweat.

Isaac whispers, "Grateful I be to depart this place of torment. Me feeble body can take no more." He begs, "Promise to see me family, should ever ye gets back to London. Live near Black Raven Alley." Dying, Isaac makes frequent exhortations to God. "Leave me go. Best off I be with ye." On Monday, he dies.

Two days later William follows Isaac in death. By the third day, a total of four have crossed the bar after several days of sweats and high fever.

"Barbados fever. Best to die quick," Mo declares with a shake of his head, standing as far away from the stricken men as the length and width of the brig allows.

John affirms, "Glad I am that I have been captive on the brig. They must have contacted the fever while ashore."

Wrapped in shrouds and weighted down by shot, the pirates unceremoniously throw the victims overboard.

"Deep harbor, room for many bodies," theorizes Weasel. He sighs. "Sad to note, many bodies already rest there."

"The sea will cleanse," responds Mo. "Not wise to get too friendly with any. Could be dead tomorrow. Death never far away."

Night breezes drift across the deck but do little to dissipate a heat intolerable to those suffering with fever. If enough men die John suspects the hunt will begin for replacements. An armed brig requires many recruits to man the cannon and tend the sails. *How will Morgan manage?* he wonders.

Unbeknownst to his crew, Morgan secretly appeals to the governor for assistance in obtaining men to supplement the number who have died or will die. Raising his wineglass in a salute to his dinner companions, he says, "With luck, also be able to set up a crew for a sloop to go north with us."

"That should be no trouble at all," replies his host, and so the deal is struck.

*   *   *

John is sitting upon an overturned bucket when, after six weeks in the harbor, Morgan returns to the brig.

"Get ready to go ashore, lad." Morgan laughs. Seeing the surprised expression on John's youthful face, he warns, "Mo shoulders the responsibility for ensuring you do not escape.

"Keep your eyes open," he cautions Mo. "The lad needs time off the boat before we leave here. His punishment will be yours if he escapes. Successfully manage him, and your reward will be great."

"'Tis as safe a place as any," agrees Mo.

Pointing a well-manicured finger at John, Morgan warns, "Trust me, mate, 'tis no place to jump ship. Just end up caught by another pirate looking for crew. Any attempt to escape be futile, but should ye try, severe the penalty will be."

With a menacing squint, Morgan places a curled index finger next to his small, pointed beard. "If ye value life, stick close to Mo. Try to escape and death will be slow by my hand or ye will be killed by some fearsome creature in the jungle." Sneering with great relish, he adds, "The choice be with ye. Ye decide. Ye do not look a fool."

*   *   *

Mo, Weasel, and John row ashore with six other pirates. As the tender touches the beach, John's

155

excitement overcomes him. Following the example of the other sailors, he leaps out of the boat. Landing on his right foot, he immediately staggers and falls, dropping to his hands and knees.

Laughing, the others shout, "Need to gits your land legs. On solid ground ye be."

Standing, John takes a shaky step on the beach, finding it almost impossible to place his right foot in front of his left. Swaying, he rocks from side to side as if crossing the deck of a ship in the middle of a storm. Mo and Weasel, their gait steady, quickly outdistance him. Looking to the ground, struggling to walk a straight path, John does not see his companions turn and come around behind him. A sharp whack to his back lands him flat on his face.

Laughing, Weasel and Mo yank him into a standing position. Pulling John along, they shout encouragement. "Come now, lad, keeps up! Lime Street be ahead."

John's gait quickly steadies, and he manages to take increasingly longer strides, soon catching up with the pirates. Near the end of a short, dusty street, the trio veers right into a narrow lane. Halfway down Lime Street two- and three-story buildings hang high over the cobbles. Blocking the sun, they throw the end of the street into a deep impenetrable gloom. As his pupils dilate to compensate for the change in lighting, John's throat constricts with dread as they enter the ominous unlit alley.

Surrounded by deep shadows, four women stand around a well caught in the shaft of light caused by the sinking sun peeking between two buildings. Using a winch and pulley they bring water to the surface in heavy oaken buckets. The arriving men capture the attention of a slim-waisted young maiden. Smiling, she pulls back her long blonde hair, using a graceful hand to knot it close to the back of her head. The cut of her blue diaphanous blouse clings to the curve of her shoulders and drapes over her ample breasts. John unexpectedly feels heat rise in his cheeks, an increase in the beat of his heart, and tension in his groin. Embarrassed, he averts his eyes. Not daring to stare, he whispers, "Lovely."

"Me duty to keep ye close," Mo grumbles.

As the men grab John's arms to keep him from lagging, loud, screeching laughter rips across the courtyard. The tars turn as one, looking for the source. A plump arm waves a white handkerchief out of a window. John winces, his upper arm caught in Mo's viselike grip, which does not loosen even while the pirate scans the buildings for more women.

"Values me neck, I do. If'n ye values yours, best not try to slip away. Responsible for ye. Seek ye out no matter where ye go. Certain."

Mo abruptly frees John. Stunned by his apparent freedom and sobered by Mo's warning, John does not attempt to run. With a single motion Mo shoves John up against a rough, uneven wall. Sharp edges of stone cut into his back through the thin gauzy shirt.

Mo issues a harsh demand. "Stays here till we returns, lad. Be warned—stays till we be back."

Scampering up the irregularly worn stone steps, Mo and Weasel halt on a partially concealed landing. Lingering under a tree pregnant with large bright red flowers, Mo pauses to smell the blooms. Impatiently Weasel surges ahead, clutching at the generously endowed woman who waved the handkerchief.

Spying, striving to determine the source of the laughter, John moves close enough to see that a room is situated above the tavern. Visible through one of the windows, their arms tightly entwined around two appreciative females. Mo and Weasel are eagerly exchanging kisses with the willing ladies. Face crimson, John lowers his eyes to the brightly colored sign hanging over the open door. A picture boldly displays the pleasures available on the second floor— for a price. He has never before seen such a sign, not even in London, but John immediately understands it designates a place where men pay coin to spend time with prostitutes.

He remembers a word the preacher had used— *depraved.* "Such behavior would produce a scowl on the faces of respectable people." John sees a man leave the tavern. Never having seen the governor before, he does not recognize him.

John freezes after noticing a figure lurking in the shadows. Fearful, he moans, "Oh, precious Father, be too risky to run." Nervously biting his index finger, he murmurs, "Could be from the *Revenge.* I dare not go. Who knows what demons dwell in the jungle?" Looking at the shadowy figure, he whispers, "If'n I did, what foes will follow me there?"

*   *   *

John senses that evil dwells everywhere in Port Royal. Bawdy women, pirates, and mariners from many countries roam the streets. He will not attempt an escape until he can flee to the safety of a king's ship. He is certain His Majesty's officers will protect him. After all, he has been kidnapped against his will. Another possibility occurs to him. "Mayhap I can buy passage on a ship. Soon will have some coin in my pocket. I will wait until Morgan distributes the prizes."

Stopping short, John considers the first serious moral dilemma of his young life. Guilt seizes him at the thought of accepting misbegotten money. Stoutly, he declares, "Ill-gotten gains, money earned in gore."

He will not to go into a house with the painted ladies—that's an easy decision—but he blushes when the girl he saw on his way into town proposes to him.

"Come with me, mon. Loverly room I have."

She appears to be his age. Not soiled. Her closeness brings with it the scent of tropical flowers. The sight of her clean, long blonde hair, neatly combed, makes it difficult for John to stick firm to his resolve. Swallowing hard, the vision of his mother's face lined with strict disapproval dances before him. Grateful that his poor condition saves him from temptation, he declares, "Have no coin." Walking away, gracefully swinging her hips, she pauses and looks back with a hopeful look on her face, as if he might save her.

When the girl disappears, John begins to think about the prize money. "More ships will be captured, lives lost. 'Tis not virtuous to share in profits they take as easily from others as a holy man receives a sacrament from God." Knowing God would severely punish him if he robbed others; he swears to be done with it. "Simple as that.

"Options be few. I need passage on another ship; else I cannot escape these dogs. Sadly, I may not be rescued by a king's ship." Caustically he reminds himself, "Indeed, fool, how many king's men have ye seen during these past months at sea? None! The truth is clear—with prize money I can escape, but to use these ill-begotten gains is an affront to God."

Mo and Weasel return from the bawdyhouse, each with a buxom painted lady on his arm. "Come, lad, continue on round the town. Lots to see."

They shove their companions away. Surprisingly clean hair falls across their faces as they gallantly bow, sighing. "Farewell, fair harlot. Return at dark, true."

Turning to John, with a wink Weasel sighs. "Most unlikely."

"'Tis strange," John considers. "Both Mo and Weasel have both bathed and have yet another clean suit."

Turning to John, Mo says, "Wise move, lad. Smart not to run. Wouldst not make it far." He neglects to tell John a lookout has been watching him from across the square, sword ready to run him through should he decide to escape.

*   *   *

Leaving Lime Street and its many brothels, the trio begins to look into the many shop windows on Main Street.

"Place swarms with English faces," Mo observes. "More 'n last time I be here, I freely wager. Moved in here like bees, when the English captured this isle of sin."

Mo points to the third shop. "Here be the shop I needs. A cobbler. 'Tis all right to be barefooted on ship, wear rude sandals in Port Royal, but we needs protection in Boston. Takes time to be fitted, for certain. Ye needs foot covers too, lad. Cold weather be comin'."

Expressing surprise, John inquires, "Boston? Be that our next stop?"

"Well, first clean the ship's bottom, then takes on cargo to trade." Rubbing his hands, Weasel thinks of the money to be made in Boston.

Mo continues, "'Tis the logical place, once we careen, shape her up. Before we leave here we takes on sugar, molasses, and tobacco. Pirate along the way. Other ships, slavers, bring cloth, salt, weapons, hardware, beads, and rum to trade in Africa. Picks up bound men to bring here. No slaves on the *Revenge*, 'cept them we kidnap to sail the ship, like you. Slavin' be dirty business, even for pirates." Warming to his subject, Mo adds, "Here we pick up sugar, molasses, tobacco to take to Boston. Not much, though. Too much honest enterprise not be good for pirates. Makes life dull."

"Some in Boston be Puritans," says Weasel. "In London, some be Protestants, some Royals. No matter. All enjoys the pleasure of wine and rum."

"Be most careful," Mo adds, "not be drunk in the streets of Boston. Whip or fine ye they do. End in the stocks ye will."

To further demonstrate the course they will follow, Mo makes a great circle with his arms. "Trade goes round and round: London, Africa, Jamaica, then New York, Boston. Back to London. Round and round. Calls it the triangle route. Profitable. We make no Africa stops. Boat too small."

"Forget not the fun," Weasel adds. "On way to Boston town, picks off such merchants as we can. Steal treasure."

The thought of attacking more merchant ships sickens John. He mocks, "Maybe ye can get a grand pair of boots, like Morgan's. Maybe a hat with a big feather too. Hoot, ye be grand, certain."

John considers Mo's dark look. *There be my chance,* he thinks, secretly vowing to escape in Boston. *Even if I be shot doing it.*

* * *

Reaching the corner of Lime Street, the three men wander up High Street, pausing at each of the brick and stone buildings.

John gasps. "Truly surprised there be a church in such a place."

"Spanish built," Mo simply states. "Catholic, once. Now, be Protestant."

"St. Peter's," Weasel utters.

John is so intent in his scrutiny of the church, he almost bumps into Mo, who has stopped in front of another shop.

A red irregular plank hangs above the door. Crude letters spell out "Simon Bennings" in black letters. Ten items sit in the window.

John sighs. "Me mam once had a pewter dish. Said it came from her mam. Pa sold it for drink. Broke Mam's heart, but she be strong. Never said nothin'." Frowning, he sighs again. "There was always a sadness in her eyes."

Disinterested in John's talk about his mother, Mo scornfully adds, "Such a plate be useless. A square wood plate be all ye wants. 'Tis the food what matters." After a pause to reconsider, he adds, "Though a cup to hold rum be a fine thing to own." Looking closer at the plate, he asks, "Why print them circles on the bottoms? Why not on the top for everyone to see?"

Putting his nose to the dusty, uneven glass, John inspects the plate. "Mark of the pewter maker. Saw such on a plate in a shop on Fleet Street. Made wonderful elegant things."

"Now me thinks on it," Mo mulls, "seen a fruit once. Just like that. An apple pine, or maybe a pineapple, someone said. In some port, someplace. Not sure where."

"Never seen such a fruit," John admits, "but have seen such marks. See there, there's a *S* and a *B* on either side of it. The sign says 'Simon Bennings': *S* be for Simon, *B* be for Bennings." After a slight hesitation, he went on. "A trademark declares who made it."

Mo sniffs, distracted. Disinterested in pewter, he continues along the street, hoping to find something more interesting. A porcelain dog catches his attention.

"Look, mates. Odd-lookin' dog, me thinks. White shiny stuff, like glass. Never seen another, in any port."

"Hmm," murmurs John. "Sign says 'tis a porcelain Foo Dog. From China." His smooth, tanned brow wrinkles in thought. "Wonder how it came to be here. Goods from China come off ships near the Customs House in London." He pauses. "Nothing like that, though." He looks back over his shoulder as they continue down the street. "Mam would love the whiteness of it."

A small tear squeezes from the corner of John's eye. His right hand gently touches the small pouch with the lock of his mother's red hair. He is comforted. "Yes, 'tis safe. Will bring me luck. Have no intention of being murdered by these vile men." He remembers the fate of a crewmember who had tried to unite the men in a mutiny. Fatal error. As a lesson to all, they left him hanging from the yardarm.

* * *

John idly listens to Weasel's continuous chatter about life in the colonies, being careful not to strike the cobblestones with his bare feet.

"A common man can gits his own land," Weasel blathers.

"Talk such like that can gits ye hung. Never ye mind the land," advises Mo with a sidelong glance at John. "Don't ye listen to such crazy squawk. 'Tis on the ship, here in the Indies that a man hath real freedom. Where else can a man elect his captain?" With a sneer, he adds, "Not in the king's navy. Nay, nowhere else in this world. Nay, not never!"

Sweeping his arm toward shore, Mo continues, "Here, hath choice of women, and shillings to pay for her. Easy life on this ship, or a bigger one, should we catch one. Which we will."

"I be a prisoner," argues John. "No freedom for me."

"Can foller your own inclinations when we trust ye not to run off." Scornfully, Mo persists, "Like to be on a ship of His Majesty's Navy, would ye? Ha! Soon see this life be better." He boasts, "King don't pay so richly. Your foolish religion gits in your way of real treasure. Wake up, young fool!"

Seeing no English warships in the harbor, John miserably shrugs his shoulders. "Guess I'll never know."

*   *   *

In the next hour, the men pass dozens of stone houses on the dusty road to the wharf. Suddenly, a loud explosion pierces their ears as flames burst forth from a brigantine, *Flora,* anchored less than a hundred yards away from the *Revenge.* Horrified, the crew of the *Revenge* vault into a shore boat and quickly row through choppy waters toward their ship. Reaching the brig, they clamber up the ropes to the main deck, where they speedily help their mates wet down her deck and sails. With a fire at such close quarters, all neighboring vessels are in danger of sparks igniting flammable items on their decks.

Across the taffrail they have an unobstructed view of the inferno. Tongues of fire lap at the *Flora*'s masts, vigorously destroying sails and rigging.

"Lucky we be," shouts Mo. "With the wind blowing away from the *Revenge,* mayhap we can at least save her."

Small explosions rip out the Flora's sides. John can see and hear screaming men grab ropes, poised and ready to jump ship.

Sweat pours down their backs as the men on the *Revenge* toil at the pumps, wetting down the sails and deck with water from the harbor. Within minutes of the great explosion the *Flora* sinks, taking her unfortunate brotherhood with her beneath the surface. The danger over, the men of the *Revenge* stow their sponges and buckets while others row out the small boats to retrieve survivors from the *Flora.*

*   *   *

Even during shore leave in Port Royal the pirates were aware of the jobs that must be performed to keep the *Revenge* seaworthy and make her ready for the next voyage. When Morgan returns to the ship, he urges the men to begin preparations. "Stop grumbling. You have enjoyed six weeks of leisure. Time to get on with it. Great wealth awaits our labors."

"Jeb, gather the crew. Time to tip her over on a hard piece of beach. Prepare to weigh anchor."

Most are secretly relieved to return to the sea. Nonetheless they grouse while the *Revenge* slowly slips anchor.

"Set topsail."

Under light sail, the crew uses two small boats to tow the brig to a small deserted beach west of Port Royal. Jeb orders the men to work the topsail and to maneuver the brig toward shore.

"Furl!"

*   *   *

Fortified by rum, the men begin the necessary jobs that precede beaching—staying the ropes and setting the anchors as counterweights. Cargo is placed near the untidy piles of rigging being repaired on the edge of the shore.

"Heel her over, lads. Heave!" Jeb calls out. Pulling together, using two powerful relieving tackles as leverage, the men tip the brig over to an angle sufficient to repair her bottom.

Bending over, John runs his finger into one of the hundreds of holes breaching the integrity of her bottom, postulating, "Ah, clear! Here be the reason so much water seeped into the hold during storms. Hard to believe she didn't sink."

"No ship be free of puddles." Mo laughs, barely making himself heard above the shouting men as they direct their energies to completing the job of chipping off barnacles and scrapping off accumulations of crustaceans on her sides and bottom. "Wage war with the Devil of the deep, we do. It be our solemn duty to keeps her afloat. To our benefit, after all."

True to Mo's prediction, sharp barnacles lacerate John's hands. Blisters and eventually calluses follow. Never before have his hands been so rough and raw.

Slowly the drudgery of caulking seams and filling gaps between the planks is completed. Grinning, John applies hot pitch, thinking how pleased the surgeon will be to keep the small surgery area dry during rough Atlantic storms.

Standing at the edge of the jungle, Jeb maintains surveillance, ensuring John does not attempt to escape into the jungle or Blue Mountains. Another week passes.

Painting completed, they prepare to return the brig to her upright position but are stopped by a shout from Morgan. "Belay. One task further, ere we roll her out—then she goes back to sea."

Jeb's strong body glistens with sweat under the tropical sun as he plunks a cask of gunpowder on the top of a pile of goods. "With respect, Captain," Jeb admonishes, "time we gits underway. Needs arrive Boston afore winter storms flail us about. Be tight as ever she be."

"Not be a problem with her sturdiness. We must do honor to the governor's lady. A change well worth our time," Morgan decrees. "A fine new name to grace the stern."

*   *   *

After weeks of traversing stormy seas, and enduring sunless days without end, after arriving in Jamaica John now suffered from days of incessant sun. As much as he hates his confinement, there appeared to have been no avenues for escape, even during his one-day furlough ashore. The ship was careened, refitted inside out, her bottom repaired. Now there will be one more change to this ship on which he has lived for over five months. Watching the ship's carpenter at work on the transom, his curiosity is piqued.

"Does the governor really have that much influence over the name of this vessel? It's just one of hundreds moored in the harbor. Appears a special relationship exists between this barbarous ship's captain and the governor of Jamaica. Morgan does not seek favors lightly."

"Aye, the governor be most powerful," returns the sail maker.

John had long ago realized that Morgan's predilection to deviousness influenced his every gesture. Like some Machiavelli, he believed that any means justified his end purposes. John believes the governor will be severely taxed with some enormous favor in return for the somewhat vague salute to his wife. "Well, perhaps my luck will turn with the new name."

Sand rubbed across stern sends shivers up and down John's spine. The muscles in his chest and neck tighten with each grating stroke across the wood grain until the name *Revenge* is but a faint shadow. Sanding complete, the ship is blocked at a seventy-five-degree angle.

"Stand back, gentlemen," Morgan recommends without rancor. "Allow our artist elbow room whilst he paints a proud new name upon the board." Ten pirates admire the fancy yellow letters spelling out *Lady Luck.* Not all can read or understand the meaning of the letters.

"Uncommon beginning for our new enterprise," Morgan announces, satisfied with the elegance of the scroll. "New name, new game, new fortune." He turns to Jeb. Do not share this," he murmurs, "but Governor be giving us six new crew. Volunteers, of course." He winks, and his laugh is harsh. "Urged me to christen her *Governor's Lady.* Most respectfully declined that unfortunate choice. Too unique, too easy to recall past the heat of battle. True, might have realized even richer rewards with such a name, but 'tis not smart to be too obvious about our sponsor. Aye, disastrous if remembered later in London—to us and to him."

After a momentary pause, Morgan continues, "Now, on to the christening. Governor plans a grand party, fit for gentry. All be invited. Extra, there be another surprise, especially for Mo." He lays a hand on Jeb's shoulder, saying in a soothing voice, "Not to be distressed. Need you alongside of me. No man I trust more. Mo takes the greater risk, truth be known."

*   *   *

Jeb ponders Morgan's enigmatic words. Their intent is not apparent. Jeb rarely considers alternative ways of accomplishing any given order. A man of limited speech, he blindly follows his captain's commands without question. He trusts in Morgan's navigational skills to transport them safely to each port. Jeb rarely speaks to Mo, although they share a closely confined space below deck. Jeb has served Morgan for years; he knows not how many. It doesn't matter. He has discovered Morgan always backs him up. It takes but a few words to intimidate Mo or any other man. They always get the job done, 100 percent. The pirates understand their fortunes lay in following the directions of someone schooled in navigation who understands the skill of attack. Since their arrival in Port Royal, Jeb has noticed a dramatic change not only in Mo's appearance but also in his mood. Another dramatic change: in recent weeks it has appeared to Jeb that Mo performs every necessary task, getting things done before Morgan or Jeb gives an order. "Truth be known," Jeb reflects, "Mo be best leader. Better than me self."

*   *   *

With glasses of rum, the pirates roar approval for the new name that has been painted in beautiful scrolling characters. It is the rare sailor who can sequence the necessary letters and turn them into words. In fact, most are unable to decipher the cursive symbols. After much good-natured prodding, Josh patiently spells it, slowly—one letter at a time. He understands the importance of using a name approved by the governor, one that promises extra supplies, food, and wine in quantities large enough to assure that the next leg of their voyage is as luxurious as feasible. Most of the pirates have already squandered their money on gambling and women. Few have been prudent enough to purchase any personal items for the journey. Excitedly they anticipate the upcoming distribution of prizes that they will receive as the brig leaves Port Royal. Anxious to get under way, they know there will be ample money to spend in Boston. They also understand that they will appropriate prizes along the way. Certain.

"Josephine be a-waitin' for me in Boston," brags Weasel, already forgetting that his boasting about Mary came to naught.

"And Boston be home to sinners?" asks Mo derisively. "Not likely." He shakes his head in disbelief that Weasel can be assuming enough to believe any woman would be waiting for his return. "Puritan ladies. Certain," he whispers to John. "None be his kind."

*　*　*

"One last celebration afore we sails," the men cry. Mo and Jeb agree. The brig's small boats complete the transport of wine, beer, and grog to the *Lady Luck*. A plentiful supply of meats, fruits, and vegetables is brought aboard for the few visitors finding space aboard her narrow upper deck. John is curious—the same boats are apparently supplying another ship anchored close by.

Mo's clothing is more elegant with each passing day; tonight is no exception. His fancy boots rival any worn by Morgan. His scant hair is covered with a broad-brimmed hat. Astonished, John wonders how Mo found the money for such finery. Even Weasel is wearing a new shirt with fully bloused sleeves. Flax trousers replace his blue-striped, wide-legged trousers. The prize money has not yet been distributed—how did they come upon such finery? Perhaps Mo receives special treatment, spending his prize money before the other men.

*　*　*

John pokes at a soggy leaf Joshua places in his hand. Pointing across the water to a beach fire, he urges, "Try this, me boy! Fish cooked in a frond atop hot coals."

John inhales the distinct odor of coconut, moist and warm to the touch. Peering around, remembering the joke the pirates played with the banana, he wonders who might be watching, ready to laugh—playing him for a fool. He rips off a small piece and pops it into his mouth, satisfied with the hot, sweet taste. It is unlike anything he has ever before tasted. Prowling the deck he looks for more exotic food.

"Food of the gods," Morgan raves. John nods in silent agreement. He is amazed at the baskets of foods and strong, pungent spices, many brought to Jamaica in ships from Far Eastern ports—foods he could never have experienced in London. London! With sadness, he wishes his mam and brothers were able to enjoy the warmth, music, and food. He reminds himself, "Dead, all dead. Certain."

Leaning against the main mast, worn smooth by the hundreds of men who have sat there before him, John fills his hands with nuts and mangos, absentmindedly using his tongue to push the soft mash of a ripe banana around in his mouth. Reveling sailors dance on the shore, taking advantage of a rare opportunity for merrymaking.

"Dancing to the Devil's music. Listening to the Devil's tunes," John sputters. "Not sober. Not proper to enjoy themselves so excessively."

* * *

Funding Morgan's next venture with money, men, and supplies, the governor is pleased with his investment. He knows Morgan's reputation for successful endeavors.

"Always some risk, of course," the governor tells his wife, "but not an unreasonable one."

"Do as you will. Ye have free access to my father's money, but do not expect me to set foot upon that barge of his."

"Named in your honor, me love. We must pay a brief visit. Ye be expected, if for but a brief appearance. The brig is completely repainted. Morgan expressed his satisfaction ye have agreed to come. Be not fooled—'tis certain he wants but to impress. Our lovely daughter be most excited about the prospect of yet another opportunity to flirt with our guest."

"Her eyes be fooled by his elegant clothing, her mind taken in with his grand promises of life in London. What sort of a life would she have with such a man? I forbid it. She needs not a man of the sea."

"Morgan plans to retire from the sea. Needs but one more profitable voyage. He has agreed to take rich cargo to New England. It will make all our fortunes." Rubbing his hands together with glee, he boasts, "Not be unreasonable to assume we may all end up quite comfortable in London."

"Oh, to return to civilization. Plays at the Drury, afternoons with ladies of quality. A proper society for Priscilla. I insist marriage plans be delayed till we be properly settled in our new quarters in London. Do not put fanciful ideas into her head."

"My dear, I assure you that Morgan hath no need for our funds. He has more than sufficient riches. Loves the adventure of the sea. 'Tis to our advantage to provide extra capital for this venture. Riches will be ours."

Out of the governor's hearing, his wife expresses her qualms. "Men be such fools. An imposter be our Mr. Morgan. False airs. False promises. Most likely will end up hanging in a gibbet."

Pressured by his wife, the governor spends only ten minutes aboard the *Lady Luck*. After Morgan salutes the couple and their daughter, and they return the salute to Morgan with a glass of wine, two crewmembers row the governor's party back across the harbor.

"Filthy ship," mutters his wife. "Although his cabin be not bad."

*   *   *

Following the governor's departure the enthusiastic party continues onshore and aboard the *Lady Luck* for a full day and night. Guests crisscross the harbor from ship to ship at all hours. The men toast Morgan, then the governor, and again Morgan, far into the night.

Mo and Weasel whisper to John, "Did ye notice her? What a beauty. Most attentive Morgan be to the Lady Priscilla."

"Indeed, he stood close watch," said Weasel. "Glared at any man what stared at her, he did."

"Think he be smitten?"

John silently reflects on Priscilla's beauty, remembering her long blonde hair swept away from her face and artfully piled high above her forehead with wavy tendrils hanging in front of her tiny ears.

"Looks too pure. Be not suitable for Morgan." Secretly John thinks she resembles the pretty young prostitute in Port Royal, though Priscilla's clothes are of finer material, more skillfully styled. He grumbles, "The prostitute be more properly of Morgan's class." Recalling the day they allowed him to visit Port Royal, he does not regret scorning the girl. "And yet there is longing. Be it so sinful? No, it would have been improper to talk to her, touch her, let alone use her services. Let the others debase themselves. Such behavior not fall to me."

*   *   *

"Huzzah to Morgan. Huzzah to the gov'nor," the men cry out, raising their mugs in a toast. "Thankful we be for food and drink aplenty." The pirates take every opportunity to refill their cups. Few have the ability to plan past the next glass of wine, let alone for the future. All know they will be severely punished if they are drunk at the time for setting sail.

"Who knows if we be alive next week?" a seagoing philosopher recites. "Best to eat, drink this day."

"Salute to Morgan and his gov'nor."

"To Morgan and his gov'nor," they sing out, grateful for the extra portions of brew.

John listens to the music of the fiddler but does not recognize the music of France. A few English country songs follow. An occasional Irish tune drifts across the air. The night is calm, without wind, and heavy as if before a storm. John takes several deep breaths in appreciation, smelling the fresh offshore wind. The fiddle's music carries over the water, intertwined with laughter, lewd jokes, the distant sound of drums, and an occasional flute. Very few other sounds escape from the shore—as if all the men, women, birds, and animals are reluctant to compete with the handcrafted instruments that accompany a beautifully played violin. The governor's guard prevents any altercations from breaking out onshore. John hears the sharp report of a pistol. "Has someone been shot?" Forcing himself to look through the shadows, he asks, "Who?"

In the early morning hours, after many of the guests have retired to shore, a pirate quietly sneaks a woman aboard, against Morgan's orders. The couple spends a brief time in the shadows, quickly followed by the splash of a hastily released boat as the prostitute leaves for shore under the robe of an unlit sky. Before the first rays of sun sculpt streaks through the darkness on the horizon, all guests have returned to shore. As the sun breaks the blackness of night Morgan returns to the ship, clothing somewhat disheveled, his coiffure windblown. Morgan needs but one final day to check their supplies and to ensure their readiness. On the outgoing tide they will be gone. The men await the order to hoist the sails.

*   *   *

Whisper by whisper, the pirates spread the rumor.

"Made fight with tavern keeper. Jeb not yet back," confides Weasel.

"No thought where he be?" queries John, extremely hopeful Jeb will not return. He doesn't see Mo, either. Is he also missing?

Weasel rejoins, "Bad fight, though fair, d'ye know. Witnessed it meself. Jeb and the keeper both had knives. Course, Jeb's arms, they be longer, his knife sharpest. Used his cutlass. Slashed the keep in the gut, he did." With a hearty laugh, he adds, "Course, innkeeper's gut be great target. Hung six inches over his sash. Squishy fat. Blood all over. Terrible sight, even for pirates to see."

Stunned, his spirits bolstered, John asks, "Jeb? A fight? Arrested?"

"Sure 'nough. Police come quick. Course, Morgan gits him out, quicker than your ax can chop oft a chicken's head."

"Talkin about me, be ye?" Jeb jeers, swinging his leg across the rail. His mouth is pressed into a tight line of fury, his face black as ebony. Most frightening, his bloodshot eyes glare at Weasel, who becomes the focus of his anger and contempt. Walking directly up to Weasel, Jeb knocks him on the side of the head with the flat of his pink, callused hand, threatening, "Ye little weasel, find somethin' else to gossip about, or dead ye be!"

Brave enough to snicker behind their hands, none of the pirates dare to comment. Remaining calm, John is less alarmed by Jeb's actions than when he was first kidnapped.

* * *

Spirits flagging, John's frustrations grow at his inability to sneak away aboard one of the small shore boats. Having slept through most of the merrymaking, he suspects someone drugged his wine. Josh has shadowed him for the past three days and watched him intently each time a transport boat was tied up to the brig. Sensing Josh nearby, John boldly turns to face him.

"Sorry, mate, I be ordered to ensure ye escape not," the sail maker blinks in embarrassed astonishment.

It is clear that a successful escape will place Josh's own life in peril.

Though frustrated, John is careful to not express his feelings to anyone. "Must keep mutinous thoughts to myself," he grumbles. "Try to fool them. Should they get a notion of my intent, my life be shortened. Certain."

*   *   *

The sun, a colossal orange sphere, sinks in the west. A brief twilight and darkness follow.

The splash off the oars of a small boat rowing furtively from the shore raises John's hopes, followed by a crushing emotion when it does not tie up to the *Lady Luck*. Quietly a rope is cast to the crew aboard a sloop anchored in the lee of the brig.

Only three lanterns illuminate the two-masted craft. Spectral shadows creep across the deck, not quite concealing the clandestine activities of the governor, whose rotund shape can be seen preparing to board.

"Shape of the man I saw leave the tavern in Port Royal. Consorted with the loose woman in Port Royal," John glumly realizes.

CHAPTER 6

DECEPTION

November 1666

The moon's brilliance carves bright streams of light into the dark harbor. Squinting his eyes to improve his night vision, John concentrates on the scene before him. Dark forms of men and women suspiciously move about the deck of the nearby sloop. A small man with a large feather protruding from his hat stands by the foremast.

The governor turns and strolls toward the shadows of men forced out of a small boat and then pushed to the center of the sloop. A whip cracks, sending the crouched shadows quickly below deck. John is not able to determine the content of the whispers drifting across the water toward the brig. After a brief stay the royal entourage drops back into the small boat and then rows to shore. The dark shadows remain hidden below deck.

* * *

A harsh shout alerts the crew, and the men begin the preparations for departure. Barrels and food supplies are stowed; belaying pins, lines, sheets, masts, and yardarms are reinspected for any damage that might endanger their long journey to Boston. Tasks completed, Morgan calls the crew together.

"Well, lads, we settle up the prizes. Our hard work hath paid us well." Standing in the light of the full moon, beaming broadly, he boasts, "The Devil hath given us his due. Handsome purses for all!"

Calling for the key from his cabin, he gravely instructs Mo, who has suddenly appeared on deck, to help a solemn Jeb bring forward a large wooden chest. Jeb presents the chest with an outward sweep of his right arm and a deep bow. In the light of the lanterns the chest is one of the most beautiful objects John has ever seen. Bold Oriental figures stand out against a black shiny surface. The patina of the wood glows in the flickering lights, profiting from being rubbed daily for many years. Standing as part of a semicircle in front of Morgan, each pirate solemnly maneuvers himself for a more prominent view of the informal ritual. Morgan rubs his hands with relish while the excited crewmembers behave as if they are about to receive promotions in addition to rich rewards. With an elaborate display of bravado, Morgan makes a great show of struggling to open the chest. A loud grunt accompanies a slap on the cover. It opens. Slowly, waving his manicured hands over the contents, Morgan takes a deep bow. Pointing to each pirate with his right index finger, he beckons each to come before him, one by one.

"Two hundred pounds each, gentlemen. More than ever you would see in a lifetime of hard labor in England."

Keeping one and one-half shares for himself, Morgan gives one and one-quarter shares each to Jeb, the carpenter, the surgeon, and Mo. The rest of the pirates receive equal shares in gold and silver coins, distributed one bag at a time.

Attempting to stay out of sight by hiding in the shadow of the main mast, John tries to be excluded from the ceremony, but Jeb roughly brings him to the fore. Extending a fat purse, Morgan swaggers, "Well, me boy, makes your months of suffering well worth it, does it not? A fine purse. Spend it when ye get to Boston. Aye, more to be earned on the way. Ye have learned well the ways of the ship. Take the half share, lad. A full share will be yours after our raids off the coast of America."

Withdrawing his hand, John tucks it firmly behind his back, presenting the pirates with his rehearsed speech. "I cannot accept this ill-gotten blood money."

It is a dangerous moment. Morgan has shown his mistrust of John by confining him to the boat, with only one day of well-guarded shore leave during all the weeks they had been in Jamaica. Morgan has no understanding of or patience for anyone who does not plunge himself into the piratical life. By refusing the prize money, John knows he will never be trusted and will be watched ever more closely. If John accepts the money he will appear to be a committed member of their brotherhood. He does not want that to happen—however, with money it would be easier to survive when he does escape.

"A curious lad, ye are. Stark foolish." Walking away and then turning for a second look, Morgan spits out, "Have seen ye watching me. Superior, are ye?"

"Oh, no, sir." John gives a spontaneous response, not daring to look Morgan in the eye. "Just cannot take gold that is not mine. God would disapprove."

"I'm the only God ye have to worry yourself about in this devil's den. None other." As if reflecting inwardly, Morgan calls out to the men, waving them toward him with a derisive grin. "I once believed in his God. Dead he is to me, now. Died when me mum died." With a look of danger, he adds, "'Tis watching ye, we be. Don't try anything foolish, or overboard it is. For now, an extra hand be needed. You've done well learning the duties of ship. Realize there is no other place for ye to go." Fluttering his long fingernails toward the sea, he warns, "Jump, and a great feast for the sharks ye be. D'ye hear?"

John turns away, holding his breath he slowly strolls to the starboard side of the brig. He can almost feel the thrust of a knife piercing his back he is so certain it will be thrown.

* * *

An hour later the small sloop anchored next to the *Lady Luck* prepares to leave. Mo stands on the deck wearing a pair of handsome leather boots from the shop in Port Royal. His hair is tied in a clean pigtail and hangs over the left shoulder of a beautifully tailored long-sleeved white shirt; gray trousers are tucked into his orange boots. A black hat sits atop his head; its wide brim covers his bald patches. With an epiphany, John suddenly understands the motive for the improvement in Mo's appearance. The look fits his new station in life: captain of the sloop. Mo animatedly gives orders to his crew as they move about the deck performing their assigned duties.

"Them to follow us. Lovely vessel—be most sea worthy. A fine tender," Weasel explains. "Them six guns will come in handily. Mo be in charge. Captain trusts him."

Quickly crossing the deck, John anxiously calls out to Mo that he wants to sail with him, not Morgan. He is certain he would have a better chance of escaping from a smaller ship with fewer hands to guard him. Placing his foot on the taffrail, John prepares to jump. A sudden sharp pain causes him to wince, restricting his forward motion. John reflectively grabs at the strong hand gripping his left shoulder. A sharp knife pricks his ribs and a rough shove propels him across the boat. Quickly following John's erratic path, Jeb grabs him by his tarred pigtail, forcing John against the rail.

"Tries to git away, eh?" An upward thrust of Jeb's right hand presses the knife against John's throat. "Captain needs ye to stay here under guard. A most generous act. Should throw ye to the sharks, ye piece of scat. Not be so generous, meself. Hasten below, afore he changes his mind."

Determined to stay out of Morgan's path, John passes by stored bales of sugar cane and hogsheads of molasses to find the dour old surgeon sitting on a barrel while sharpening his surgical knifes. A man of few words, the surgeon has well-known sympathies with the pirates. John knows it would be unwise to confide in him.

"Well, come below to see me, have ye?" asks the surgeon. "Be glad ye be here, not rotting in the hold of the sloop. For there ye see God's blasphemy—fifteen black men and women. Dirty business."

"Why be they in the hold?" John asks, surprised and disgusted at the thought of enslaved men contained in a boat that rides in their company, even though not on the *Lady Luck*.

"For transport to Virginia, ye fool." He snickers. "Our fine captain may not approve of trafficking in slaves but took these slaves as a favor to the governor. Out at sea they be out of his vision. Out of memory."

"Thought they had use for slaves in Jamaica."

"Right they do. But these be not so strong. Needs them powerful built for the fields in Jamaica. Worse than the eternal fires in that place. These go to the Virginia colony. Find use for them there. Morgan gits a tidy sum. Riches for our coffers. Plus, earns a friend forevermore in Jamaica. Governor be thankful for the favor."

Staying in the shadows, John makes his way toward the ladder. Standing near the hatchway, he hears Morgan conspiring with Jeb.

"'Tis a fine plan. One ship for pirating, another for trade." He points toward the west, his deep voice rising above the flapping of the yards against the mast. Morgan calls out, "Brig is in good condition. Time to sally forth. Send the signal to Mo."

*   *   *

Before dawn, after four months in port the *Lady Luck* weighs anchor with a crew most anxious to get under way.

At first the pirates were divided in their opinions about which route to take. Some voted for a direct route to Boston, while others wanted to sail along the American coast line. Nothing but confusion seemed to attend all their schemes. Standing at the aft rail, his arms crossed over his chest, Morgan listens to their dissenting positions.

"Now, lads, a right ye have to vote on what course our journey will take, but have ye considered the wealth that will be sailing south from Boston for the Virginia colony? A bounty flows from Virginia to the north. There may even be gold traveling to Spain. Don't mean to pressure you, but a meandering course is something to consider."

Encouraging the crew, Jeb advises, "Captain be most bold and daring. Not yet steered us wrong. I votes we follow him."

Agreeing Morgan is the superior knave, the best to lead them into battle, the men unanimously vote to track the course he has laid out to Boston. The possibility of severe spring storms is of no consequence; they welcome adventure.

Sailing to the outermost reaches of the harbor, the foretopsail fills with wind. Port Royal falls off the stern, and the blue color of the deeper open water and fresh sea air greet the crew. The crew slowly but steadily increases the amount of sail that welcomes the breeze into the main topsails. Morgan orders a course to the west, eight points off the wind.

*　　*　　*

"All hands make sail," commands Morgan. Sails unfurled, the *Lady Luck* makes her way out of the harbor on the outgoing tide. The sloop, crewed by Mo and twelve of Morgan's men, follows closely behind. By midmorning, under a clear azure sky they pass into the open waters of the Caribbean Sea. They are relieved to escape the sultry air so pervasive in the harbor. A moderate southwesterly wind sends the brig along on currents toward the Windward Channel between Cuba and Espanola. Ten to eleven leagues off the starboard side lies the coast of Jamaica. Sails unfurled and ropes secured, they temporarily tack along on an east-by-northeast course.

*　　*　　*

Curious about the night sky and concealed by the cover of night, John creeps along the deck. The now-familiar constellations appear higher in the sky than those he remembers off the south coast of England. Hearing the voices of Morgan and Jeb, he slinks back into the shadows.

Gazing out on the open sea, his hair blowing in the wind, Morgan expresses satisfaction with having two sturdy boats under his command.

"The hold of the *Lady Luck* be filled with silks and wine." Morgan laughs. "Look like respectable merchants, we do. Till they face our guns. By the heavens," he brags, "if'n we run into the Royal Navy, likely be able to fool them into thinking we have legitimate business. Mo will take the sloop directly to Virginia while we sail off the far shore. Keep the gunports closed. Then none will suspicion our purpose till we be ready." Twirling his long mustache with his finger he smugly offers, "Too late to escape their reach."

Strolling aft to the quarterdeck, Morgan commands, "Signal Mo. Ensure gunports on the sloop be also closed."

With great confidence, he informs Jeb, "We can safely return to London from Boston without a hint of gossip. Our secret dealings will not be suspected, as there will be no trail of witnesses to our acts of piracy and slaving."

Jeb responds, "With luck, no one will suspect."

"Yes," Morgan declares to the wind, slamming his fist on the taffrail for emphasis. "With so many friends in London we will be safe." Satisfied, he shrugs his broad shoulders. "And if any catch the sloop, Mo will be taking the blame. He be the one who hangs. None will touch us!"

Jeb is now grateful that Mo has the most dangerous job.

*   *   *

Before learning the character of cargo to be transported to Virginia in the sloop, John briefly dared to fantasize about someday sailing with Mo. He had quickly learned the tasks necessary to run a ship and was confident in his abilities to perform all necessary duties. After discovering the content of the sloop's secret cargo, he was grateful that he would not be subjected to sailing on the same vessel with enslaved men. He could only imagine the suffering in the hold. There would be few, if any, opportunities for fresh air. The poor quantity of the food would barely be enough to keep them alive. As for the trip to Boston, he had little fear.

Weasel assured him, "No storms be like them months past." He nodded. "Wild they were off the coast of Africa. Be summer before more hurricanes hit."

Once again time seems endless. Monotonous. With no chance of escape, John's renews his plan to escape in Boston. Glancing aft he is heartened when he catches a glimpse of how close he is to Mo, although no longer close enough for protection.

Northeast of Jamaica the pirates seize a small craft and its cargo of green turtles. Stacked on their backs in the hold, the turtle's legs wave helplessly in the air. Thus positioned, it is assured they will be unable to move. The pirates are assured of fresh meat for weeks. The transfer of the turtles completed, there is hilarity and great amusement when Morgan orders the crew members of the captured boat to be tied back to back. Thus immobilized, the men are thrown into the sea. Their small boat is left to drift aimlessly on the currents. No witnesses.

"If I had more crew to spare, would take her for a tender," Morgan informs Jeb.

* * *

June 1667

"See! There she be, lad. Coast of America," rejoices Weasel. "Wager we be just south of Virginia, off the Carolinas. Them colonies destined to produce much wealth, someday. Mean to have me some of it. Aye, gits rich, I will."

Hovering off the coast, John's hopes for escape, inactive for weeks, rise up in his consciousness once more. Morgan is paying less attention to him. Maybe Weasel has a plan for escape. He will watch. With luck, he will follow him.

Once again, luck seems to have attached itself to the pirates. Off the starboard bow Weasel espies a sloop bound out to Boston. Anticipating an easy prize, Morgan orders one shot across her bow. No fire is returned.

"The *Lady* brings us fortune," Morgan brags. "A wise choice of names."

The unarmed merchant is loaded with bread, flour, and rum, which the crew quickly transfers to the pirate's brig. Again, to the pirates' surprise, Morgan releases the crew.

"'Tis too generous a gesture," John mutters, suspicious of such nobleness. "A concession I find difficult to believe. What perverse plan can he be hatching?"

* * *

As they sail on a long reach before a fair southeast wind, no other potential victims materialize. At four in the afternoon Weasel whoops.

"Slow movin' ship to the northeast. A merchantman bound for London, I wager," he declares from his place in the tops. "Fifty-ton at least. Low in the water, heavy burdened."

"Hard about, gain a starboard tack," Morgan orders. The men quickly respond, changing to a tack that will allow for pursuit of a fully rigged ship.

"Low in the water. An easy mark." Morgan laughs. "Signal Mo. Should be able to catch her before the sun sets."

Following the change in signals, Mo changes course, following abaft the starboard stern as the *Lady Luck* closes to less than a quarter mile of her prey.

A shot erupts from the starboard side of the brig hurtling across the fugitive's bow. A second shot finds its mark on the intended victim's larboard side. Mo, in the more maneuverable sloop, sweeps up on a port tack to threaten the merchant on her starboard side. With two vessels bearing down, and frustrated that he carries but two guns, the captain of the merchant quickly makes the decision to surrender. Fourteen men hastily cross over the bow onto the fifty-ton sloop. The invading pirates cheer, "Carryin' indigo, fresh water, food."

"Grand booty to trade in our next port," cries a triumphant Morgan. "Quickly now, let's be on our way. Pass Mo a generous supply of food and water."

The crew stares at Morgan, shocked he has allowed their quarry to sail off without sinking the ship or killing the crew. John shakes his head in disbelief as he watches it slowly glide away into the darkening sky of the northeast. Squinting in an effort to improve his vision, he watches it diminish into the distance. Consumed with horror and foreboding he sees the merchant flounder, suddenly list to larboard. John complains to Weasel, "She be sinking."

Slapping his knobby knee, his protector laughs. "Now see there. Must be cannon puncture near the waterline. Water sink her fast. Soon be swimmin' with the sea monsters."

Without concern or remorse, Morgan leisurely resumes his tack to the northwest, away from his latest victim, just off the American coastline.

"Continue on a larboard tack," Morgan bellows up to the lookout. "Keep a sharp lookout for another merchant."

John is filled with sadness as he imagines the terror consuming the minds of their latest victims, impotently attempting to stop the leak yet aware of the certainty they will soon sink into the depths of the ocean.

* * *

Trimming the sails, allowing the wind to fill them from the larboard, the crew makes fast the ropes about the belaying pins.

"A profitable trip," the surgeon comments to Jeb.

"Aye, true. But in spite of it, unrest be most evident," warned Morgan. "There be trouble afoot."

"Whatever is the cause?"

"Some be unhappy Mo has command of the sloop."

The report of a pistol ruptures the air, shockingly audible above the noise of the wind and the chanting of the men. All hands not in the ropes run aft.

Glancing about, John catches a glimpse of the sloop one mile distant. No smoke rises from her deck, and no other boats are present on the horizon. Before John has time to discover the cause of the disruption, Jeb shoves past him as he hurries toward the quarterdeck, striding with the full length of his long legs.

"Where be the captain?" Jeb screams. Relief spreads across his dark face when he sees Morgan casually standing with his arm draped over the taffrail, smiling. More than any of the other pirates, Jeb understands the importance of Morgan to the success of their enterprises. He also understands Morgan's vanity and unfettered cruelty. Although Morgan has led them to riches, unrest aboard the brig frequently leads Jeb to worry about Morgan's safety. Morgan's moods and actions cannot always be anticipated, but he still feels surprise at what he now sees before his eyes.

John lets out a gasp, staring at what grips Jeb's attention. Although Morgan's unpredictable violence no longer surprises him, nothing has prepared him for the shock of seeing the body of one of the most able topmen lying on the deck, blood flowing from chest and neck wounds. John instinctively glances at Jeb.

Jeb stares at Morgan, puzzled. His large dark lips purse as he slowly, audibly lets air whistle out of his lungs.

"Heard a shot."

Contemptuously, Morgan smirks at Jeb, his stare unwavering. After a momentary halt, he insolently stares into the eyes of each man within his line of vision.

"Bloody twit," he jeers, spitting down at the body. "Warned him, just an hour past. Drunken fool! Fell into me, grabbed me with his filthy hands. Look here, dirt on my best pink cloak." Spitting on the fallen crewmember, he hisses, "An insult not be tolerated. Let this be a lesson to each and every one. Exceeding the ration of drink increases a man's passion. Passion increases stupidity. Throw the fool overboard. Shark bait. That's what he was born to be. So be it."

While Morgan continues his tirade, Jeb, flanked by Weasel, moves to stand protectively at Morgan's side, daring anyone to challenge their position. Tension permeates the air as grumbling swells through the line of men. Pirates do not sanction the killing of their own, even by the captain. During the attack too many ropes had been dropped midtack. Now the only sound to be heard is from the flap of sails overhead as the ship threatens to stall from a bow dangerously close to the wind. Everyone's attention is focused on the dead man, his dark red blood oozing onto the deck.

"Fools," roars Morgan. "Pay attention. Bring her about. We're about to go into irons. Tend to business."

Jeb counters, "Square off main and mizzen. Sheet headsails."

John mutely watches the threatening figure of Jack creep up behind Morgan. His skin is the dark color of a weathered oak tree from years in the sun. A patch covers an the absence of an eye lost during a distant onshore fight. His remaining watery blue eye settles on the body of the dead pirate. Slowly, without anyone else noticing, Jack withdraws a long curved knife from the black sash tied about his waist. His lips are drawn firmly across his mouth in a horrific grimace. Anger flashes in his lone eye. He does not attempt to suppress his fury. Jack stands with his feet spread apart, even though there is little need for maintaining his balance in such a light breeze. No waves rock the boat. He squints through his one good eye as his slow mind tries to decide on his next action. The dead man was his best mate since Jack lost his eye defending him during a fight many years ago.

*　　*　　*

From the maintop, an excited warning cry breaks the turgid spell. "Sails off starboard," Weasel calls out.

"Run up the Dutch flag," orders Morgan. "Signal the sloop to do likewise." Returning his full attention to commanding the brig, he gestures toward the cannon and sharply orders, "Gunports to remain closed."

Foolishly disregarding imminent danger, Morgan crosses the deck to the starboard bow, passing within two feet of the one-eyed pirate. Morgan ignores the consuming fury following his every move.

"Bring her about. Helm to larboard, prepare for a starboard tack."

Jeb, calls out, "Braces there. Let go and haul."

"Hit her fast." Morgan laughs through cupped hands. "She be low in the water. Heavy-burdened." Rubbing his hands together, he blusters, "Easy mark."

Quickly the pirates change tack, almost in unison with Jeb's orders. Winds now to their advantage they begin a tack toward the lone ship moving lugubriously to the northeast.

*   *   *

The chase begins. "Smartly, now. She's slowly changing direction."

The merchant ship appears to be attempting a change in bearing, trying to maintain her distance ahead of the two ships as she moves to the northeast. The pirates' vessels seem to be more maneuverable than that of their prey, less laden and faster through the water.

In less than an hour the distance between *Lady Luck* and their intended victim closes until the *Lady* glides within a quarter mile off the merchant's larboard bow.

The sloop follows less than a half mile behind, attempting to hang back in the lee of the larger ship, keeping out of sight.

"Best keep our presence dark," calls Mo to his crew. "Keeps us back from the merchant."

* * *

"Quarter mile off the starboard," declares Weasel. "She be carryin' a French flag." Silently counting their prize of pieces of gold in his head, he asks Morgan, "Change colors?"

"No, get close enough for one across her bow as we slide past her. Keep the gunports covered, but prepare for firing. Everyone to their job. Spring the guns through the holes. Immediately we open them."

John, doing as instructed, carries powder cartridges up from below deck, laying them on the windward side of the piece. The linstocks are placed to leeward. Seeing the approaching ship, he dares to hope, "Maybe we be beaten at last. Pray God, let me off this ship, escape from these devils."

As the pirates continue to gain on the slower French ship, Morgan commands, "Continue past on the larboard side. We'll fire; then we board. May be a smidgen bigger but no evidence they have guns."

The *Lady Luck* sails a length past the French ship. "Spill the sails. Sharply!" orders Morgan. The air spills from the mizzen topsail and foretopsails, sucking the sails against the mast. The heavy canvas flaps like thunder in the no longer still air.

"Now, mates! Black flag!"

*　　*　　*

In the space of a heartbeat, the French ship swings in behind *Lady Luck*, guns aimed at her vulnerable stern.

Too late, Jeb realizes what is happening. He shouts, "Hard a-lee!"

Morgan watches in surprised horror as the French flag is lowered. The king's colors spring up the halyard. Gunports spring open. Ten bronze throats burst menacingly out of dark gun holes. Weighted barrels that had been dragged aft of the ship to slow her speed and lower her in the water are quickly cut loose. The navy warship rises in the water, now capable of unfettered maneuverability and speed, spilling her sails. Devastated, Morgan sees ten guns aimed directly at *Lady's* transom. Taking advantage of the element of surprise, a navy gunner's hand claps a linstock to a touchhole as the ship moves on the downward roll. An infinitesimal moment of hesitation precedes the loud thunderclap filling the air. Morgan and the brig shudder as the transom receives a shot just above the waterline. Firing on the upward roll, the British ship dispatches a second shot that fractures the ship's mast. Splinters fly through the air. Shards of oak pierce the bodies of several pirates unfortunate enough to be standing at the guns nearest the quarterdeck. In the heat of the day, blood, flowing from many wounds, turns gummy on the deck.

John, turning from his position at the cannon amidships, looks aft over what's left of the transom, for a glimpse of Mo and the sloop. Reacting quickly, Mo has already set sail for the northwest. He does not see a far-off ship change tack for the same direction.

* * *

Rankled, brandishing his sword, Morgan screams, "Curse ye for a rogue. Who be ye?"

"Our colors be true. Surrender, or feel our fire most severely," calls out the English captain.

"Lucifer's fire! Will give no quarter."

"Be not a fool. We have the superior ship. Superior numbers," the captain shouts across the water.

Quickly, Morgan recovers his wit. "Sir, I also sail for the king—have the required letter of marque."

"Come aboard, then. Show these papers, lest your ship sink." Turning to the master, he orders, "Take the long boat and twenty seamen across to the pirate brig."

Outnumbered in both guns and men, Morgan, seeing the futility of his situation, orders the small boat to be lowered and hurries to his cabin. Donning his fancy pink silk jacket and his finest red leather boots, as he leaves the cabin he snatches the black hat with its large ostrich feather. He has no intention of leaving it for any of the pirates or His Majesty's seamen.

Leaving the *Lady Luck*, Morgan loudly warns his men, "Hands off all weapons." More secretly, with a wink he whispers to Jeb and the pirates standing nearby, "We may fool them yet, lads." Briskly he climbs into the small boat.

Loud commands from the English captain drift across the short span between the two ships. "Smartly, Mr. Tompkins. Take charge."

His Majesty's shore boat and Morgan pass each other at the halfway point between the two vessels. The men of the navy ship, hands on their weapons and backs rigid, stare straight ahead. Expressionless, they will not be indecorous—will not give recognition to a pirate such as Morgan. They have captured dogs of sea before.

*   *   *

Morgan bows as he presents his papers to Captain Pells.

"These papers, sir, do not appear to be in order," censures the English captain. "Where be the proper signatures? None?" he haughtily asks. Pointing to the bottom of the page with a beefy hand, he reiterates, "Sir, I see there be none. And since we are not presently at war with France, ye had no privilege to attack what ye suspected to be an unarmed French ship." Turning toward his blond Lieutenant, he laughs, saying, "Mr. James, appears we have caught ourselves some pirates. Prepare to throw the lot into the hold." Turning with a slight bow, he addresses Morgan, "We will take ye to Boston and then on to London for trial. Your crew made poor judgment when they signed on with you."

"Sir, kindly allow me to return to my ship. I have other papers there."

"Ye take me for a fool, sir? I believe ye not. Fancy clothes and fine manners fool me not. True, it may be that ye have had some advantages over others of your crew. I be referring to your fancy speech. Therefore, I hold ye as a gentleman, not to pull any chicanery. I mean to have ye stay upon this ship."

"I humbly beg your pardon, sir. I believe I might satisfy your doubt, prove I carry the necessary papers. Waving his hat toward the *Lady Luck*, he continues, "If you will but generously allow me to go across."

Captain Pell's officers watch this exchange with undisguised delight, certain the arrogant pirate will not fool the crusty old captain.

Therefore, there is great disbelief when the captain answers Morgan in a quiet voice, "With reluctance, I will allow ye that request. You will have but a moment's time whilst we imprison your men. That completed, Master Tompkins will take charge of your brig. I must warn you—do not attempt to conspire with your crew. I will not hesitate to hang you here at sea. Back in London we will speak of your sad accident at sea, nothing more."

Seeing Morgan draw back and hesitate, Pells assures the pirate, "Oh, a trial ye will certainly have. Do not be concerned."

Two of the more senior English officers fail to hide their delight. The wind is suddenly calm. Snickers are heard from the taffrail.

As suddenly as a smile appears on his face, a twinkle lights up his aging eyes. Just as quickly the look of amusement turns to a snarl. "A trial for certain, but quicker than the sun drops in the tropics."

Turning to his lieutenant, Pells orders, "Mr. Fitzgerald, kindly take Mr. Morgan across." Fitzgerald hides his frown as he turns away to perform Captain Pells's bidding.

"A vicious pirate addressed as 'mister,'" Fitzgerald complains. "A title best reserved for gentlemen, which Captain Pells most certainly is not. If well bred, he would not believe this charlatan's lies."

*   *   *

The crew of the *Lady Luck*, each with his hands behind his back, stands about the deck. A few, secured to masts, sneer at John's discomfiture when approached by Tompkins. John shivers. Certain he will be thrown below deck with the others, he mutters, "I must pray for mercy. I must try."

Tompkins's blond hair blows in the breeze, making him appear even larger than his six-foot height. At his approach, John blurts out, "Please," but further remarks are cut off when the officer holds up his hand, palm facing his young prisoner. With a shake his head, Tompkins silently instructs John not to speak. Fearful death will be certain if he does not explain his position, John softly utters, "Please, sir."

Interrupted by urgent shouts of profanity, both John and Tompkins look starboard in time to see Captain Pells hurry toward the area of commotion.

*   *   *

Hat sitting on the back of his head, Morgan has returned to the brig. Sensing the tension among the men, he hesitates. Wary, he looks to his right and then left. Confident that he stands alone, Morgan turns his back amidships, glances over the edge of the rail and hides his smile as he watches the lieutenant climb out of the long boat.

*   *   *

Morgan's anguished scream crescendos as a look of astonishment creeps across his face. Seizing the right side of his neck, he is horrified to see it covered with his own blood. Morgan instinctively tries to scream but the attempt pierces the cool sea air before decaying into a moist sputter. Doubled over, he is aware of a knifelike pain penetrating his chest. Lungs burning, he is unable to fill them with air. Sliding to the deck, the sensation of drowning engulfs him.

Shouts of anger fill the air. Lieutenant Fitzgerald runs toward the commotion, toward Morgan and the man standing above him. Sailors struggle to remove Jack's inelastic grip from the bloody dagger he has plunged into Morgan's chest. As he wrestles with His Majesty's men, the patch over Jack's eye slips off. A long, ugly scar, whitened and puckered by time, makes a remarkable line across his flushed face. During the skirmish the pirate Tom gets free of his bindings. Grabbing his knife, he jumps into the middle of the brawl.

John stands helpless as he sees Tom raise a clasped knife high above his head and then lunge forward, the knife disappearing into Jack's chest. Before the knife silences him forever, with tears streaming down his face, Jack cries out, "Killed me mate, he did! Cast his soul to the Devil."

* * *

Tompkins orders, "Belay. Step back, I say. Step back," he warns, "or we'll throw all ye scum into the sea. Belay this minute." When there is little response to his threats, he easily forces his way into the middle of the fray, using his strong hands and long arms as a wedge.

Lieutenant Fitzgerald and six other of the king's men lunge into the skirmish. In less than a minute there is a sudden calm. Maneuvering for a better view, John can see six pistols aimed at the pirates. No longer hesitant to speak out, John pronounces, "Just end for one so foul."

*   *   *

Although pleased there will be no further need to transport the pirate back to London, Pells's face betrays no emotion when he learns of Morgan's death, secretly elated time will not be wasted on a sham trial. Morgan's influence over the others has been carved away by the swift slice of a knife. Pells's control over the pirates is now complete.

"Excellent, excellent," Pells mumbles. Then, for the benefit of his officers, he demands, "Who is responsible for not seizing the knives?" A barely distinguishable smile crosses his pocked face. Graying red hair waving in the breeze, he slaps his gnarled hand on the side of the man-of-war. "Sirs, sever the outlaw's head from his body." Grimly, he adds, "Hang it on the bowsprit."

Exuding confidence, Pells struts to the most elevated section of the quarterdeck. Taking advantage of an uninterrupted view of the pirate ship, he watches the myriad activities on its forward deck, including the hanging of Morgan's detached head. Softly he snorts, "Each man should serve God daily, love one another, keep good company. A just warning to you who do not."

*   *   *

Pells watches the lieutenant supervise the hanging of the knife-wielding pirate, Tom. Firmly, Fitzgerald places the noose around Tom's neck, calmly taunting, "Barbarian. Assaults among civilized men are not tolerated."

Before they string him up, Tom proclaims, "Had me knows me life would end so quick, would have killed me more than me did."

Determined to avoid further risk to the lives of the king's men, Pells and his officers decide they will not take the pirates to England for trial. Spurious trials completed, guilty verdicts seal the pirate's fates.

"Death by hanging."

All will be summarily hanged. Death will be slow, by suffocation, for the victims' necks will not break when hoisted from a block placed below the end of a yardarm.

Pells blares, "Proceed."

Looking across the water at Tom's swinging body, Captain Pells comments on the assassin of one-eyed Jack. "Thoroughly evil fellow. Most surely will slowly roast in Hades. Feel a bit of remorse for the one-eyed fellow. Did us all a favor when he struck down Morgan."

Within an hour all of the pirates except Weasel and John have been dispatched. After each body is cut down His Majesty's navy throws it disdainfully into the sea.

*   *   *

"Lieutenant Fitzgerald, perhaps ye might speak with this young man," Mr. Tompkins says, bringing John before him. "Last one in the hold, constantly proclaiming his innocence. Lamentably so! Claims to be an unwilling participant in the pirates' evil exploits."

"Lad, state your age," demands Fitzgerald.

Standing tall, trying to show respect, John answers, "Sir, I be sixteen. I know not today's date. Perhaps I am now older."

Unfettered tears flow down his face as he tells the officer of his kidnap. "Sir, they knocked me well out. Drugged me, they did. Took me out of a small boat from whence I took refuge from the plague. When finally fully awake, I found myself on this pirate ship."

Trying to judge the effect of his claims on the officer, John hurries on, "If ye please, sir, give me the opportunity to serve the king on an English ship. Let me show my worth. I can be of use in a hundred ways." Not realizing most of the pirates are dead, he continues, "Surely one of the pirates will tell you the truth of my kidnapping. I desire only to serve our king."

Laughing derisively, his disbelief evident to all who watch, the lieutenant points to the two bodies still hanging from the yardarm, asking, "I say, will any of ye fine gentlemen speak up for the lad?" Laughing, he inquires again, "A chance to repent past sins, so to speak." Pausing, he looks at each of the dead pirates. "Is there none with the compassion to speak the truth? Oh, the truth has died with you. I say, you cannot take it with ye. The Devil wants it not."

Weasel, quietly standing with a wide noose around his throat, bows his head and utters as best he can, "He tells the truth, sir. Fought all attempts to make him a pirate. Fine lad."

John sighs, overcome with relief and gratitude at the positive turn in events. Weasel is a friend, after all. The lieutenant expresses surprise and suspicion at the revelation.

Forcing John to enter the long boat, Fitzgerald ferries him back to the English ship. Once aboard, he repeats John's story to Captain Pells. Not daring to speak, John squints as he looks up into the older man's weary blue eyes.

John's hand searches for the small pouch tied inside his trousers, the bag holding a lock of his mam's red hair, the color of which not unlike that of Captain Pells. Holding fast to the hair, he prays. Although John realizes that swinging from the yardarm almost guarantees a slow death, he prays Weasel's death will be quick. He is sorrowful that Weasel will not be able to escape to the colonies.

"The Devil controlled his life. Certain."

*   *   *

Captain Pells paces. Deep in thought, he appears to give John's fate due consideration.

"Ye have no weapon, no money. Appear to be the narrow side of seventeen. Display your back, lad," he commands. John slowly uncovers his back and shows Pells the scars from his many beatings. Pells knows many of the men on his ship have more severe scars. Men pressed into service commonly present with more scars than do those who volunteer for service. Stooping to authority takes longer for some men than for others. Life aboard ship is difficult, but so is life on land. On ship a coordination of effort and intent is most critical.

Pacing, Pells considers what is best for his ship. Short of hands, he decides to allow the lad to join the crew, but he will make it sound like a favor. In truth, the lad is more willing to serve than a pressed man—might conceivably present with fewer problems to be managed.

Pells does not explain the reasons for his decision. He sternly states, "For the present I will accept this dubious story that you tell. I generously grant you this wish to serve on His Majesty's ship. Do not doubt for a moment that you will be watched most critically. There will be no time for leisure. More than enough labor to fill the day. Some on this ship have been pressed into service, as apparently thou hast been. Do not attempt to conspire with them." Pells thinks back on his own youth, when he first sailed as a servant to an officer. He advises, "Work hard at whatever needs to be done. Report immediately to Mr. Simms, our midshipman. Earn your way. No doubt you will find we be strict. Only reward for compliance is to avoid the sting of the cat. Quick now, we will see how ye fare in the tops'l." Unknowingly, he mimics Morgan when he gruffly warns, "Obey orders, or face the consequences."

*   *   *

The executioners have completed the hangings. None of the condemned expressed remorse even as they faced death. Given an opportunity for prayer, most declined. A few oaths are heard in protest, denying the presence of God or Devil. Finally, the grisly work of hanging and throwing bodies into the sea complete, Captain Pells commands, "Now, on to Boston, Mr. James. If ye please, set a north-northwest course. Signal Mr. Tompkins to follow in the brig."

* * *

As the ship tacks to the north-northwest the days lengthen with the impending summer solstice. They experience light winds, few blows, and few high seas. During one rare summer's gale, John takes his turn assisting the gunners to man the elm tree pumps to force water out of the bilge. On an aging ship, strict discipline is required to keep the ship tight, clean, and afloat.

Working in the topsails there are moments for private thoughts, but memories of his time on the pirate ship intrude through any available rare moments of silence. Pondering Weasel's fate, John recollects his grand plans to escape to Jamestown or Plimouth— plans forever suspended by the executioner's noose. Pressed into piracy, Weasel had chosen what appeared to be the best of the few options available to him, eventually falling into evil habits even while dreaming of the day when he would escape to the colonies.

"Pity for Weasel. He imagined he could read far better than he did. In truth, could read very few words."

In spite of these gloomy intrusive thoughts, John smiles at the irony of Weasel's situation. "Dream he

did, with less than a caged bird's chance of being free."
Over the next few weeks, John dwells on memories of
Weasel and Mo. "Both from London," he reminisces,
"their beginnings barely different from mine. Like me,
destined for poverty. They craved excitement, tried to
find a better life."

*   *   *

Relieved to have secured a place on a king's ship,
John is grateful for Captain Pells's acceptance of his
story. Anticipating a life of adventure and service, he
feels great pride. "I be certain to receive rewards for
my faithfulness. After the English officers learn to
trust me, more freedom will be mine. I will use it to
my advantage."

His Majesty's 140-foot frigate carries twenty-six
guns and a crew of 250. Though more spacious than
the brig, the sleeping quarters are tight. Instead of
sleeping topside John has a hammock on the latched
and crowded gun deck with the rest of the crew.
Only six feet of wall separates the gunports from the
waterline. If not kept latched, water can flood into the
gun deck through the gunports during high seas.
There is little natural light, with the exception of a rare
beam wafting down through the main hatch. Rare
small breaths of fresh air drift into the sector, doing
little to dispel the cumulative odors of one hundred
unwashed sailors. When not rotating to duties on the
weather deck, they sleep and eat their meals in the
same space. During the first week the rope of his

hammock, slung from the beams of the deckhead, digs into John's raw back. Fresh stripes cross his back from the flogging he just received. Curious if he could see land, he had climbed up into the rigging without being ordered to do so. Streaks of dried blood run down his back, absorbed into the tops of his breeches. The rules of the Royal Navy are curious to him. Isn't he supposed to be a topman? Then why was he denied access into the tops?

John believed there would be strict discipline but mistakenly thought that on His Majesty's ships it would be fair. Not so. Beatings are commonplace aboard the man-of-war. The food is vile and always in short supply.

"With Morgan, I knew to be wary. But there were often second chances."

The form of punishment changes daily, depending on who metes it out. When he does not address a midshipman as "sir," John is sent aloft, amazed to learn that a twelve-year-old is considered a naval cadet and a young gentleman.

*   *   *

In England, generally the second or third sons of gentlemen are bequeathed none of their father's money or property. Inheritance falls to the oldest son under the custom of primogeniture. Many younger sons are destined for the ministry, but others are sent to sea to serve as a midshipman for at least one year before applying for a commission. John feels no satisfaction in learning the midshipman also suffer dire consequences if he fails to follow the orders of his superior officers.

* * *

John is surprised at the severe punishment meted out on a ship of His Majesty's navy. After months of enduring the raw language of the pirates, he is surprised when the captain places a topman, Robert Tufts, into leg irons for cussing.

"What say you in your defense?" the captain censures Tufts. Mute, the condemned man stares at his feet.

"Well, well. Nothing to say? Then strip him to the waist," Pells orders.

"Strip," the boatswain demands. At a nod from the captain Tuft's manacles are temporarily removed. Tufts removes his shirt, shocking John when a multitude of healed ridges are revealed streaking across his back.

"Seize him. Make fast his hands," Pells demands. "Place his legs in irons." Pointing upward toward the wind and rain, Pells orders, "Up there, to the top deck with him."

Anticipating the order, members of the crew drag the accused man to the foredeck. Throwing Tufts across the grate the boatswain chains him on his back and reports, "Seized up, sir."

The sailor does not struggle. Amazed, John tries to analyze his reactions. Perhaps Tufts has seen what happens to crewmembers that foolishly rebel. It appears most prudent to be compliant, not to resist.

As he lies exposed to the forces of nature for more than twelve hours, a constant rain pricks at Tuft's face. He snarls when his drenched hair plasters like mucus to his head. At eleven the following morning, the shriek of the boatswain's pipe accompanies a roll of drums, summoning all hands to witness Tuft's flogging. Officers stand on the quarterdeck in full formal dress uniform; fists grip the hand guards of swords hanging in the scabbards at their sides. The master-at-arms stands before the crew with two sturdy boatswain's mates standing rigidly at his side. Hats are removed as the captain reads the appropriate passage in the Articles of War. Turning to the boatswain's mate, he commands, "Do your duty. I'll not have profanity on His Majesty's ship."

The bos'n raises his arm above his head and snaps the knotted cat-o'-nine-tails down on the condemned man's back, ignoring the whispered plea of "You scratch my back and I'll scratch yours."

Afraid of what his own punishment will be if he does not sharply apply the whip, the mate whispers, "Not likely, mate. They'd chain me up next, then give me twice the amount as was ordered for ye."

The first lash leaves a pattern of livid red welts running along Tufts's back, marching beside raised scars like wheel ruts in a muddy road. The next few lashes cut more deeply. A dozen more lashes turn his flesh into a spongy, dripping mass. The mate pauses to run the cat's tails between his fingers, clearing away the blood; flicking it onto the deck.

Holding his head high, John considers, "Life as a pirate, for all of its shame, offered more freedom. Though not freedom for me," he regretfully admits. "A pirate claims more rights, has more to say about his everyday life than any in the navy." Ruefully he adds, "A fine life for some, before death by beating or scaffold. Pirates eat better. He who signs the Articles be rarely whipped. True, their scandalous behavior would never be condoned by any God-fearing man." For all their kindness to him, Mo and Weasel, both willing participants in their crimes, zealously robbed and murdered innocent victims. "Weasel wanted to escape, but rather than resist, he followed the easy path into robbery on the seas. Why, indeed, had he followed Morgan from London only to suffer a violent end to a brutal life?" Saddened, John realizes he will never know Mo's fate. "Possible he made it to Boston. But not likely."

*   *   *

Within days of joining the navy, and after three beatings, like a cold spray of ocean water, his situation hits John with full force.

"I must escape," he laments. "Forever imagined me existence would improve, but things be worse here than with the pirates." *In truth, inferior by far,* he thinks as he uses his fingers to follow the welts from his latest whipping. *No more hesitation!* his mind shouts. *Escape! First chance.*

It has been several months since the ship was last in any port, another month since it captured the pirates' brig. There has been no fresh fish in several weeks, and they have completely consumed most of their food, including the cache taken from the pirate's brig. Again, John's primary diet consists of hard biscuits made from salt and flour. "If not soaked in beer or grog, 'tis certain would not be able to eat it." He knows the officers eat well even though the crew do not. He remembers with delight the wondrous variety of the food in Port Royal. The food on the pirate ship had been the best that he had ever experienced in his life—shared by all, equally. John does not wish to return to the evil, uncertain life of the pirates, but he can see its advantages over life in His Majesty's navy.

"Always thought them striped shirts to be handsome," he mutters, thinking of the clothing worn by the sailors who passed by on the Thames. Up close, they smell of body odor, grease, and tar. "The odors almost suffocate me on the gun deck. We eats below deck too," he mutters. "Sits down there on a trunk and partakes of me food with the smells of animals insulting me nostrils."

The odors are ever present, day and night. John is determined to sneak up to the main deck whenever possible. In the past year he has matured, gained courage. It is time to get on with it, no matter the risks.

CHAPTER 7

ESCAPE TO THE CITY
ON THE HILL

July 5, 1667

Passing abeam Halfway Rock, the ship tacks toward the passageway between Baker's Island and the Miseries. Recognition of familiar landmarks provokes *huzzah*s throughout the ship. Crudely built colonial vessels float at anchor, boats never before seen by John, even in London. A ship measuring at least ninety feet, of the type occasionally used to trade goods in Port Royal, passes out of the harbor.

"Surely her breadth be over twenty-five feet," estimates the new visitor to colonial Massachusetts.

Amazed at the variety of craft, John spots a small sloop silhouetted against the sun as it sinks below the small hills of Boston. A slight swivel of his head brings into view a one-masted ship with fore-and-aft sails and a ship carrying a gaff mainsail, two headsails, and square topsail sailing out of the harbor. Built in a small yard near the mouth of the Charles River, it will be sold in London after the sale of its colonial goods is completed.

"Look there," shouts the first mate. John supports his hands on the rail, air swooshing out of his lungs as he propels himself into the air for a better look.

"There! On the north shore. Just like Wapping."

Unable to pull his eyes away from the repulsive sight, John feels chills run down his spine. Vomit rises in his throat. What is left of a rotting body sways in the wind, a seductive treat for scavengers. Thin scraps of orange leather cling to where boots once cupped the victim's feet. One eye socket is vacuous, picked clean by the beaks of voracious birds.

The ships carpenter leans close to John. With a deep chuckle he taunts, "Tarring be not always successful. Crows, gulls, other garbage pickers find ways to tear off the decaying meat."

Though putrefying, the body is held together within a harness of wide iron hoops. Such scenes serve as strong reminders of the fate awaiting those who rob and raid for a living. John is reminded of the blackened heads hanging on stakes near the Southwark stews. He spits into the water to clear the bile rising to his mouth.

Mesmerized by the body's slow, elliptical swing in the breeze, John whispers, "Mimics a flag hanging from the quarterdeck on a ship." Twisting and turning, the corpse pivots around on its hook. Colorful clothes peak out from the coating of tar. Stunned by the orange leather boots, John gasps, "Mo—can it be Mo? Oh, as God is my witness, they caught and hung him."

John is amazed that no one had thought to steal Mo's beautiful boots. In London they would have been nabbed without hesitation. "Some might have thought it a waste of a good pair of boots," he tells the carpenter.

While the ship slips into the harbor John strains to keep the rotating giblet in sight. "Certain I am, the body be Mo. He had hidden motives but treated me well. Certain." Smiling, he remembers the subtle protection Mo and Weasel extended to him. Now he is on his own and responsible for each and every decision. The rules are different on the English ship. John fears what his fate will be if he stays aboard. He is weary of long months at sea. Certain his family is dead, John makes the decision to immediately escape. "Though I risk hanging for desertion." He takes heart—"At least there be no jungles here. No monsters."

Not wavering in his resolve, he decides, "I go tonight. Beatings be too brutal to suffer for even one more day."

*   *   *

One hundred ship's crewmembers and officers are gathered topside to relax and listen to music, comforted by the calmness of the night and the millions of lights that radiate from the Milky Way. The ascending moon sends a vibrating path through the water—straight to shore. John prays that a fog bank creeping silently toward the ship will protect him from being detected during his escape. Within moments the stars segue from sparkling on a black backdrop to being muted by the gray blight that creeps in to snuff them out of existence.

*   *   *

Ignored by sailors attentive to the shifting rhythms of pipe and fiddle, John furtively searches until he finds his tormentor, Captain Pells. Standing next to one of his lieutenants, he appears bent over, as if in pain, but his feet tap to the pulsing tempo of tunes impossible to resist.

The music is an abstract background to John's thoughts. *I be in Captain's direct line of sight—looks ready to put his hand on his ivory stocked pistol. Watching me, certain.* Waiting for trouble, John silently admits, *perhaps just my imagination. Captain's face be in the dark.* John reassures himself, *Can't see the captain's eyes. Fear be eating me up. Confusing me. Lucky to escape from Morgan, now forced to flee from the English. Most difficult.*

*   *   *

Like a moth near a flame, the captain senses that something is about to breach the serenity of the evening. He is attuned to every creak of the ship's aging timbers. Little escapes his notice. Survival depends upon meticulous attention, and something is different this night. On this he would wager a month's salary at a gaming table in Paris.

224

*   *   *

John hopes the fog will hide his presence in the water. Sliding into the shadows on the larboard side, he wriggles closer to the foremast. Finally he successfully places the mast between himself and the captain's line of vision. Other than the soft glow of a few scattered lights onshore, there are few reflections that successfully fight their way through the creeping fog.

Swallowing his fear, he hopes to grab a piece of wood to hold on to so that he can paddle his way toward the lights of a settlement onshore. Perhaps then it will be possible for him to quietly sneak away. Then, at the moment that John is poised to drop over the side, an explosion jolts the air.

A dazzling flash of light precedes the shockwave of sound that crosses the spaces between the ships. Heads snap to attention, looking for the source of the disturbance. The captain gapes in alarm, his concern about the sailor slinking away on the far side of the ship fading.

Clapping hands pause midbeat. All animation is suspended as flames shoot skyward. Across the water a ship is seized in an inferno.

After a split second of hesitation, one hundred of His Majesty's sailors rush in a wave to the rail—stare in awe at the fiery sight.

Crewmen compete to be first to identity the casualty.

"The *Sea Dog.*"

"No, no, the *Elizabeth*."

"Bless me if 'tis not the *Mary Rose*," calmly remarks the captain. "Her powder barrels appear to have blown all 150 tons of her to pieces."

"A judgment of God, no doubt," sneers a lieutenant.

"Or sheer carelessness," amends the captain.

A surge of intense heat radiates across the water, reddening the skin of those nearest to the gunwale. Staring in horror at the unfortunates struggling to escape, they are mesmerized by the screams. Several men instinctively cover their ears against the tortured shrieks calling out to God for help. Others howl invectives blaming both God and Satan for their suffering. As the water and fog engulf the victims, the sudden deadly silence lends a spectral effect to the scene.

After a brief hesitation John rushes to take advantage of the unexpected opportunity. Unable to help the victims of the explosion, he is determined to help himself. Without a backward glance he squirms over the gunwale, grabs an anchor line, and slides downward past the top two decks. The harsh scarping of his hands on the prickly rope makes it difficult to maintain his grip, but he dares not drop into the water. A splash would surely betray him. Finally his raw hands come into contact with slime, enabling him to slip down the remainder of the cable into the cold waters of Boston Bay. The fate for deserting a king's ship is certain: the same end Weasel and the rest of the pirate crew suffered. It makes no difference if it were a different crime, theirs of piracy, his of desertion—all crime is against the king. Thoughts of Mo swaying in the giblet fill his mind. Fear quickens his flight.

*   *   *

Shivering, chilled by the water, John immediately begins to swim in an attempt to warm his body. He is aware that excited chatter and shouting have replaced the music and singing on the ship. He prays the diversion of the fire, the fog, the water lapping against the hull, the groans of the ship's timbers, the screams of the unfortunate sailors, and the sound of the breeze through the rigging will cover any sounds he might create. In the distance the master is commanding his men into the boats, shouting a myriad of rescue orders. Head low in the water, kicking slowly beneath the water's surface, John is optimistic that no one will discover his absence before the coming of dawn.

On the leeward side of the ship John is protected from the open sea. Just a few stars and the light of a small fire onshore guide him. Struggling through the evening mist, he is able to see the silhouettes of several large long boats anchored offshore. A funeral tune by a lone Irish fiddler drifts over the water.

In the darkness he doesn't see the drifting log until a sharp pain sears through his head. Biting his lip to suppress a cry of pain, John tightly grasps the log. Continuing toward shore, he waits for the discomfort to pass.

*   *   *

Two men quietly drift by in a small boat. A strong hand grips John's shoulder and then swiftly submerges him beneath the water. Gasping for air, John is hauled back to the surface by a faceless figure.

"Hush, laddie. Not a sound," his assailant whispers, clasping a powerful hand over John's mouth. Overpowered and unable to call out, John quickly realizes the futility of struggling. Vigorously shaking his head, John indicates he understands the necessity for silence but involuntarily gasps when muscular arms drag him over the side of the boat. He fears that he will attract the attention of the men on the ship, but they seem to be a long ways off.

"Me and me brother be willin' to help ye. Willin' to help anyone who tries to flee from a king's ship." After a slight hesitation, the man asks, "Not be off a ship from New York, be ye?"

Gulping for breath, spitting salt water out of his mouth, John informs his rescuers, "Nay, from Jamaica." Holding his tongue, he says nothing more. The darkness of night hides their faces; John is unable to guess their size or appearance. The moon, now almost hidden behind the fog, sends a thin spectral beam across the water.

"Yella fever in New York, so we hear," comes a muffled reply. "Would not favor it to come to Boston." Sighing in resignation the voice adds, "Not certain we can stop it from coming in through the harbor."

Muffling the oars, the men quietly row the shallop toward shore. Its fore-and-aft sail hangs useless, furled in the still air. John hopes safety is but a short ways off. He relaxes, huddled quietly in the bottom of the boat. The two men do not appear ready to harm him.

After a few minutes the men guide the boat into the gently swaying reeds lining the shore, quietly dropping a small anchor to secure the boat. Climbing over the gunwale into the cold water, they creep through a salt sea marsh. The strong, rank odor irritates John's nose. Exhausted, he stumbles toward solid ground. With each slip of his foot the men pull him upright and quietly half drag him through the rough beach grasses. Within a few minutes they have crossed an area of scrub to a sandy path. About a mile inland they reach a crude log cabin. The men inform John that they are north of the village of Boston.

Following an order to strip off his wet clothes, John is grateful to absorb the heat from a small fire. Cautiously keeping his almost-naked body turned from them, he tries to hide the small sack containing the lock of his mam's hair. Noticing the small pouch, the Puritans mutely nod to each other.

Time passes. After more than an hour in each other's company, the taller and older of the two men tells John, "Me name be Richard. Here be my brother James. Not likely the king's men will look for ye this far from shore tonight. With the ship's fire and all, not likely they miss ye before dawn. We be north of their usual anchorage."

Responding to the worried crease in John's brow, Richard continues, "Even if they come lookin' in this area, the fog will hide the smoke of the fire. We leave before dawn's light and head to the south. James and me will take ye across the peninsula. Then ye be on your own. Ye would do well to continue along the way south after we cross over."

"Will be forever grateful for the kindness," John responds with a slight bow, finally looking Richard in the eye. "My trust in ye be total, but I know not why ye have taken interest in a deserter."

Handing John a long, dark cloak and a high-crowned broad-rimmed hat, Richard assures him, "Anyone who leaves old England, for whatever reason, must be nurtured, cherished as one who can strengthen our colony. All who come here have equal opportunity to succeed. Our colony stands to be a beacon to the world. Only through charity can a man receive his predestined salvation."

"So by good works, each man is saved?" John asks.

"Live by two rules: justice and mercy. In this life, no one knows who will receive salvation; it be God's domain to decide." Patiently, Richard explains, "We win salvation by our good works, but in the final moment, only God decides who be saved."

Troubled, John reflects, "Seems to be no guarantee of salvation no matter what path I follow."

Returning to the matter at hand, Richard continues, "Here be some clothes. Make ye less conspicuous if'n the king's men look for ye. Not a doubt the captain now knows he be short a crewmember." Self-consciously, he adds, "Bread in the pocket. 'Tis near the time of harvest—plenty of fruit to eat along the way."

*   *   *

Cresting over the horizon, the first rays of the sun glimmer across the black cloaks and steeple-crowned hats of two Puritans. Standing in the doorway of the cabin and turning to John, Richard pulls a cloak off a peg. "Possessed by my father," he explains as he hands it to John. "Recently dead of the sharp cough and wasting disease."

Strolling toward the door, Richard opens it and pauses to let John and his brother to pass through. The three men begin to tread their way south through the early morning fog, shrugging their shoulders under the brims of their black hats in an effort to keep the morning dampness off the napes of their necks. Following a path toward the narrow neck of the peninsula, they plan to hurry through the village of Boston. The rising sun breaks through the fog. The silhouette of the hill that had been visible from the ship shimmers in the distance.

"Our city on the hill," Richard explains. "Journeyed here to build a city independent of old England—a place where we be free to go our own way, worship our own way, without King or Parliament, without clerics. A new Jerusalem. Proud we be that King Charles signed the charter afore they axed off his head. South of here be the Plimouth plantation. A compact gives them self-rule. Ye may pass that way. Perhaps linger there."

John ponders, *Is it possible for men to maintain self-rule? Weasel thought so, but I wonder. With such an act be they still loyal to the king? The pirates were loyal to none but themselves. I will listen to these people of New England. Perhaps stay here.* Without a doubt, John senses he has the opportunity for freedom. He knows in England, with its class structure, he has no hope of ever owning land. Mayhap he could, here.

Somewhere in the distance, the occasional mournful bark of a disturbed dog lends a sense of eeriness to the scene, an edge to their nervousness. John, who had never worn a hat of any kind, constantly pokes at it, tries to keep it straight with his right hand. The loose trousers and shirt are comfortable.

*   *   *

The rays of the morning sun filter through tall maple trees, bouncing off the rough, irregular, overlapping clapboards of a timbered house. Eager to see what wonders the new world offers, John quicken his pace to keep beside his new friends. The frames of heavy timbers have dried to a natural gray, and their thatched roofs remind him of England.

"Ideal, to keep out rain and snow," Richard says. "Along the way be a house with gables, another with more than four. Our people profit by the selling of goods to England. Show their wealth by their houses. God approves of honest profit."

"Humph," inserts James, "be more profitable if the king neglected us, let us follow our own impulses."

Surprised that James has spoken, John makes no reply.

*   *   *

Entering the village at a steady pace, cautious to keep out of sight, they walk on the side of the road under the shadows of large oak trees. True to his word, Richard points out a large house with beautifully formed gables overlooking a large grassy square.

Richard tells him, "The villagers refer to the area as a common. Belongs to everybody, just like the sea is common to all. A place where villagers graze their milk cows. Me parents did the same in their village in old England, afore they arrived here thirty-five years past. I be just a wee lad."

John points to a wooden pillory. In it sits a lone man, shivering in the early morning chill. "Blasphemed on the Sabbath," Richard explains. "Punishment to remind him to avoid uttering profanities in the future. Fined forty shillings, he was."

"Are women reproved likewise?" John asks.

"Over there, at the edge of the Frog Pond. See the ducking stool? 'Tis where they punish wives who nag their tolerant husbands. Occupied frequently. Some women be tools of the Devil."

John momentarily agrees. Remembering the salacious women in Port Royal he can see the logic in Richard's claim. Then his mind floods with his mother's goodness. The Devil did not reside in her. Far from it.

Sounding the day, the cock's crow follows the men south along the dusty road until they come to a radiant fieldstone path meandering off to their right. Like sentinels, a stand of tall trees guards the entry to the church at the path's end. Close to the back of the church stands a single-story house. A dying candle reflects through the uneven glass of the kitchen window. An elderly woman tugs at the white hood covering her head as she bends to tend a small garden. Long plaits of hair snake over the shoulders of her dark brown dress. John slows, absorbed by the tranquility of the scene. Grabbing his arm his companions firmly encourage him to keep pace.

Farther down the street there is a store—and, yes, a tavern, which reminds him of London. Wondering if Hocke survived the plague, John sadly thinks of his small family. Did any of them survive?

Next to the tavern stands an old jailhouse, its huge dark oak door fastened to the frame with large rusted hinges. A rustling movement behind a four-foot-high slatted fence makes John jump. Grabbing the Puritan's arm, he whispers, "The soldiers of the king have discovered my absence. They will drag me back to the ship."

Preparing to run, he is hushed by his rescuers into silence. His blue eyes twinkling, Richard softly laughs at John's nervousness.

"Just some livestock stirring, lad. A cow, most assuredly."

Church bells sound as they hurry past a two-story house, more spacious than any John has seen thus far.

"Seems there might be three rooms on the first floor," John estimates. "Much finer, by far, than our family rooms in London. Great riches. Not crowded. Surely no more than one family lives there." Tall grasses separate the house from the street. A wild rose bush grows beside the door; its powerful fragrance reaches his nose.

Hardly containing his excitement, he observes, "It appears that here a man can have a house for his family."

"Yes, we have prospered here. Freemen own property. Look over there, lad—a man who owns two cows, a horse, chickens."

After a year at sea, John sees hope of an improved future. "I pray never to go to sea again."

"Many here make a fine living, fishing in the ocean—a fine living. Others do well building boats."

*　　*　　*

Irregular spiny petals surrounding a pink flower attract John's attention. After a transitory touch, he pulls back, his eyes filled with tears.

"Burdock." His companions laugh. "Well, lad, everything beautiful not always be safe."

"I will well remember your wise counsel in the future," John dryly agrees, making a great display of pulling tiny burrs out of his finger and thumb.

Pausing in front of a two-gable structure, Richard remarks, "Lives there an industrious pair. Built a plain sensible house. Just two doors, one exit from each end of its long sides."

Two men are busily replacing the thatch on the roof. With smooth, coordinated movements they lift heavy three-foot bundles of thatch above their heads, skillfully placing each to overlay the one beneath it.

"Neighbor helping neighbor," observes Richard.

"This appears to be a land where a man can live in a godly spirit," answers John.

"True, lad, but be aware—there be witches and demons about ready to entrap you. Man hath either one of two natures, good or evil, godly or satanic. A few men seem to be both, depending upon whom they be dealing with. Walk humbly with your God, lad. 'Tis the right path to follow."

An hour passes in silence. As they pass free of the village, each man reflects on his own thoughts and concerns. John has never before been in such a pastoral setting. Instead of liveried carriages driving through narrow streets, here farmers guide their oxen and carts over deeply rutted roads. Instead of crowded wooden buildings of multiple stories with shops and mean living spaces, small homes sit upon orderly farmlands.

"As the Bible commanded, we founded our city on the hill, but already crowding in Boston be as bad as in old England. People move out, away from the village, away from the control of the main congregation. At one time all the farmers lived in town and walked to their fields. Now a few build on their land. Being closer leaves more time for labor—use less time wasted walking there."

"Did most who came here stay here?"

"Sadly, some five hundred have returned to old England, some to Lincolnshire. Difficult to conceive of such a choice, where there be constant strife between King and Parliament. Here we have autonomy, our own set of laws. King be far distant. He be wise to let us alone. Takes months to get a message to England and a response back to Massachusetts. We did send representatives last year."

"Most in London be satisfied to have a king, after the restrictions of Cromwell. Me mam found King Charles most handsome," John declares.

Richard, acting as if he had not heard John, goes on. "We banish those from the colony we deem not wanted, who be of a different belief. Our church alone prevails."

Responding to the look of surprise on John's face, he says, "Oh, we recognize new churches, if they be orthodox. Have, on occasion, executed those whose faiths we considered to be unorthodox. Hanged them, don't ye know. All for the best." Firmly, Richard adds, "Not able to sanction those not of our belief."

Reciting as if by rote, thoughts quickly become words, and words become a sermon: "Without the interference of Parliament or King, we created our own judiciary, plus a system of taxation. Our magistrates sit and enact our business. Let King and Parliament fight their battles. We have our own charter and our own covenant with God. Those who share this covenant be made freemen.

"Some remained less than a year," Richard adds. "Did not find their Christ when they followed Governor Winthrop to Salem, then to Boston. A few moved south toward Plimouth and to islands off the coast. Others became dissatisfied when our government restrained and punished their excesses. Some feared famine but were reluctant to provide honest labor to feed themselves. Gratified to be rid of them, we were."

"A spoiled plan for some, but appears to have worked for others?" observes John.

"When the Winthrop fleet came," Richard interrupts, warming to his subject. "they desired a holy commonwealth in the New World. 'Tis not only a religious colony—in theory it be a commercial enterprise to exploit the sea, land, and other resources of the land. Worked well for Father. Though not a member of the Bay Company, he became a freeman in 1630 at the first meeting of the General Court in Boston. Fortunate he not be a papist or Anglican. Becoming a freeman gave him a right to own land, not possible for him in old England."

Weasel believed this land would be paradise. Mayhap it is, thinks John. *Some colonists seem to act independently, go their own way. Appears to already be dissension between England and her colony. Had he not been hanged, would have been a good life for him.*

Breaking John's reverie, Richard says, "Everything planted here prospereth. More fruit than we can eat."

"Appears it be heaven on earth."

"Not perfect for everyone. So many of our worthies have left, and we have sent more than one man on his way back to England. Now we have our own colony, some speak of divorcement from the English church and its papist ways. Our preachers be men like us. We pray not to saints, nor kneel. Our communion tables be of unpolished oak."

Nodding his head, John turns to scrutinize James, who is eating a handful of delicious scarlet berries, wondering if the man ever spoke more than a few words. "His head just nods in agreement with everything Richard says. Well, at least he hears," John murmurs, looking at the bald little man with bulbous eyes. "Seems dependable. Not given to idle prattle."

"Land disputes happening in Salem village," Richard informs John. "Such things lead to evil ways."

As Boston town recedes into the distance, they continue on a footpath toward the Shawmut peninsula and the mainland. The sound of bleating attracts John's attention to a pastoral scene of five white sheep grazing near a small farmhouse protected by a split-rail enclosure.

Richard says, "Shawmut be the Indian name for the land Boston sits on. Best hurry—peninsula becomes an island at high tide."

The three men walk in a silence broken only by the occasional screech of a jay. Near the path are fields tall with corn. In the distance lies the dark ebony of a forest. The trees stretch upward, straining to touch the low gray clouds of heaven. The early morning chill burned off by the sun is warm in comparison to the coldness of last night in the bay. Remembering his time in the water sends shivers through John's body. Hurrying southward, he strives to increase the distance between himself and the English ship, praying they will not be induced to follow him for so great a distance.

John notices the lack of dead leaves and underbrush, a scene completely different from the lush green of Jamaica and the woods of England.

"Indians burn it off in the fall," Richard explains. "Enriches the land."

"Be there Indians nearby?"

"Most certainly, but many have moved inland, away from the newcomers. Disease hath reduced their numbers."

For a time the men walk in a silence, conscious only of the crunching noise of their shoes following the path. From directly above, a beam of sunlight shines down, as if sent to lead them. Reaching the throat of land connecting the peninsula to its neighbors to the south, they rejoice. It is low tide; a remarkable land bridge spreads before them.

Shouts and screams distract the trio, causing them to slowly turn toward the direction of their origin. They peer into the dark shadowy woods toward the sounds of distress.

*　　*　　*

"Someone be gettin' a thrashin'," Richard bellows. Charging forward he drags John behind him. "Come, lads, if not be the Devil, we must assist as we can."

Hurrying ahead they hear screams of protest accompanied by thumping fists and repetitive blows hitting the soft tissue of a human body.

"A robbery, for certain," Richard calls out. "Hurry now." Entering the woods they slow their steps to allow their eyes to adjust to the diminished light caused by the dense foliage.

Unexpectedly Richard halts John with a fist to his chest. A finger to his lips warns Richard's companions to silence. The men slow, trying to lessen the crackle of their feet stomping across the broken twigs and branches in their path.

Richard points in the direction of the conflict. "There, just out of the shadows," he whispers. Fearful the attackers might see them, they stop to hide behind a large uprooted tree. Less than fifteen feet away, exposed in the filtered light coming through the branches of a tall maple, they see two men trying to beat their victim to the ground. Holding his quarterstaff out in front, the man defensively tries to ward off the knife and fists directed at his head and stomach.

"Two against one," hisses Richard. "Two great men against a wee one."

"He's tiring! Not able to protect himself forever," John exclaims. "Let's go."

Light reflects off the metal blade as one of the attackers raises his arm to plunge it into the victim's chest. Rushing forward, the men instinctively yell, waving their arms in an attempt to scare off the attackers. A stabbing seems imminent.

Remembering how skillfully smaller sailors used belaying pins as weapons, John grabs a heavy stick, using it to force an attack on the knife-wielding villain.

"Belay," John yells as the startled men turn to run.

"Halt," shouts Richard, as the would-be thieves escape deep into the darkness of the woods.

Satisfied that the rogues are no longer a threat, the three rescuers turn back to assist the man, who has crumbled to the ground. Seeing the amount of blood on his face and clothing, John thinks the victim is mortally wounded. On closer inspection he finds the attack was not deadly.

"Just enough time to box us around, brothers. Not fatal. Thankful ye come as ye did. Almost lost the fight to keep our pistol," he adds, patting the weapon carried in a sash around his waist. "Lucky our musket was in the woods, safe. Unfortunately, didn't get a chance to fire upon them. Not even able to get our powder bag open," he adds with an English accent John has never heard before, a singsong rhythm from an era long past.

"Glad for your assistance, kindly sirs. Our name be Willem."

Willem's nose is bloodied, and the skin around his eye turns to a dark blue as they speak. Full of confidence, Willem declares, "We be more frightened than hurt."

Kindly, Richard helps Willem to a sitting position and then helps him drink water from his doeskin bag. Grateful, Willem takes deep gulps.

"Again, we thank ye, friends." John and Richard each grab an arm to help him to a wobbly upright position. Willem struggles to brush dust off his loose gray trousers and the sleeves of the homespun red vest he wears over his oversized white shirt. Seven wooden black-powder tubes hang on the wide leather straps crisscrossing his chest.

"This young lad be John," Richard says, pointing to his young friend. "I be Richard, and this here be me brother James."

"Honored to meet ye," Willem exclaims, bowing from the waist, his face brightening into a broad smile. "Allow us, sirs, may we offer a feast to share with ye? But first allow us to retrieve our valuable hat," he says as he reaches over to pick up a broad-brimmed hat made out of the fur of some animal that John does not recognize. After he places the hat on his head, a shadow almost hides his face, making his thin white beard less prominent. Turning his back to them, Willem begins walking to an area of sunshine at the edge of the woods. Beckoning them to follow, he indicates a crop of wild strawberries, some almost two inches around. "Taste these, an elegant repast, certain. We had just begun to eat when those fiends attacked us. Tried a run into the woods, but we could not escape."

John quickly realizes that there is no *we*. Besides the three of them, Willem is the only other person within view. As he wonders why Willem refers to himself as *we*, John reaches out his hand, gratefully accepting a handful of strawberries from his gracious host. Enjoying the delicious sweetness, John reciprocates by handing Willem a piece of the bread from his coat pocket. Hesitantly he inquires, "Where be ye going, Willem?"

"Come north upon a ship from Virginia. Helped to load the tobacco we carried. Captain needed extra hands, so came aboard, jumping off in Plimouth. Thought to look about this colony." Willem pauses, waving his arm to the east and the ocean. "Coast now beckons us back. Needs find another ship to take us south."

Richard spoke up, "John here needs to travel south. Barnstable—or Plimouth, for that fact—be a fine place for him to go. Look for work to do."

Turning toward John, Willem again expresses his appreciation, "Glad for your most kindly assistance. Our gun and loading staff would cost us one pound fifteen shillings to replace. Hard to come by in these times." With a slightly more formal bow, he adds, "Be honored if ye come along. Two be safer than one, as evidenced by these late activities."

"Be there Indians along the way?"

Richard interrupts Willem's attempted reply. "Not so many anymore. Few years back, many died of smallpox."

With a determined look on his face, as if looking inward and seeing the value of a land without the natives, Richard perseveres. "We must wrest these unused and undressed lands from the heathens. The proper thing to do. They just roam from place to place, waste any land they might have. We can make better use of it."

Surprised by Richard's apparent loathing of the Indians, Willem comments, "Met with friendly Indians on the way. Nothing to fear, so far as we can see. The praying Indians along Long Island Sound have been taught the words of the Lord. At times we trade with them for food when we fail to shoot some game with our gun. But game be plentiful. A trade be not often necessary—'tis why I feared losing our musket. Not easy to replace such a loss."

John asks, "Will we mostly see just men? Or are women and families likely to be visible?"

"Eh, sure. Indian women be very alluring with black hair, high foreheads, out-breasted, small-waisted figures. Beheld a beauty just the other day. She didn't see us. Sang like a beautiful bird, she did, whilst rocking her wee babe in her arms."

Uncomfortable with William's intimate description of the Indian woman, Richard returns the discussion to John's escape from the Royal Navy. "If'n ye take unfriendly to Plimouth, ye can move south to the village of New York or on to the southern colonies— though ye must beware of the fever. Might even sail around Cape Cod to New York. There be ships readily available, though at times can be a rough sail with harsh winds coming out of the northeast. Might work for your passage, though not a long walk if you follow the Bay Path to the south coast. A final choice would be to go west, to land the king has lately secured from the Dutch."

John looks at Richard, reluctant to respond. Assuming his silence indicates the possibility that John has changed his mind and now wants to return to England, Richard kindly suggests, "Not a few have gone back to Old England, disappointed in our experiment. Some have thought a church-run state unlikely to work. If ye make the decision to stay—or, for that fact, to leave—ye should be able to find a ship to work."

"Had enough of beatings by men who see their power as divine right. Will avoid ships for a bit."

"'Tis certain that ye dare not go back to Boston whilst the English ship remains. Most likely be more than a month in port. Whatever ye decide, we must leave ye. My sister lives out there," he says, pointing toward the west. "Just the other side of that woods."

"Aye, 'tis true, I must leave," agrees John. "Your kindness will be forever remembered. Without it, certain the king's navy would have caught me, sentenced me to inescapable death. Not pleasant to think of ending me life swinging at the end of a rope, body tarred, wrapped in a metal brace—food for the gulls." Shaking his head in misery, he continues, "Nothing more."

"Had not the slightest hesitation about rescuing you," Richard tells John. "We help each other. Make each other's condition our own." Waving his hand as the two men walk away, Richard calls out, "Farewell to ye, lads."

"Farewell to ye," answer John and Willem in unison, turning one final time to wave good-bye to their friends. For a few minutes he and his new companion walk along in a comfortable silence, broken only by the occasion song of a meadowlark and the sounds of their feet along the path.

After a few moments Willem returns to the subject of Indians. "Aye, might well see natives along the way. Mostly friendly. Well, some be, at least. Look close— now and then ye will glimpse one, most likely with a knife suspended around his neck in a scabbard of wampum, a form of money they use for trade. Most likely not be a menace."

John follows Willem along the bay path, occasionally finding treackleberries and hurtleberries to eat. The sweet tastes are exquisite to John's palate. Never has he seen fruits the likes of these. When hungry, they plan to shoot an occasional pheasant or grouse.

The two men travel southeast, toward the coast. Somber, John utters, primarily to build up his wan spirits, "Fate brought me here to Massachusetts, to a place where independent thinking is encouraged. I will trust in God's plan."

Nodding in agreement, Willem pauses at the edge of a swiftly running river. "Here, lad, try our hand at catching a fish for our repast." Taking twine to construct a snare, he inquires, "Truth be known, did ye live with pirates? Seen what they do to men on captured ships. Unsavory."

"With them most of a year. Fearful every minute, but one thing to be said, the pirates, though cruel, understand well how to live a life of freedom. They elect their leaders and unelect them if they do not satisfy."

Straightening his back, John stares straight into Willem's eyes, hesitant to continue. Gathering his courage, John goes on. "The people in Boston honor God, have established their own independent lives. Seem to fear not the king or Parliament. Believe their lot to be determined by God himself. I believe and honor God, but I also revere the king."

Willem, who had never seen the king and felt no relationship to him, nodded his head. He did not argue.

*   *   *

Under a maple tree, worn out by the adventures of the past two days, John sleeps soundly for the first time in a more than a year. A gentle shaking of his shoulder awakens him to Willem's offer of an alternative to returning to England.

"From Plimouth, the path continues on to Falmouth. There be small vessels that fish and trade with small villages along the bay. Settlements, headed by a few missionaries, are also being developed out on the small islands in Vineyard Sound. Perhaps ye can find a sponsor, earn land in some manner."

"How long might that take?"

"Depends on the master's needs. Sometimes you can trade fur or livestock for land. Ye will find a way, but may take time."

"Certain I am my family be all dead. Will stay here, try to erase the past year from my mind. I have no desire to go back to sea, no thoughts of returning to Jamaica or to England." He proclaims, "A piece of land is all that a man needs to be his own master. Where will you go, Willem?"

"Return to Virginia. Grow tobacco. For now, I've seen enough of the world."

MARTHA'S VINEYARD

Spring 1006

A soaring osprey flies above the high hill. His whistle splits the stillness like a sharp knife. The screech of an owl further breaks the silence. The island appears uninhabited. It is not. An Algonquian Indian lurks in the shadows, the lone witness to the movement of a ship threading its way past the sea grasses and vines that choke the hundreds of budding oaks. The Vikings do not land at Noe-pe, the land amid the waters.

Returning to his village, the tall native spreads his arms and tells his tribe the story of the great canoe with the head and tail of a serpent. "From its bowels grows a tree without branches. Reaching for the sky, it catches the spirit of the wind in a large skin that speeds it across the great pond."

Six hundred years later, in April 1602, Captain Bartholomew Gosnold leads a ship of Englishmen on a voyage of exploration. Landing amid thick vines, they name the island Martha's Vineyard. In the next century, Thomas Mayhew purchases the island, hiring missionaries to educate and teach religion to the natives. The ruling sachems of the island exchange their lands for English goods and money, and by 1700 seventy-three persons live on Martha's Vineyard. The island produces farmers, but it's the mariners, whalers, and fishermen who frequently cross the waters to other islands and the mainland. Some disappear, presumed drowned in the turbulent currents.

Through the eighteenth century, fog, rain, and unfavorable winds often force sailors of many nations to seek protection in the island's many bays and coves. When the winds of political dissension blow, some islanders remain loyal to King George of England. Others, influenced by Massachusetts's rebels, determine the American War of Independence to be a just cause.

CHAPTER 8

JOHN AND SAMUEL

Martha's Vineyard

July 1736

"Grandpapa, Grandpapa," beseeches five-year-old Samuel. Clutching the hem of his grandfather's jacket, the child is carried along as the pair walks home along the shore of the great pond. Stopping in front of the home of Thomas Poole, John Hillman gazes down with affection and pride at his beloved grandchild.

"Reminded of my own wee brothers. Dead roughly seventy years," he whispers. Stiff with arthritis, he slowly bends to peer into Samuel's serious dark brown eyes.

Samuel, puffing from his recent exertions, leisurely fans his young face with a clump of dried ferns. Squinting into the glare of the bright sun, he finds it impossible to fully return his grandfather's gaze.

"Wise lad," John comments. "Splendid way to keep both sun and bugs out of your eyes." Adjusting the ferns on Samuel's forehead, he suggests, "See here, to best provide shade, hold the fern just above your eyes. Aye, just there."

"A story, Grandpa, a story," pleads Samuel.

Diverting the child's attention, John points to a sleek animal playing on the shore. "Look, Samuel, the river otter be frolicking in the stream. Just like you, lad. Everything be a game. A time for play."

Samuel glances at the shiny, furry body wiggling along the riverbank. Although the boy is momentarily fascinated, the ruse to redirect his attention does not work for very long. Once again, Samuel continues his insistent demands for a story.

"Please, Grandpapa! A story about pirates."

In an effort to put off the inevitable, the eighty-nineyear-old grandfather tries another tack. Gently removing Samuel's tight grip on the hem of his homespun gray jacket, which, except for its size, mimics his grandson's, he whispers, "Shush, Samuel, mustn't distract Thomas from his work. See, over there. He be cutting down the great oak tree."

"Belay," Samuel bellows. Releasing his grandfather's coat he dashes toward the tall man preparing to cut down the tree, indignantly crying out, "Want to climb it. Leave it! Belay, I say!"

With an indulgent smile the grandfather asks, "Now, just what be this word, *belay*?"

"Belay your teasing, Grandpapa. Make Mr. Poole stop."

"He just be cutting down trees to make more pasture for his horses and cows. Wager you'd like to help Thomas feed and care for more horses."

Plaintively, Samuel pulls away from his grandfather's restraining grip, raising his voice. "Don't care. Don't care."

"Hush, lad," John insists, pulling Samuel back. Then, calculating the quieting effect a promised story is certain to bring, he adds, "Abide, over there by the wall. Shall I tell you about the pirates?"

Anticipation crosses Samuel's face. Joyfully he realizes that his grandfather is about to relent—to tell his favorite story. Remembering the oft-told tale, a smile spreads across his face. He asks, knowing well the answer, "How didst you git away?"

Taking a short break to enjoy a story he has heard many times before, Thomas Poole stops sawing and rests against the aged stone fence built by his father thirty years before.

Momentarily distracted, John Hillman ignores his grandson and, greets his neighbor. "Good day to you, Thomas. Ready for an oft-told tale of the sea?"

Settling his back against the rough, cold stone, John briefly reflects back to the time that he and other neighbors had helped Thomas's father cut down trees to build a one-story house. "Stacked the wood over in the clearing," he reminisces. "Used oxen to haul the trees over to the cutting pit. Hard work it was. Each log had to be individually cut, so we worked over a pit. Why, some trees measured out at three feet around. Neighbors all worked together to cut the planks."

"Good friends all. Many sadly gone," recalls Thomas.

"Sometimes took me turn standing in the pit," John laughs at the distant memory. "Covered all over with sawdust. Then took me turn standing above the pit, working the upper handle of the saw. Got the job done. We cut the planks, then raised the house. Worked as a community, each helping the other. Good times."

"Did pirates help you, Grandfather?" Samuel interrupts with an air of pretend innocence. When he does not seize his grandfather's full attention, he insists, "Tell me about the pirates. Now, Grandpapa." Quickly perceiving his grandfather's disapproval at his insistence, he amends with an engaging broad smile, "Please."

Teasing his young grandson, John makes his face as neutral as possible and deliberately puts off telling Samuel the story of his time with the pirates, persisting with his reminiscences of early Martha's Vineyard.

"All the neighbors worked together. First built the house. Then we used horses and ropes to drag the large stones out of the pasture, laid them by to build this here fence." Solemnly nodding his head, he adds, "Happened long ago. Long after me escape from the pirates." Trying to capture Samuel's interest, he points to the house, "Why, in that very house, Thomas and his brothers were born. The new houses were a great improvement over the wigwam houses of the Indians, superior to the log houses built by the first settlers. Your daddy be but a wee lad when it was built. Not much older than ye be now."

A loud screech interrupts John's reminiscing. Glancing up, he watches a young osprey make ready for flight. Flapping its wide wings to grab a pocket of air, it prepares to soar out over the salt marsh toward the ocean. Then it gracefully rises into the afternoon sky. Its flapping creates a negative pressure over its wings, providing lift. "Note the osprey, Samuel. It be heading for the ocean. Pirates lurk there to this day."

*   *   *

"The ocean," John whispers, slipping back into a frequently recurring reverie where memory blends with the present. "A place deep in my memory. Remember it more clearly than yesterday."

John nods his head, his mind drifting back over the years to those confused, unhappy days when he was a captive aboard the *Revenge*. Vigorously rubbing his forehead, John tries to bring his mind back to the present. Images of the English navy arise and recede in his memory. At times the sequence of events becomes confused, but the impressions of the men and ships he served, good and evil, are never jumbled.

The past sixty years on Martha's Vineyard were good years. The times with the pirates are best forgotten. Ah, but the stories are so entertaining to his grandson. He nods in agreement with his innermost thoughts.

"Has it been only a few years since I last sailed out of Holmes Hole to Boston? Old I be. More 'n likely will never sail again. Reluctant to go back to sea at my age, in any event." Sadly, he thinks, *Why, this aged body no longer has the energy to even climb the short path up Peaked Hill. The osprey soars up there for me, delights in the magnificent views. His eyes be my eyes as he soars out over the water. He watches the English ships sail around the cape to Holmes Hole, then onto the Elizabeth Islands—his view not blocked by trees.*

Turing to face Samuel, the grandfather explains, "Oak and pine covered the island when first I came from Barnstable. Long time past since trees were cut down to use as timber for houses." Rubbing Samuel's diminutive fingers between his rough, arthritic ones, he adds, "And as firewood to warm your wee hands.

"Just a few families resided here when I first arrived. Thanks be to the Almighty, old Thomas Mayhew purchased the island from the Indians. He insisted they receive fair payment, so we didn't have the Indian problems that some of the other colonies had. Now pastures exist where once stood stands of hardwood trees. Allows you to see far across the water, especially from Peaked Hill—a view to behold.

"On clear days the point at Gay's Head shines in the distance. Lad, your legs be gettin' longer and stronger—soon be running up the hill quick as a deer. Peaked Hill be not high as hills go, only three hundred foot or so. Three times higher than the mast of a ship. From there ye can watch ships sail across Vineyard Sound out to the ocean, see them pitch upon seas that surge and pass beneath them. One minute a ship be visible, next she be quickly swallowed up in a blowing fog." Then, attempting to discourage Samuel from a life at sea, he adds, "Ye will find out for yourself, lad. Storms ashore can be frightening but are naught compare to a tempest at sea."

Returning his thoughts to the land, John dwells on the short time he suspects he has left to live. Wistfully, he thinks, *If only me final resting place could be atop the hill, where the earth around me feels the sun's warmth and the trees whisper secrets into the wind. From such a spot I could watch the events that come to this island. But I will have to settle for the community burial grounds a few hundred feet lower, unaware of who, if any, visit me.*

"When were you kidnapped?" demands Samuel, trying to bring his grandfather back to the pirate story. "Was you bigger than me?"

"Oh, forgive me, Samuel, me mind wanders. When be I kidnapped by the pirates? Why, over seventy years ago, in me sixteenth year, directly out of the River Thames." He muses, "Can it really have been so long ago?" Taking the small pouch out of his trousers, he is reassured by the lock of his mother's hair, now stiff and darkened with age.

Has it been over seventy years since I last saw her and Tristram and Samuel? In those days I was certain that I would never see eighteen, let alone survive to such a respected old age. How young Samuel loves to hear my tales. Well, I must make him appreciate the land; the sea be much too dangerous.

"Why, young fellow, the year I arrived here, young Bethia Folger and John Barnard drowned while coming to Martha's Vineyard from Nantucket."

Samuel had never heard these names before, so John explained, "She was Peter Folger's daughter; he being a surveyor and a preacher. Not many folks lived on Nantucket at that time. A sudden wind out of the northeast must have tipped them into the water out of their craft. Terrible currents flow in that part of the sea. Sad time, just afore I took possession of me first half lot—right down the road, on the east side of Old Mill Brook. Paid with a good sheep and a fattened lamb. Later, hired the lot of Simon Athearn at the Red Ground." He pauses to remember. "He, Athearn, came close to fighting the praying Indians to keep them from taking it back."

Distracted from his impatience with his grandfather's wandering thoughts, Samuel interjects, "Who be the praying Indians, Grandpapa?"

"Indians taught to pray by Mayhew's hired missionaries. Peter Folger was also a teacher. Plan was to send the Indians to Harvard, near Boston."

John felt another tug on his sleeve, a gentle reminder from Samuel to finish his story. "'Nough of the Indians. Tell 'bout the pirates," Samuel insists. "Please, Grandpapa, finish the story. Make him finish, Thomas."

"Ha! Pray excuse my wanderings, lad. Back to the sea, to the pirates, as ..."

"... you promised," finishes Samuel.

Focusing his mind's eye on scenes from long ago, John continues, "The pirates bind to no homes, no land. Commit crimes most grievous. Life at sea gets you whippings. Early death."

Samuel's excitement at the story's continuation is short-lived.

"Here on the Vineyard, the sea provides for us, protects us, serves as a link to the mainland. But me boy," John exhorts, "the land is what's solid. Requires great industry to keep it tended. Trees to be felled. Pastures maintained. Good, honest work." Trying to instill a love of the land in his grandson, he stresses, "A good way to feed your family."

Thomas chimes in. "Small towns provide a place to exchange goods—all that a man and his family require. Why, almost seventy families live in Holmes Hole."

John adds, "Only a few lived there when I arrived. The town fills with islanders on market day to exchange surpluses of grain, meat, or milk for things needed. Ships from Boston bring supplies not available here on the island. Fortunate we be to have the strength of such as community of solid friends. There be strength in binding together."

Samuel jumps up and down with frustration when John's mind again wanders away from the story, returning to familiar themes about the land.

John absently watches the osprey ride a thermal and then returns his gaze to Samuel. The strong wrinkles in his face soften as he speaks so softly the boy must struggle to hear. "Sailed to many a strange shore, lad."

Reaching into his trousers, John idly pulls out the small pouch sewn by his oldest granddaughter, a receptacle for the treasured strand of his mother's hair.

"See here, Samuel, me mam's hair. Bright red, it was. Protected me."

Samuel's eyes grow large with this new, unanticipated information. "Someday you can carry it. Will protect you too. Truly believe her spirit protected me from death on the pirate ship. My love for her lies undiminished to this day. Her spirit protected me from a demon ready to take me away whilst I suffered from intense thirst. Beckoned me with a long, thin finger, laughing at me from a thin face. The vision had large white teeth in a thin mouth above a small, pointed beard. Remember it well. Me mam came into the vision, shoved the apparition aside."

Samuel remains silent. He knows of ghosts and is frightened. He can tell by the look on his grandfather's face—a look that comes more and more frequently of late—that his thoughts are leaving him, going far away.

If I abide a bit, Grandpapa will come back. He's done it before.

Finally John whispers, "Soon, my God will find me a place on one last shore, a final port—the one that no man sees till his passing." His brow furrows, and his head nods as if in agreement with silent thoughts. "Always guided me well, He did."

*   *   *

Breaking his musing, John calls out to his neighbor, "Winter be a-comin'. Cold winds soon to fly out of the northwest. Ye ready, Tom?"

"Goin' to be a hard one," Tom agrees. "Imagine that Jonathan is well prepared. Least he had best be."

"My son be prepared. A great help to me, certain. More 'n twenty acres to take care of. Both he and Benjamin take care of the land now. Granted it over to them some years back." Patting Samuel on the shoulder, he comments, "Someday be yours, Samuel."

"Oh, no, Grandfather. If ye please, I will to go to sea."

Before John has time to reply to Samuel's remark, Thomas calls out in a tone disguised to appear stern, "Say there, Samuel, lad, get home and grab an ax. Big strong boy like you should be able to cut down a tree. Six years old, is it?"

With the respect in his voice reserved for his elders, Samuel calls back, "No, sir, just five."

"Five, is it?"

"Soon I be five."

"Well, big ye are for your age. Next year, then. Then is when we'll sharpen the ax for ye." With a strong voice that gives emphasis to his words, he adds, "Yes, sir, you know I will. Then you can help cut wood."

*   *   *

Preparing to swing the ax, Thomas mutters, "Old John spends excessive time spinning tales of the sea to the young one. The boy won't want to stay on this island, I'll wager." Shaking his head with a soft grunt of discomfort, he curls his gnarled fingers around the smooth, worn handle of the sharpened ax. "Each season it's more difficult to grip it. How many years have I swung this old friend? How many hundreds of trees have we cut down?"

"Most difficult to imagine, Tom," John calls back.

Using his hands and shoulders to exert control, Thomas swings the ax over his head and then brings it down with a power that would make many a younger man stare in awe. Another downward stroke creates an even deeper cut.

Forgetting his previous protest against cutting down the tree, Samuel claps his hands and jumps up and down with approval. "In a few years I be able to cut down a tree. Won't I, Grandpapa?"

"Few more chops and this one be down," Thomas calls back. "Abide. Have a hot drink." As he turns his body into the next swing of the ax, his powerful arms give strength to the downward stroke, imbedding the edge of the ax deep into the core of the tree. The tree crashes.

"Exactly where ye charted, Thomas," hails John. "Good man."

But Thomas does not hear John's voice above the thunder reverberating through the woods as the tree breaks branches in its fall, smacking the ground five yards from the clay-filled exterior walls of the one-story, center-chimney house. Flying bark and dirt spread in all directions. Wiping his brow with a large, soiled white handkerchief, Thomas walks to the house where he has lived alone since the death of his wife the previous winter. He motions for John and Samuel to follow.

"Wish I had a fine lad like Samuel," Thomas considers, rubbing his smoothly shaved chin. "Amazing child. One day will make his family proud. Smart as a whip. Dark straight hair just like his mother's. Her disposition too. Not easily swayed. He'll be a leader when we need one. There's restlessness in the air that will burst one day. Sentiments against England be growing. Disagreements between King George and the Parliament assure it."

"Come inside, Samuel," Thomas calls. Grabbing a rough cloth from a peg outside the front door, he swabs his sweaty brow and laughs. "Your grandfather can spin his tales whilst we have a cup of tea, a most wonderful brew. Introduced into the colonies about twenty years ago, if my mind serves correctly." The trio enters through the front door. One man stands straight and tall; the other is bent with age. The child follows them, bouncing with each step.

Sweeping his arm to show off his house and belongings, Thomas says, "This be superior to our first dwelling, which was just a log hut. Filled the cracks and chinks with clay to keep out wind and weather."

"Aye," agrees John. "My first house had a thatched roof of salted hay. Most houses were like that till the island got a carpenter to split shingles for us. Many a house topped with a thatched roof burned to the ground caused by a spark jumping from the fireplace or a strike of lightning."

"Pleased to have glass windows to replace oiled paper," adds Thomas. "Allows in purer light, indeed."

Before Samuel settles in for an extended visit, John states firmly, "Well, Thomas, we can sit but a minute. Samuel's mother be wanting us home for the evening meal. A lovely pious woman, but sanctions no deviations from mealtime. She be fixin' a special treat—ox cheek. Bethia often reminds me that not attending to fixed times for the meals takes precious time away from other duties. Fine woman. My Jonathan be lucky to have married her, a gift from heaven. Seven children, none on the way for a change." After a moment's reflection, he adds, "At least, not so I know."

An eight-by-seven-foot fireplace monopolizes the center of the room. Taking the iron kettle from the trammel, Thomas transfers it to the kitchen table, pausing momentarily to watch Samuel trace the outline of a scorched area in the planked table with his finger.

Excitedly he calls out, "Look, Grandpapa, a pirate's head. Right here in the table."

Smiling, John nods.

Remembering his grandfather's promise, Samuel again tugs on John's sleeve. "Please, Grandpapa," he pleads, "the pirates. Mr. Poole desires to hear it, too, whilst we drink our tea." Fearful he will be punished for his rudeness, he stops and stares at the floor.

Patiently, John replies, "Samuel, child, it's been many years since I escaped from the pirates. Drink your tea."

"How did they get you, Grandpapa?"

"Dear Samuel, have already told ye. Snatched me from the river in London. Drugged me; hauled me off.

Woke upon the deck of their brig, eyes bleary from the grog."

"Did they wear patches over their eyes? Carry guns?"

"Some had patches on one eye or the other. All carried guns, 'cept for me and two others." Wrapping Samuel in his arms, John takes his index finger and makes a circle around the child's eye. "Right here be where one wore his patch. No eye under it. Lost it in a fight."

Samuel pushes away. He runs around the kitchen and slides under the table. Squinting his dark brown eyes as if peering down the barrel of his make-believe gun, he brags, "Bang, got me a pirate."

"Not be so easy. A frightening time," John chides him. "Feared for me life. Horrified each time we attacked another ship. When guns be fired, people die. Here we use guns to hunt for food, protect ourselves." Musing again, he adds, "Parliament requires we provide an armed militia. Might regret that decision someday." Noting the impatience in the child's eyes, John returns to the story.

"The pirates intimidated other ships to gain ill-gotten goods for the benefit of none but themselves."

"Were there no good pirates, Grandpapa?" questions Samuel.

"Fortunate I be. Safeguarded by two who be good to me, Mo and Weasel, till I be rescued by the English and taken upon their great ship of war."

"Did the pirates whip you, Grandpapa? Did the English stop them?"

"Oh, I be whipped all right, when I refused to rob, kill, or sign their Articles. Being a good topman saved me. In the end the pirates all died, some hung by the English, right from the yardarm. At least those I knew of. Cruel men, but they had an honor amongst themselves. Their leader, Morgan, was a cold, hard man. Studied him to determine possible ways to escape, but the English rescued me 'fore I did." With a grim expression, he adds, "Then I discovered that the English navy had a cruelty of its own. Wasn't long before I determined to escape from them in Boston Harbor."

"Tell 'bout Jamaica, Grandpapa."

"Why, Port Royal has since disappeared in a great earthquake—at least 'tis what I heard. Happened just a few years after I came to Martha's Vineyard. Just payback for the evil that went on there. A place of evil merrymaking and corruption."

"What is corruption, Grandpapa?"

"I just hope that you will never have to know about how men manipulate each other to get what they want for a few years of satisfaction and glory. Morgan be one of the worst of them. No godliness in him or his men."

"But you said the food was good. Was that not so?"

"I tell ye this, my lad, didn't always have enough to eat and drink. When water ran out, I got so thirsty I became delirious. A ghost with a thin, leering face beckoned me with a long, thin finger. Mocked me, gnashing his gapping white teeth above a small, pointed beard." Then, remembering he had just told

Samuel this tale, he murmurs, "Guess you don't want to hear of the ghost again."

"Be scaring the lad, Samuel," Thomas censures.

"Well, the experience made me aware of evil. To know there be ghosts." Not noticing the fear in Samuel's eyes, he wraps the boy's hand in his. "Time to be off, lad. Cow requires milking."

"Grandpapa, please stay by me in the woods." Then, with a youthful ability to quickly forget problems, he asks, "Can we sail to Boston soon? Be pirates there?"

Making their farewells to Thomas, John warns Samuel, "Season of storms be upon us. Speak to your father, lad. He might take ye there to visit cousin Josiah. Should imagine there be pirates in Boston— pirates who no longer sail the seas, who now earn money in more honest ways. Perhaps some have even changed their ways, joined in church meetings."

Walking toward their farm, John calls back to Thomas, "Prepare for a game of cribbage when the first snow hits."

Dictionary

Backstaff: A navigational instrument that was used to measure the altitude of a celestial body, in particular the sun or moon.

Barque, or bark, is a 3 masted vessel with the foremast and main mast square- rigged and the mizzenmast fore-and-aft rigged.

Beak or beakhead: A small platform at the fore part of the upper deck; the part of a ship forward of the forecastle. In warships, the sailor's lavatories, or "heads," were located here.

Beat: To sail toward the wind on successive tacks.

Fo'c'sle: A short raised deck at the fore end of a vessel, originally for archers to shoot arrow into enemy vessels.

Mainsail (pronounced *mains'l*): A ship's principal sail; on a square-rigged ship, the lowest and largest sail on the mainmast.

Ratlines: Small lines made of tarred rope and fastened horizontally to the shrouds of a vessel, forming steps by which seamen climbed up the rigging.

Starboard (pronounced *st'rb'rd*): The right-hand side of the vessel when facing the bow (as opposed to larboard, or port, side).

Yards: Long and narrow wooden spars slung at their centers from before the mast in a square-rigged ship and serving to support and extend a square sail that is bent to it

These definitions are from *A Sea of Words: A Lexicon and Companion for Patrick O'Brian's Seafaring Tales* by D. King. 1995, An Owl Book by H. Holt & Co. NY

CPSIA information can be obtained at www.ICGtesting.com
Printed in the USA
BVOW041015170613

323509BV00001B/1/P